Why You'll Love This Book

by Vivian French

I can't remember how old I was when I first read *Jennie*, but I do remember I couldn't put it down. I told my friend Alison how brilliant it was and asked her if she wanted to borrow it, but she shook her head. "That's a story for people who like cats," she said, "and I like dogs."

"But it's a story about a boy called Peter," I told her. "His mother's always busy, and his father's away a lot, and he's lonely."

Alison looked more interested. "Does he have adventures?"

"LOADS," I said. "He gets into fights, and he goes travelling on a ship with an extraordinary crew, and he catches the most enormous rat—"

"YEUCH!" Alison made a face. "Why does he do that?"

"Didn't I tell you?" I put the book on the table. "He runs after a kitten and gets knocked down by a coal lorry, and when he opens his eyes he discovers he's a cat... but he doesn't know how cats behave, so he has to learn. It's Jennie who teaches him – and they have adventures together."

Alison picked the book up, and flicked through the pages. "'When in doubt – any kind of doubt – WASH!'" she read out loud, and laughed. "My brother HATES washing!"

"So did Peter," I said. "But it's different for cats. And it tells you why."

"Is it a teachy book?" Alison looked suspicious. "I mean, does it pretend to be a story, but really it's so you learn about cats?"

I thought about it. "No," I said. "It's much more about a friendship. Sometimes they get things wrong and get cross with each other, but they sort it out. You don't learn stuff, but you do end up knowing exactly what it's like being a cat, because of all the detail – like how they stretch and twist and jump, or how they clean themselves, or fight each other. It makes you really and truly feel as if you've lived in the world of cats, and understand the way they think. It's so clever. And it's funny, too."

"Who's your favourite character?" Alison wanted to know.

"Jennie, of course." I was surprised she'd even asked. "And Captain Sourlies. He's the captain of the ship they stow away on, and he weighs twenty-two stone, and he hates the sea. And big Angus, with fingers like sausages, who does embroidery. And Mr Grims— "

Alison held up her hand. "Don't spoil it for me!" Then she turned to the begining of the book, and started reading... and I never ever got my book back.

I've read Jennie lots of times since then (my mum bought me another copy!) and I enjoy it just as much – if not more – each time. These days, I'm sometimes reminded by a phrase or an expression that the book was published in 1950, but the story still grips me. At one point in his life Paul Gallico had twenty-three cats, and he obviously studied them with a real passion; that passion pours into his writing. He was also passionate about people, and the way they interact one with another. Every time I get to the end of the book (even though I've read it so often) I have to go and find a hanky. And I know exactly what I'd do if I was a cat, and someone saw me looking just a little bit silly...
I'd wash!

Vivian French

Vivian French is the author of over 200 children's books, including the hugely popular *Tiara Club* series. She is also a playwright, storyteller and teacher of creative writing to children and adults.

Jennie

Paul Gallico (1897–1976) was born in New York City and studied at Columbia University. After serving in the First World War he became a journalist with the *New York Daily News* where he enjoyed particular acclaim for his sports writing. Among Paul Gallico's best known books are *The Snow Goose* (1941), a classic story of Dunkirk, and *The Poseidon Adventure* (1969), which was made into a very successful film. His magical stories about animals, particularly cats, are also enduring favourites. These include *Jennie* (1950) and *Thomasina* (1957).

In 1936 Paul Gallico moved to Salcombe in South Devon where he lived in a house on a hill with his Great Dane and twenty-three cats. In later life he settled in Monaco.

essential modern classics

PAUL GALLICO

Jennie

HarperCollins *Children's Books*

First published in the USA as *The Abandoned* in 1950
First published in Great Britain by Michael Joseph in 1950
This edition published by HarperCollins *Children's Books* in 2011

HarperCollins *Children's Books* is a division of HarperCollins*Publishers* Ltd,
77–85 Fulham Palace Road, Hammersmith, London W6 8JB

The HarperCollins *Children's Books* website address is
www.harpercollins.co.uk

1 3 5 7 9 8 6 4 2

Text copyright © 1950 by Paul Gallico. Copyright renewed 1978 by Virginia Gallico,
Robert Gallico and William Gallico
Why You'll Love This Book copyright © Vivian French 2011

ISBN 978-0-00-739519-4

Typeset in Bembo by Palimpsest Book Production Ltd,
Falkirk, Stirlingshire
Printed and bound in England by Clays Ltd, St Ives plc

To the late Simon of the Amethyst

Contents

Poussie, Poussie, Baudrons

"Poussie, poussie, baudrons,
    Whaur hae ye been?"
"I've been tae London,
    Tae see the Queen."

"Poussie, poussie, baudrons,
    Whit gat ye there?"
"I gat a guid fat mousikie,
    Rinnin' up a stair!"

"Poussie, poussie, baudrons,
    Whit did ye dae wi' it?"
"I pit it in ma meal-poke,
    Tae eat tae ma breid."

OLD SCOTTISH NURSERY RHYME

CHAPTER ONE

How It Began

PETER GUESSED THAT he must have been hurt in the accident although he could not remember very much from the time he had left the safety of Scotch Nanny's side and run out across the street to get to the garden in the square, where the tabby striped kitten was warming herself by the railing and washing in the early spring sunshine.

He had wanted to hold and stroke the kitten. Nanny had screamed and there had been a kind of an awful bump, after which it seemed to have turned from day to night as though the sun were gone and it had become quite dark. He ached and somewhere it hurt him, as it had when he had fallen running after a football near a gravel pile and scraped nearly all the skin from the side of one leg.

He seemed to be in bed now, and Nanny was there peering at him in an odd way, that is, first she would be quite close to him, so close that he could see how white her face was, instead of its usual wrinkled pink colour, and then it would seem to fade and become very small like seen through the wrong end of a telescope.

His father and mother were not there, but this did not

surprise Peter. His father was a Colonel in the Army, and his mother was always busy and having to dress up to go out, leaving him with Nanny.

Peter might have resented Nanny if he had not been so fond of her, for he knew that at eight he was much too old to be having a nurse who babied him and wanted always to lead him around by the hand as though he were not capable of looking after himself. But he was used by now to his mother being busy and having no time to look after him, or stay in and sit with him at night until he went to sleep. She had come to rely more and more upon Nanny to take her place, and when his father, Colonel Brown, once suggested that it might perhaps be time for Nanny to be leaving, his mother could not bear to think of sending her away, and so of course she had stayed.

If he was in bed, then perhaps he was sick, and if he was sick, perhaps his mother would be with him more when she came home and found out. Maybe now they would even give him the wish he had had for so long and let him have a cat all of his own to keep in his room and sleep curled up at the foot of his bed, and perhaps even crawl under the covers with him and snuggle in his arms on nights that were cold.

He had wanted a cat ever since he could remember, which was many years ago at the age of four – when he had gone to stay on a farm near Gerrards Cross, and had been taken into the kitchen and shown a basketful of kittens, orange and white balls of fluff, and the ginger-coloured mother who beamed with pride until her face was quite as broad as it was long, and licked them over with her tongue one after the other. He was allowed to put his hand on her. She was soft and warm, and a queer kind of throbbing was going on inside of her, which later he learned was called purring, and meant that she was comfortable and happy.

From then on he dearly wished for a cat of his own.

However, he was not allowed to have one.

They lived in a small flat in a Mews off Cavendish Square. Peter's father, Colonel Brown, who came home occasionally on leave, did not mind if Peter had a cat, but his mother said that there was enough dust and dirt from the street in a small place, and not enough room to move around without having a cat in, and besides, Scotch Nanny didn't like cats and was afraid of them. It was important to Peter's mother that Nanny be humoured in the matter of cats, so that she would stay and look after Peter.

All of these things Peter knew and understood and put up with because that was how it was in his world. However, this did not stop his heart from being heavy, because his mother, who was young and beautiful, never seemed to have much time for him, or prevent him yearning hungrily for a cat of his own.

He was friends with all or most of the cats on the Square, the big black one with the white patch on his chest and green eyes as large around as shilling pieces, who belonged to the caretaker of the little garden in Cavendish Square close to the Mews, the two greys who sat unblinking in the window of Number 5 throughout most of the day, the ginger cat with the green eyes who belonged to Mrs Bobbit, the caretaker who lived down in the basement of Number 11, the tortoiseshell cat with the drooping ear next door, and the Boie de Rose Persian who slept on a cushion in the window of Number 27 most of the time, but who was brought into the Square for an airing on clear warm days.

And then of course there were the countless strays who inhabited the alley and the bombed-out house behind the Mews, or squeezed through the railings into the park, tigers and tabbies, black and whites and lemon yellows, tawnies and brindles, slipping in and out behind the dustbins, packets of waste paper, and garbage containers, fighters, yowlers, slinkers, scavengers, homeless waifs, old 'uns, and kittens, going nervously about the difficult business of gaining a living from the harsh and heedless city.

These were the ones that Peter was always dragging home, sometimes kicking and clawing in terror under his arm, or limp and more than willing to go where it was warm and there might be a meal and the friendly touch of a human hand.

Once in a while, when he evaded Nanny, he managed to smuggle one into the cupboard of the nursery and keep it for as much as two whole days and nights before it was discovered.

Then Nanny, who had her orders from Mrs Brown as to what she was to do when a cat was found on the premises, would open the door on to the Mews and cry – "Out! Scat, you dirty thing!" or fetch a broom with which to chase it. Or if that did not work and the stowaway merely cowered in a corner, she would pick it up by the scruff of the neck, hold it away from her, and fling it out into the street. After that, she would punish Peter, though he could not be worse hurt than he was through losing his new friend and remembering how happy it had been safe in his arms.

Peter had even learned not to cry any more when this happened. One could cry inside of one without making a sound, he had found out.

He was feeling that way now that he was sick, only this was different because he seemed to want to cry out this time, but found that he could not utter a sound. He did not know why this should be except it was a part of the queer way things had been since whatever it was had happened to him when he had darted away from Nanny who was talking to the postman, and run across the road after the striped kitten.

Actually, it was a coal lorry that had come speeding around the corner of the Square that had struck Peter and knocked him down just as he had stepped off the kerb without looking and had run in front of it, but what happened after that, the hue and cry, the people that gathered after the accident, Nanny's crying and wailing, the policeman who picked him up and carried him into the house, the sending for the doctor and the trying to find his mother, and later, the trip to the hospital, Peter was not to know for a long, long time. So many strange things were to happen to him first.

For, unquestionably, events seemed to be taking an odd turn what with night appearing to follow day at such rapid intervals that it was almost like being at the cinema with the screen going all dark and light and Nanny's face seeming to be on top of him first and then sliding away into the distance only to return once more with the lenses of her spectacles shining like the headlamps of an approaching motor-car.

But that something really queer was about to take place Peter knew when after Nanny had faded into the distance and his bed had seemed to rock like a little boat in the waves and when she had begun to return again, it was no longer the face of Nanny, but that of the tabby striped kitten that had been washing itself by the park railings and that he had wanted to catch and hug.

Indeed, it was this dear little cat now grown to enormous size, sitting at his bedside smiling at him in a friendly manner, its eyes as large as soup tureens, large, luminous, and shiny, and resembling Nanny's spectacles in that he could see himself mirrored in them.

But what was puzzling to him was that although he knew it to be himself reflected therein, still it did not seem to look like him at all as he was accustomed to seeing himself when he passed the tall cheval mirror in the hallway, or even in Nanny's glasses in which he could frequently catch a reflection of his curly head of close-cropped auburn hair, round eyes, upturned button nose, stubborn chin, and cheeks as red-and-white and rounded as two crab-apples.

At first Peter did not try to make out exactly who or what he looked like because it was pleasant and soothing just to lose himself in the cool green pools of the kitten's eyes, so calm and deep and clear that it seemed like swimming about in an emerald lake. It felt delightful to be there bathed in the beautiful colour and surrounded by the warmth of the smile of the kitten.

But then soon he began to notice the effect it was beginning to have upon him.

Sometimes the picture would be hazy and then for a moment it would grow quite clear so that he could see how the shape of his head had altered and not only the shape but the colour. For whereas he was familiar with the reddish-brown curly hair and apple cheeks, his fur now seemed to be quite short, straight and snow white.

"Why," said Peter to himself, "I said 'fur' instead of hair. What a strange thing to do. It must be looking into the cat's eyes that is changing me into a cat, if that is what is happening."

But he continued to look there because he found that for the moment he could not take his gaze elsewhere, and when it grew hazy, his image seemed to quiver as though things were happening to it from inside, and each time it grew clear he noted new details, the queerly slanted eyes that were now no longer grey but a light blue, the nose that had changed from an uptilted little sixpenny-bit into a rose-pink triangle leading to a mouth that was no more like his than anything he could think of. It now curved downwards over long, sharp white teeth, and from either side sprouted sets of enormous, bristly white whiskers.

The head was square, the slant-set eyes large and staring, and the sharp-pointed ears stood up like dormers. "Oh," thought Peter, "that is how I would look if I were a cat. How I wish I were one." And then he closed his eyes, because this queer, unusual image of himself was now so clear and unmistakable that it was a little frightening. To wish to be a cat was one thing. To seem very much to be one was quite another.

When he opened them, it seemed for a moment as if he had broken the spell of the cat's-eye mirror, for he was able to avoid staring into it and instead managed to look down at his paws. They were pure white, large and furred, with quaint, soft pinkish pads on the underside and claws curved like Turkish swords and needle-sharp at the end.

To his astonishment, Peter saw that he was no longer lying in the bed, but on top of it. His whole body, now long and slender, was just as soft and white as the ermine muff his mother used to carry when she dressed up and went out in the winter, and what seemed to be a blank and eyeless snake curving, moving, twitching and lashing at the end of it was his own tail. From ear-tip to tail-tip he was clad in spotless white fur.

The tiger-striped kitten, who with his smile and staring

eyes had apparently worked this mischief on him, had vanished and was nowhere to be seen. Instead there was only Nanny, ten times larger than she had ever appeared before, standing over the bed shouting in a voice so loud that it hurt his ears –

"Drat the child! He's dragged in anither stray off the street! Shoo! Scat! Get out!"

Peter cried out – "But, Nanny! I'm Peter. I'm not a cat. Nanny, don't, please!"

"Rail at me, will ye?" Nanny bellowed. "'Tis the broom I'll take to ye then." She ran down the hall, and returned carrying the broom. "Now then. Out ye go!"

Peter was cold with fright. He could only cower down at the end of the bed while Nanny beat at him with the broom, and cry: "Nanny, Nanny, no, no! Oh, Nanny!"

"I'll miaow you!" Nanny stormed, dropped the broom, and picked Peter up by the scruff of the neck so that he hung there from her hand, front and hind legs kicking, while he cried miserably.

Holding him as far away from her as she could, Nanny ran down the hallway muttering, "And it's to bed without any supper for Peter when I find him. How often have I told him he's no' to bring in any more cats!" until she reached the ground floor entrance to the flat from the Mews.

Then she pitched Peter out into the street and slammed the door shut.

CHAPTER TWO

Flight from Cavendish Square

IT WAS MISERABLY cold and wet out in the Mews, for when the sun had gone down a chill had come into the air, clouds had formed, and it had begun to rain in a heavy, soaking, steady downpour.

Locked outside, Peter let out such a howl of anguish and fright that the woman who lived opposite said to her husband, "Goodness, did you hear that? It sounded just like a child!"

He parted the curtains to look, and Peter cried – or thought he cried to him – "Oh, let me in! Please let me in! Nanny's put me out, me-out, me-out!"

Peter then heard the husband say as he dropped the curtains: "It's only another stray, a big white tom. Where do they all come from? You never get a minute's rest with their yowling and caterwauling. Ah there! Boo! Scat! Go 'way!"

The boy who delivered the evening newspapers came by on his bicycle, and hearing the shouting to scare away the cat outside the door, decided to assist him in the hope of earning a tip.

He rode his bicycle straight at Peter, crying "Oi! Garn!

Scat! Get along there!" and then, leaning from the saddle, struck Peter across the back with a folded-up newspaper. Peter ran blindly from this assault, and a moment later, with a roar and a rumble, something enormous and seemingly as big as a house went by on wheels, throwing up a curling wave of muddy water that struck him in the flank as he scampered down the Mews into Cavendish Square, soaking right through his fur to the skin underneath.

He had not yet had time even to look about him and see what kind of a world this was into which he had been so rudely and suddenly catapulted.

It was like none he had ever encountered before, and it struck terror to his heart.

It was a place that seemed to consist wholly of blind feet clad in heavy boots or clicking high heels, and supplied with legs that rose up out of them and vanished into the dark, rainy night above, all rushing hither and thither, unseeing and unheeding. Equally blind but infinitely more dangerous were wheels of enormous size that whizzed, rumbled or thundered by always in twos, one behind the other. To be caught beneath one of those meant to be squashed flatter than the leopard-skin rug in their living-room.

Not that the feet weren't of sufficient danger to one in the situation in which Peter now found himself, cowering on the wet, glistening pavement of the Square, standing on all fours, and not quite ten inches high. Eyeless, and thus unable to see where they were going, the shoes came slashing and hurtling by from all directions, and no pair at the same pace.

One of them stepped on his tail, and a new and agonising pain he had never felt before shot through Peter and forced an angry and terrified scream from his throat. The foot that had done this performed an odd kind of slithering and sliding dance with its partner for a moment, while down from the darkness above thundered a voice: "Dash the beast! I might have broken my neck over him. Go on! Clear out of here before somebody hurts himself!"

And the partner foot leaped from the pavement and flung itself at Peter's ribs and shoulders where it landed a numbing blow.

In sheer terror Peter began to run now, without knowing where he was going or what the end was to be.

It seemed as though suddenly all London had become his enemy, and everything that had formerly been so friendly, interesting and exciting, the sounds, the smells, the gleam of lights from the shop windows, the voices of people, and the rush and bustle of traffic in the streets, all added to the panic that began to grip him.

For while he knew that he still thought and felt like and *was* Peter, yet he was no longer the old Peter he used to know who went about on two legs and was tall enough to be able to reach things down from over the fireplace without standing on tiptoes. Oh no. That Peter was gone and in his place was one who was running on all fours, his ears thrown back and flattened against his head, his tail standing straight out behind him, dashing wildly, hardly looking or knowing where he was going through the rainswept streets of London.

Already he was far from his own neighbourhood or anything that might have looked familiar, and racing now through brightly lighted and crowded thoroughfares, now through pitch-black alleys and crooked lanes. Everything was terrifying to him and filled him with fear.

There was, for instance, the dreadful business of the rain.

When Peter had been a boy, he had loved the rain and had been happiest when he had been out in it. He liked the feel of it on his cheeks and on his hair, the rushing sounds it made tumbling down from the sky, and the cool, soft touch of it as it splashed on to his face and then ran down the end of his nose in little droplets that he could catch and taste by sticking out his lower lip.

But now that he seemed to be a cat, the rain was almost unbearable.

It soaked through his thick fur, leaving it matted and bedraggled, the hairs clinging together in patches so that all their power to give warmth and protection was destroyed and the cold wind that was now lashing the rain against the sides of the shops and houses penetrated easily to his sensitive skin, and in spite of the fact that he was tearing along at top speed he felt chilled to the marrow.

Too, the little pads at the bottom of his feet were thin and picked up the feel of the cold and damp.

He did not know what he was running away from the

most – the rain, the blows and bruises, or the fear of the thing that was happening to him.

But he could not stop to rest or find shelter even when he felt so tired from running that he thought he could not move another step. For everyone and everything in the city seemed to be against him.

Once he paused to catch his breath beneath a kind of chute leading from a wagon and which served to keep the rain off him somewhat, when with a sudden terrible rushing roar like a landslide of stones and boulders rolling down a mountainside, coal began to pour down the chute from the tail-gate in the wagon, and in an instant Peter was choking and covered with black coal dust.

It worked itself into his soaked fur, streaking it with black, and got into his eyes and nose and mouth and lungs. And besides, the awful noise started his heart to beating in panic again. He had never been afraid of noises before, not even the big ones like bombs and cannon fire when he had been a little boy in the blitz.

He had not yet had time to be aware that sound had quite a different meaning to him now. When noises were too loud it was like being beaten about the head and he could now hear dozens of new ones he had never heard before. The effect of a really thunderous one was to make him forget everything and rush off in a blind panic to get away from it so that they would not hurt his ears and head any more.

And so he darted away again to stop for a moment under

a brightly lighted canopy where at least he was out of the dreadful rain. But even this respite did not last long, for a girl's voice from high above him complained:

"Oh! That filthy beast! He's rubbed up against me, and look what he's done to my new dress!"

It was true. Peter had accidentally come too close to her, and now there was a streak of wet coal grime at the bottom of her party gown. Again the hoarse cries of "Shoo! Scat! Get out! Pack off! Go 'way!" were raised against him, and once more the angry feet came charging at him, this time joined by several umbrella handles that came down from above and sought to strike him.

To escape them, shivering and shaking, his heart beating wildly from fright and weariness, Peter ran under an automobile standing at the kerb where they could not reach him.

It was to be only a temporary sanctuary from rain and pursuit, and an unhappy one at that, as the water was now pouring through the gutters in torrents. For the next moment from directly over Peter's head, there sounded the most appalling and ear-splitting series of explosions mingled with a grinding and clashing of metals as well as a shattering wail of the horn. Hot oil and petrol dripped down on Peter, who was nearly numb with terror from the shock of the noise. Summoning strength from he knew not where, he darted off again, and just in time, as the car started to move.

He seemed to have struck a kind of second wind of panic strength, for he ran and ran and ran, bearing towards the darker and more twisted streets where there was less wheeled traffic to menace him and less likely to be humans abroad to abuse him.

And thus he passed on into the poorer section where the streets were dirtier and horrible smells arose from the gutters to poison his nostrils and make him feel sick, mingled with the odour of coffee and tea and spices that came from the closed-up shops. And nowhere was there any shelter, or friendly human voice, or hand stretched forth to help him.

Hunger was now added to the torments that beset him, hunger and the knowledge that he was fast approaching the end of his strength. But rather than stop running and face new dangers, Peter was determined to keep on until he dropped. Then he would lie there until he died.

He ran. He stopped. He started again. He faltered and kept on. He thought his eyes would burst from his head, and his chest was burning from his effort to draw breath. But ever when he came to pause, something happened to drive him on – a door banging, a shout, a sign waving in the wind, some new noise assaulting his sensitive ears, dark threatening shapes of buildings, a policeman glistening in his tall helmet and rain cape, hideous bursts of music from wireless sets in upper-storey windows, a cabbage flung at him that went bounding along the pavement like a head without a body, drunken feet staggering out of a pub door, a bottle thrown that crashed into a hundred pieces on the pavement close to him and showered him with glass.

He kept on as best he could, but running only weakly now as exhaustion crept up on him.

But the neighbourhood had changed again, the little shops and the lighted upstairs windows were gone, and Peter now entered a forbidding area of huge black sprawling buildings, of blank walls and deserted streets, of barred doors and iron gates, and long, wet, slippery steel rails he knew were railway tracks.

The yellow street lamps shone wetly on the towering sides of the warehouses and behind them the docks and the sides of great ships in the Pool, for it was to this section of London down by the Thames that Peter's wild flight had taken him.

And there, just as he felt that he could not run or stagger another step, Peter came upon a building in which the street light showed the door standing slightly ajar. And the next moment he had slipped inside.

It was a huge warehouse piled high with sacks of grain, which gave forth a warm, comfortable, sweetish smell. There was straw on the floor and the sacks were firm and dry.

Using his sharp, curved claws to help him, Peter pulled himself up on to a layer of sacks. The rough jute felt good against his soaked fur and skin. With another sack against his back, it was almost warm. His limbs trembling with weariness, he stretched out and closed his eyes.

At that moment a voice close to him said: "Trespassing, eh? All right, my lad. Outside. Come on. Quick! Out you go!"

It was not a human voice, yet Peter understood him perfectly. He opened his eyes. Although there was no illumination in the warehouse, he found he could see clearly by the light of the street lamp outside.

The speaker was a big yellow tomcat with a long, lean, stringy body, a large head as square as a tiger's, and an ugly, heavy scar running straight across his nose.

Peter said: "Please, I can't. Mayn't I stay here a little while? I'm so tired—"

The cat looked at him out of hard yellow eyes and growled, "You heard me, chum. I don't like your looks. Pack off!"

"But I'm not hurting anything," Peter protested. "All I want to do is rest a little and get dry. Honestly, I won't touch a thing—"

"You won't touch a thing," mocked the yellow cat. "That's rich. I'll wager you won't. I work here, son. We don't allow strangers about these premises. Now get out before I knock you out."

"I won't," said Peter, his stubborn streak suddenly showing itself.

"Oh, you won't, won't you?" said the yellow tom softly, and gave a low growl. Then, before Peter's eyes, he began to swell as though somebody were pumping him up with a bicycle pump. Larger and larger he grew, all lumpy, crooked and out of plumb.

Peter continued to protest: "I won't go. There's plenty of room in here, and besides—" but that was as far as he got, for with a scream of rage the yellow cat launched his attack.

His first lightning buffet to Peter's head knocked him off the pile of sacks on to the ground, his second sent him rolling over and over. Peter had never dreamed that anything or anyone his size could hit so hard. His head was reeling from the two blows, and he was sick and dizzy. The floor seemed to be spinning around him; he tried to stand up, but his legs gave way and he fell over on his side, and at that moment the yellow tom, teeth bared, hurled himself upon him.

What saved Peter was that he was so limp from the first punishment he had taken that he gave with the force of the attack, so that the big bully rolled with him towards the door. Nevertheless he felt teeth sink into his ear and the needle-sharp claws rip furrows in his side. Kick, kick, kick, one-two-three, and it was like thirty knife thrusts tearing his skin. More blows rained upon his bruised skull. Over and over they rolled, until suddenly they were out of the door and in the street.

Half blinded by the blood that had run into his eyes, Peter felt rather than saw the yellow cat stalk back to the warehouse door, but he heard his hard, mocking voice saying: "And don't come back. Because the next time you do, I'll surely kill you."

The water running in the gutter helped to revive him a little, but only for a moment. He knew that he was bleeding from many wounds; he could hardly see out of his eyes, there was a rip in his ear, and he felt as though every bone in his body was broken. He dragged himself on a hundred yards or so. There was a hoarding advertising Bovril a little further down the street, and he tried to reach it to crawl behind it, but his strength and his senses failed him before he got there. He fell over on his side by a pillar box, with the rain pouring down in torrents and bounding up from the pavement in glistening drops. And there Peter lay quite still.

CHAPTER THREE

The Emperor's Bed

WHEN PETER OPENED his eyes again, it was daylight and he knew that he was not dead. He was also aware of something strange, namely that he was no longer in the same place where he had fallen the night before shortly before he had lost his senses.

He remembered that there had been a hoarding with a poster, a pillar box, and a long, low wall, and now there were none of these to be seen. Instead, he found himself lying on a soft mattress on an enormous bed that had a red silk cover over it and a huge canopy at one end with folds of yellow silk coming down from a sort of oval with the single letter 'N' on it, written in a manner and with a kind of a crown over it that Peter found vaguely familiar.

But now he was only concerned with the wonderful comfort of the great bed, the fact that he was warm and dry, even though he ached from head to foot, and wondering how he had got to where he was.

For now that his eyes were fully opened, he noticed that he was in a dark, high-ceilinged chamber into which only a little light filtered from a small grimy window at the top with one pane out – it was really more a bin than a chamber, because it had no door and it was filled with furniture of every description, most of it covered with dust sheets, and piled to the ceilings, though in some cases the covers had slipped down and you could see the gilt and the brocade coverings of chairs and sofas. There were a lot of cobwebs and spider webs about, and it smelled musty and dusty.

All the horrors of the night before came back to Peter, the pursuit, the noises, the hounding, and the fright, the terrible mauling he had suffered at the hands of the yellow tomcat and, above all, his plight. Turned into a cat in some mysterious manner and thrown out into the street by Nanny by mistake – how was she to know that he was really Peter? – he might never again see his mother and father, his home, and Scotch Nanny from Glasgow who, except for hating cats, was a dear Nanny and good to him within the limits of a grown-up. And yet the wonderful feel of the bed and the soft silk under him was such that he could not resist a stretch, even though it hurt him dreadfully, and as he did so, to his surprise a small motor seemed to come alive in his throat and began to throb.

From somewhere behind him a soft voice said, "Ah well, that's better. I'm glad you're alive. I wasn't sure at all. But I say, you *are* a mess!"

Startled, for the memory of his encounter with the yellow cat was still fresh, Peter rolled over and beheld the speaker squatted down comfortably beside him, her legs tucked under her, tail nicely wrapped around. She was a thin tabby with a part-white face and throat that gave her a most sweet and gentle aspect heightened by the lively and kind expression in her luminous eyes that were grey-green, flecked with gold.

She was so thin, Peter noticed, that she was really nothing but skin and bones, and yet there was a kind of tender and rakish gallantry in her very boniness that was not unbecoming to her. For the rest, she was spotlessly clean, particularly the white patch at her breast, which gleamed like ermine and (along with her remark) made Peter acutely conscious for the first time of his own condition. She was quite right. He was a mess.

His fur was dirty, matted with blood and streaked with mud and coal dust. To look at him, no one would ever have known he had once been a snow-white cat, much less a small boy.

He said to the tabby, "I'm sorry. I'll go away as soon as I am able. I don't know how I got here. I thought I was going to die in the street."

"You might have," she said. "I found you and brought you here. I don't think you're very well. Hold still, and I'll wash you a bit. Maybe that will make you feel a little better."

Although Peter had acquired the body and the appearance of a white cat, he still thought and felt like a boy, and the prospect of being washed at that moment did not at all appeal to him, and particularly not at the hands, or rather tongue, of a bone-thin, scrawny tabby cat even if she had a sweet white face and a kind and gentle expression. What he really wanted was to stretch out on the heavy silk of the covers on the comfortable bed and just stay there and sleep and sleep.

But he remembered his manners and said, "No, thank you. I don't want to trouble you. I don't really think I would care—"

But the tabby cat interrupted him with a gentle "Hush! Of course you would. And I do it very well too."

She reached out a scrawny part-white paw and laid it across his body, kindly but firmly, so that he was held down. And then with a long, stroking motion of her head and pink tongue she began to wash him, beginning at his nose, travelling up between the ears and down the back of his neck and the sides of his face.

And thereafter something strange happened to Peter, at least inside him. It was only a poor, thin, stray alley cat washing him, her rough tongue rasping against his fur and skin, but what it made him feel like was remembering when he had been very small and his mother had held him in her arms close to her. It was almost the very first thing he could remember.

He had been taking some of his early running-walking steps and had fallen and hurt himself. She had picked him up and held him tightly to her and he had cuddled his head into the warm place at her neck just beneath the chin. With her soft hands she had stroked the place where it hurt, and said, "There, mother'll make it all better. Now – it doesn't hurt *any* more!" And it hadn't. All the pain had gone, and he remembered only feeling safe and comfortable and contented.

That same warm, secure feeling was coming over him now as the little rough tongue rasped over his injured ear and down the long deep claw furrows torn into the skin of his shoulder and his side, and with each rasp, as her tongue passed over it, it seemed as though the pain that was there was erased as if by magic.

All the ache went out of his sore muscles too, as her busy tongue got around and behind and underneath, refreshing and relaxing them, and a most delicious kind of sleepiness began to steal over him. After all the dreadful things that had happened to him, it was so good to be cared for. He half expected to hear her say, "See, mother's making it all better! There! Now it doesn't hurt any more..."

But she didn't. She only kept on washing in a wonderful and soothing rhythm, and shortly Peter felt his own head moving in a kind of drowsy way in time with hers; the little motor of contentment was throbbing in his throat. Soon he nodded and went fast asleep.

When he awoke it was much later, because the light coming in through the grimy bit of window was quite different; the sun must have been well up in the sky, for a beam of it came in through a clear spot in the pane and made a little pool of brightness on the red silk cover of the enormous bed.

Peter rolled over into the middle of it and saw that he

looked almost respectable again. Most of the coal grime and mud was off him, his white fur was dry and fluffed and now served again to hide and keep the air away from the ugly scars and scratches on his body. He felt that his torn ear had a droop to it, but it no longer hurt him and was quite dry and clean.

There was no sign of the tabby cat. Peter tried to stand up and stretch, but found that his legs were queerly wobbly and that he could not quite make it. And then he realised that he was weak with hunger as well as loss of blood, and that if he did not get something to eat soon he must surely perish. When was it he had last eaten? Why, ages ago, yesterday or the day before, Nanny had give him an egg and some greens, a little fruit jelly, and a glass of milk for lunch. It made him quite dizzy to think of it. When would he ever eat again?

Just then he heard a little soft, singing sound, a kind of musical call – "Errrp, purrrrrrow, urrrrrrp!" – that he found somehow extraordinarily sweet and thrilling. He turned to the direction from which it was coming and was just in time to see the tabby cat leap in through the space between the slats at the end of the bin. She was carrying something in her mouth.

In an instant she had jumped up on to the bed alongside him and laid it down.

"Ah," she said, "that's better. Feeling a little more fit after your sleep. Care to have a bit of mouse? I just caught it down the aisle near the lift. It's really quite fresh. I wouldn't mind sharing it with you. I could stand a snack myself. There you are. You have a go at it first."

"Oh, n-no... No-no, thank you," said Peter in horror. "N-not mouse. I couldn't—"

"Why," asked the tabby cat in great surprise, and with just a touch of indignation added, "What's the matter with mouse?"

She had been so kind and he was so glad to see her again that Peter was most anxious not to hurt her feelings.

"Why, n-nothing, I'm sure. It's... well, it's just that I've never eaten one."

"Never eaten one?" The tabby's green eyes opened so wide that the flecks of gold therein almost dazzled Peter. "Well, I never! Not eaten one! You pampered, indoor, lap and parlour cats! I suppose it's been fresh chopped liver and cat food out of a tin. You needn't tell me. I've had plenty of it in my day. Well, when you're off on your own and on the town with nobody giving you charity saucers of cream or left-over titbits, you soon learn to alter your tastes. And there's no time like the present to begin. So hop to it, my lad, and get acquainted with mouse. You need a little something to set you up again."

And with this she pushed the mouse over to him with her paw and then stood over Peter, eyeing him. There was a quiet forcefulness and gentle determination in her demeanour that made Peter a little afraid for a moment that if he didn't do as she said, she might become angry. And besides, he had been taught that when people offered to share something with you at a sacrifice to themselves, it was not considered kind or polite to refuse.

"You begin at the head," the tabby cat declared firmly.

Peter closed his eyes and took a small and tentative nibble.

To his intense surprise, it was simply delicious.

It was so good that before he realised it, Peter had eaten it up from the beginning of its nose to the very end of its tail. And only then did he experience a sudden pang of remorse at what he had done in his moment of greediness. He had very likely eaten his benefactress's ration for the week. And by the look of her thin body and the ribs sticking through her fur, it had been longer than that since she had had a solid meal herself.

But she did not seem to mind in the least. On the contrary, she appeared to be pleased with him as she beamed down at him and said, "There, that wasn't so bad, was it? My tail, but you *were* hungry!"

Peter said, "I'm sorry. I'm afraid I've eaten your dinner."

The tabby smiled cheerfully. "Don't give it another thought, laddie! Plenty more where that one came from." But even though the smile and the voice were cheerful, yet Peter detected a certain wan quality about it that told him that this was not so, and that she had indeed made a great sacrifice for him, generously and with sweet grace.

She was eyeing him curiously now, it seemed to Peter almost as though she was expecting something of him, but he did not know what it was and so just lay quietly enjoying the feeling of being fed once again. The tabby opened her mouth as though she were going to say something, but then apparently thought better of it, turned, and gave her back a couple of quick licks.

Peter felt as if something he did not quite understand had sprung up to come between them, something awkward. To cover his own embarrassment about it, he asked: "Where am I – I mean, where are we?"

"Oh," said the tabby, "this is where I live. Temporarily, of course. You know how it is with us, and if you don't, you'll soon find out. Though I must say it's months since I've been disturbed here. I know a secret way in. It's a warehouse where they store furniture for people. I picked this room because I liked the bed. There are lots of others."

Now Peter remembered having learned in school what the crown and the 'N' stood for, and couldn't resist showing off. He said, "The bed must have belonged to Napoleon, once. That's his initial up there, and the crown. He was a great emperor."

The tabby did not appear to be at all impressed. She merely remarked, "Was he, now? He must have been enormously large to want a bed this size. Still – I must say it is comfortable, and I don't suppose he has any further use for it, for he hasn't been here to fetch it in the last three months and neither has anybody else. You're quite welcome to stay here as long as you like. I gather you've been turned out. Who was it mauled you? You were more than half dead when I found you last night lying in the street and dragged you in here."

Peter told the tabby of his encounter with the yellow tomcat in the grain warehouse down by the docks. She listened to his tale with alert and evident sympathy, and when he had finished, nodded and said:

"Oh dear! Yes, that would be Dempsey. He's the best fighter on the docks from Wapping all the way down to Limehouse Reach. Everybody steers clear of Dempsey. I say, you did have a nerve, telling him off! I admire you for that even if it was foolhardy. No house pets are much good at rough-and-tumble, and particularly against a champion like Dempsey."

Peter liked the tabby's admiration, he found, and swelled a little with it. He wished that he had managed to give Dempsey just one stiff blow to remember him by, and thought that perhaps some time he would. But then he recalled the big tom's last words: "And don't come back. Because next time you do, I'll surely kill you," and felt a little sick, particularly when he thought of the powerful and lightning-like buffets of those terrible paws that had so quickly robbed him of his senses and laid him open for the final attack which but for a bit of luck might have finished him. Assuredly he too would steer clear of Dempsey, but to the tabby he said:

"Oh, he wasn't so much. If I hadn't been so tired from running—"

The tabby smiled enigmatically. "Running from what, laddie?"

But before Peter could reply, she said: "Never mind, I know how it is. When you first find yourself on your own, *everything* frightens you. And don't think that *everybody* doesn't run. It's nothing to be ashamed of. By the way, what is your name?"

Peter told her. She said, "Hm… Mine's Jennie. I'd like to hear your story. Care to tell it?"

Peter very much wanted to do so. But he found suddenly that he was a little timid because he was not at all sure how it would sound, and, even more important, whether the tabby would believe him and how she would take it. For it was certainly going to be a most odd tale.

Chapter Four

A Story is Told

BY AND LARGE, Peter made about as bad a beginning as could be when he said:

"I'm not really a cat, I'm a little boy. I mean actually, not *so* little. I'm eight."

"You're what?" Jennie gave a long, low growl, and her tail fluffed up to twice its size.

Peter could not imagine what he had said to make her angry, and he repeated hesitantly, "A boy—"

The tabby's tail swelled another size larger and twitched nervously. Her eyes seemed to shoot sparks as she hissed: "I *hate* people!"

"Oh!" said Peter, for he was suddenly full of sympathy and understanding for the poor thin little tabby who had been so kind to him. "Somebody must have been horrible to you. But I *love* cats!"

Jennie looked mollified, and her tail began to subside. "Of course," she said, "it's just your imagination. I should have known. We're always imagining things, like a leaf blowing in the wind being a mouse, or if there's no leaf there at all, then we can imagine one, and when we've

44

imagined it, go right on from there and imagine it isn't a leaf at all but a mouse, or if we like, a whole lot of mice, and then we start pouncing on them. You just like to imagine that you're a little boy, though what kind of a game you can make out of *that* I can't see. Still—"

"Oh, please," said Peter, interrupting. He could feel somehow that the tabby very much didn't want him to be a boy, and yet, even at the risk of offending her, he knew that he must tell her the truth. "Please, I'm so sorry, but it *is* so. You must believe me. My name is Peter Brown, and I live in a flat with my mother and father and Nanny, in a house at Number 1A, Cavendish Mews. Or at least I *did* live there before—"

"Oh, come now," protested Jennie, "don't be silly. Anybody can see that you look like a cat, you feel like a cat, you smell like a cat, you purr like a cat, and you—" But here her voice trailed off into silence for a moment and her eyes grew wide again. "Oh dear," she said then. "But there *is* something the matter. I've felt it all along. You don't *act* like a cat—"

"Of course not," Peter said, relieved that he might be believed at last.

But the tabby, her eyes growing wider and wider, wasn't listening. She was going back over her acquaintance with Peter and enumerating the odd things that had happened since she had found him exhausted, wounded and half dead in the alley and had dragged him to her home, for what reason she did not know.

"You told off Dempsey, and right on his own premises, where he *works*. No sensible cat would have done that, no matter how brave. And besides, it's against the rules." She almost seemed to be ticking items off the end of her claws, though of course she wasn't. "And then you didn't want to eat mouse when you were literally starving – said you'd never had one, and then you ate it all up at one gobble, with never a thought that I might be hungry too. Not that I minded, but a real cat would never have done that. Oh, and then, of course – *that's* what I was trying to remember! You ate mouse right on the silk counterpane where you've been sleeping, and *you didn't wash after you'd finished…*"

Peter said, "Why should I? We always wash before eating. At least, Nanny always sends me into the bathroom and makes me clean my hands and face before sitting down to table."

"Well, cats don't!" declared Jennie decisively, "and it seems to me much the more sensible way. It's after you've eaten you find yourself all greasy and sticky, with milk on your whiskers and gravy all over your fur if you've been in too much of a hurry. Oh *dear*!" she ended up. "That almost proves it. But I must say I've never heard of such a thing in all my life!"

Peter thought to himself, "She is good, and she has been kind to me, but she does love to chatter." Aloud, he said, "If you would like me to tell you how it all happened, perhaps—"

"Yes, do, please," said the tabby cat and settled herself

more comfortably on the bed with her front paws tucked under her, "I should love to hear it."

And so Peter began from the beginning and told her the whole story of what had happened to him.

Or rather he began away back before it began, really, and told her about his home in the Mews near the square and the little garden there inside the iron railings where Nanny took him to play every day after school when the weather was fine, and about his father who was a Colonel in the Guards and was away from home most of the time, first during the war when he was in Egypt and Italy, and then in France and Germany, and he hardly saw him at all, and then later in peacetime when he would come home now and then wearing a most beautiful uniform with blue trousers that had a red stripe down the side, except that as soon as he got into the house he went right into his room and changed it for an old brown tweed suit which wasn't nearly as interesting or exciting.

Sometimes he stayed a little while for a chat or a romp with Peter, but usually he went off with Peter's mother with golf clubs or fishing tackle in the car and they would stay away for days at a time. He would be left with only Cook and Nanny in the flat and it wasn't much fun being alone, for even when he was with friends in the daytime, playing or visiting, it got very lonely at night without his father and mother. When they weren't away on a trip together, they would dress up every evening and go out. And that was when he wished most that he had a cat of his own that would curl up at the foot of his bed, or cuddle, or play games just with him.

And he told the tabby all about his mother, how young and beautiful she was, so tall and slender, with light-coloured hair as soft as silk, that was the colour of the sunshine when it came in slantwise through the nursery window in the late afternoon, and how blue were her eyes and dark her lashes.

But particularly he remembered and told Jennie how good she smelled when she came in to say goodnight to him before going out for the evening, for when Peter's father was away she was unhappy and bored and went off with friends a great deal seeking amusement.

It was always when he loved her most, Peter explained, when she came in looking and smelling like an angel, with clouds of beautiful materials around her, and her hair so soft and fragrant, when he so much wanted to be held to her, that she left him and went away.

Jennie nodded. "Mmmmm. I know. Perfume. I love things that smell good."

She was indignant when Peter came to the part about not being allowed to have a cat because of the mess it might make around a small flat, and said, "Mess, indeed! We never make messes, unless we're provoked, and then we do it on purpose. And can't we just—!" But strangely enough she took Nanny's part when Peter reached the point in his story about Nanny being afraid of cats and not liking them.

"There are people who don't, you know," she explained,

when Peter expressed surprise, "and we can understand and respect them for it. Sometimes we like to tease them a little by rubbing up against them, or getting into their laps just to see them jump. They can't help it any more than we can help not liking certain kinds of people and not wanting to have anything to do with them. But at least we know where we stand when we come across someone like your Nanny. It's the people who love us, or say they love us and then hurt us, who…"

She did not finish the sentence, but turned away quickly, sat up, and began to wash violently down her back. But before she did, Peter thought that he had noticed the shine of tears in her eyes, though of course it couldn't be so, since he had never heard of cats shedding tears. It was only later he was to learn that they could both laugh and cry.

Nevertheless, he felt that the tabby must be nursing some secret hurt, perhaps like his own, and in the hopes of taking her mind away from something sad, he launched into a description of the events leading up to his strange and mysterious transformation.

He began by telling about the tiger-striped kitten sunning and washing herself by the little garden in the centre of the square, and how he had wanted to catch her and hold her. Jennie showed immediate interest. She stopped washing and enquired: "How old was she? Was she pretty?"

"Oh yes," said Peter, "very pretty, and full of fun…"

"Prettier than I?" Jennie enquired, with seeming nonchalance.

Peter had thought she had been, for she was like a round ball of fluff as he remembered, with most proud whiskers and two white and two brown feet. But he wouldn't for anything have offended the tabby by telling her so. The truth was that for all her gentle ways and the kindly expression of her white face, Jennie was quite plain, with her small head, longish ears and slanted, half-Oriental eyes, and what with being so dreadfully thin making her bones stick out, Peter felt she was really nothing much to look at as cats went. But he was already old enough to know that one sometimes told small white lies to make people happy, and so he replied: "Oh, no! I think you're beautiful!" After all, he *had* eaten her mouse.

"Do you really?" said Jennie, and for the first time since they had met, Peter heard a small purr coming from her. To cover her confusion she gave one of her paws a few tentative licks and then with a pleased smile on her thin face, enquired: "Well, and what happened then?"

And Peter thereupon told her all the rest of the story right to the end.

When he had finished with "…and then the next thing I knew, I opened my eyes and here I am", there was a long silence. Peter felt tired from the effort of telling the story and reliving all the dreadful moments through which he had come, for he was yet far from having regained his full strength, even with rest and a meal.

Jennie, undeniably taken aback by the tale she had heard, appeared to be thinking hard, her eyes unblinking, and a faraway look in them, which, however, was not disbelief. It was clear from her demeanour that she apparently accepted Peter's word that he was not a cat really, but a little boy, and the queer circumstances that had brought this about, and that it was something else that was occupying her mind.

Finally she turned her too-small, slender head towards Peter and said: "Well, what's to be done?"

Peter said, "I don't know, I'm sure. I suppose if I am a cat, I will just have to be one—"

The tabby put her gentle paw on his and said softly, "But, Peter, don't you see, that's just it! You said yourself that you didn't feel as though you were a cat at all. If you're going to be one, you must first learn how."

"Oh dear," said Peter, who never did much enjoy having to learn things, "is there more to being a cat than just liking to eat mice and purring?"

The little puss was genuinely shocked. "Is there more?" she repeated. "You couldn't begin to imagine all the things there are! There must be hundreds. Why, if you left here right now and went out *looking* like a white cat, but *feeling* inside and thinking like a boy, I shouldn't be inclined to give you more than ten minutes before you'd be in some terrible trouble again – like last night. It isn't easy to be on your own, even if you have learned to know everything or nearly everything that a cat ought to know."

Peter hadn't thought about it that way, but there was no doubt she was right. If he had been himself in shape and form and had been locked out of the house, or had got lost from Nanny at the fun-fair, or in the park, he would have known enough to go straight up to a policeman and tell him his name and address and ask to be taken home. But he couldn't very well do this in his present condition as a white cat with a slightly droopy left ear where it had been ripped by a yellow tom named Dempsey. And what was worse, now that the tabby had called it to his attention, he was a cat and didn't know the first thing about how to behave as one. He began to feel frightened again, but different from the panic of the night before – it was a new kind of shakiness as though the bed and the ground and everything beneath his four paws was no longer very steady. He said somewhat piteously to the tabby: "Oh, Jennie – now I'm really frightened! What *shall* I do?"

She thought for a moment longer and then said, "I know! I'll teach you."

Peter felt such relief he could have cried. "Jennie dear! Would you? Could you?"

The expression on the face of the cat was positively angelic, or so Peter thought, and now she actually almost did look beautiful to him as she said: "But of course. After all, you're my responsibility. I found you and brought you here. But one thing you must promise me if I try…"

Peter said, "Oh yes, I'll promise anything—"

"First of all, do as I tell you until you can begin to look after yourself a little, but most important, never tell another soul your secret. I'll know, but nobody else needs to, because they just wouldn't understand. If we get into any kind of trouble, just let me do the talking. Never so much as hint or let on in any way to any other cat what you really are. Promise?"

Peter promised, and Jennie gave him a comradely little tap on the side of his head with her paw. Just the touch of her velvet pad and the simplicity of the caress made Peter feel happier already.

He said, "Won't you tell me *your* story now, and who you are? I know nothing about you, and you've been so good to me..."

Jennie withdrew her paw, and a look of sadness came over her gentle face as she turned away for a moment. She said, "Later, perhaps, Peter. It is hard for me to speak about it now. And besides, you might not like it at all. Since you say you are a human and really not a cat at all, you would not be able to understand the way I feel and why I will never again live with people."

"Please do tell me," Peter pleaded. "And I *will* like it, I'm sure, because I like you."

Jennie could not resist a small purr at Peter's sincerity. She said, "You are a dear—" and then fell into reflective silence for a moment. Finally she seemed to make up her mind and said:

"See here, what is really important at the moment is for you to begin to learn something about being a cat, and the sooner we begin, the better. I shudder to think what might happen to you if you were alone again. How would it be if we had a lesson first? And of course nothing is more pressing than for you to learn how to wash. Afterwards, perhaps, I will be able to tell you my story."

Peter hid his disappointment because she had been so kind to him and he did not wish to upset her. He merely said, "I'll try, though I'm not very good at lessons."

"I'll help you, Peter," Jennie reassured him, "and you'll be surprised how much better you will feel when you know how. Because a cat must not only know *how* to wash, but WHEN to wash. You see, it's something like this…"

CHAPTER FIVE

When in Doubt – Wash

"'WHEN IN DOUBT – any kind of doubt – *Wash!*' That is Rule Number 1," said Jennie. She now sat primly and a little stiffly, with her tail wrapped around her feet, near the head of the big bed beneath the Napoleon Initial and Crown, rather like a schoolmistress. But it was obvious that the role of teacher and the respectful attention Peter bestowed upon her were not unendurable, because she had a pleased expression and her eyes were again gleaming brightly.

The sun had reached its noon zenith in the sky in the world that lay outside the dark and grimy warehouse, and coming in slantwise through the small window sent a dusty shaft that fell like a theatrical spotlight about Jennie's head and shoulders as she lectured.

"If you have committed any kind of an error and anyone scolds you – wash," she was saying. "If you slip and fall off something and somebody laughs at you – wash. If you are getting the worst of an argument and want to break off hostilities until you have composed yourself, start washing. Remember, *every* cat respects another cat at her toilet. That's our first rule of social deportment, and you must also observe it.

"Whatever the situation, whatever difficulty you may be in you can't go wrong if you wash. If you come into a room full of people you do not know, and who are confusing to you, sit right down in the midst of them and start washing. They'll end up by quieting down and watching *you*. Some noise frightens you into a jump, and somebody you know saw you were frightened – begin washing immediately.

"If somebody calls you and you don't care to come and still you don't wish to make it a direct insult – wash. If you've started off to go somewhere and suddenly can't remember where it was you wanted to go, sit right down and begin brushing up a little. It will come back to you. Something hurt you? Wash it. Tired of playing with someone who has been kind enough to take time and trouble and you want to break off without hurting his or her feelings? Start washing.

"Oh, there are dozens of things! Door closed and you're burning up because no one will open it for you – have yourself a little wash and forget it. Somebody petting another cat or dog in the same room, and you are annoyed over *that* – be nonchalant; wash. Feel sad – wash away your blues. Been picked up by somebody you don't particularly fancy and who didn't smell good – wash him off immediately and pointedly where he can see you do it. Overcome by emotion – a wash will help you to get a grip on yourself again. Any time, anyhow, in any manner, for whatever purpose, wherever you are, whenever and why ever that you want to clear the air, or get a moment's respite or think things over — WASH!

"And," concluded Jennie, drawing a long breath, "of course you also wash to get clean and to keep clean."

"Goodness!" said Peter, quite worried, "I don't see how I could possibly remember them all."

"You don't have to remember any of it, actually," Jennie explained. "All that you have to remember is Rule 1: 'When in doubt — WASH!'"

Peter, who like all boys had no objection to being reasonably clean, but not *too* clean, saw the problem of washing looming up large and threatening to occupy all of his time. "It's true, I remember, you always do seem to be washing," he protested to Jennie, "I mean all cats I've seen, but I don't see why. Why do cats spend so much of their time at it?"

Jennie considered this question for a moment, and then replied, "Because it feels so good to be clean."

"Well, at any rate I shall never be capable of doing it," Peter remarked, "because I won't be able to reach places now that I am a cat and cannot use my hands. And even when I was a boy, Nanny used to have to wash my back for me…"

"Nothing of the kind," said Jennie. "The first thing you will learn is that there isn't an inch of herself of himself that a cat cannot reach to wash. If you had ever owned one of us, you would know. Now watch me. We'll begin with the back. I'll do it first, and then you come over here alongside of me and do as I do."

And with that, sitting upright, she turned her head around over her shoulder with a wonderful ease and grace, and with little short strokes of her tongue and keeping her chin down close to her body, she began to wash over and around her left shoulder blade, gradually increasing the amount of turn and the length of the stroking movement of her head until her rough, pink tongue was travelling smoothly and firmly along the region of her upper spine.

"Oh, I never could!" cried Peter, "because I cannot twist my head around as far as you can. I never know what is going on behind me unless I turn right around."

"Try," was all Jennie replied.

Peter did, and to his astonishment found that whereas when he had been a boy he had been unable to turn his head more left and right than barely to be able to look over his shoulders, now he could swivel it quite around on his neck so that he was actually gazing out behind him. And when he stuck out his tongue and moved his head in small circles as he had seen Jennie do, there he was washing around his left shoulder.

"Oh, bravo! Splendid!" applauded Jennie. "There, you see! Well done, Peter. Now turn a little more – you're bound to be a bit stiff at first – and down the spine you go!"

And indeed, down the spine, about halfway from below his neck to the middle of his back, Peter went. He was so delighted that he tried to purr and wash at the same time, and actually achieved it.

"Now," Jennie coached, "for the rest of the way down, you can help yourself and make it easier – like this. Curve your body around and go a little lower so that you are half sitting, half lying. That's it! Brace yourself against your right paw and pull your left paw in a little closer to you so that it is out of the way. There… Now, you see, that brings the rest of you nicely around in a curve where you can get at it. Finish off the left side of your back and hindquarters and then shift around and do the other side."

Peter did so, and was amazed to find with what little effort the whole of his spine and hindquarters was brought within ample reach of his busy tongue. He even essayed to have a go at his tail from this position, but found this a more elusive customer. It would keep squirming away.

Jennie smiled. "Try putting a paw on it to hold it down. The right one. You can still brace yourself with it. That's it. We'll get at the underside of it later on."

Peter was so enchanted with what he had learned that he would have gone on washing and washing the two sides of his back and flanks and quarters if Jennie hadn't said, "There, that's enough of that. There's still plenty of you left, you know. Now you must do your front and the stomach and the inside of your paws and quarters."

The front limbs and paws of course proved easy for Peter, for they were within ample reach, but when he attempted to tackle his chest, it was something else.

"Try lying down first," Jennie suggested. "After a while you'll get so supple you will be able to wash your chest sitting up just by sticking your tongue out a little more and bobbing your head. But it's easier lying down on your side. Here, like this," and she suited the action to the word and soon Peter found that he actually was succeeding in washing his chest fur just beneath his chin.

"But I can't get at my middle," he complained, for indeed the underside of his belly defied his clumsy efforts to reach it, bend and twist as he would.

Jennie smiled. "'*Can't*' catches no mice," she quoted. "That is more difficult. Watch me now. You won't do it lying on your side. Sit up a bit and rock on your tail. That's it, get your tail right under you. You can brace with either of your forepaws, or both. Now, you see, that bends you right around again and brings your stomach within reach. You'll get it with practice. It's all curves. That's why we were made that way."

Peter found it more awkward to balance than in the other position and fell over several times, but soon found that he was getting better at it and that each portion of his person that was thus made accessible to him through Jennie's knowledge, experience and teaching brought him a new enjoyment and pleasure of accomplishment. And of course Jennie's approval made him very proud.

He was forging ahead so rapidly with his lesson that she decided to see whether he could go and learn by himself. "Now how would you go about doing the inside of the hindquarter?" she asked.

"Oh, that's easy," Peter cried. But it wasn't at all. In

fact the more he tried and strained and reached and curved, the further away did his hind leg seem to go. He tried first the right and then the left, and finally got himself tangled in such a heap of legs, paws and tail that he fell right over in such a manner that Jennie had to take a few quick dabs at herself to keep from laughing.

"I can't – I mean I don't see how…" wailed Peter, "there isn't any way…"

Jennie was contrite at once and hoped Peter had not seen she had been amused. "Oh, I'm sorry," she declared. "That wasn't fair of me. There is, but it's most difficult, and you have to know how. It took me the longest time when my mother tried to show me. Here, does this suggest anything to you – Leg of Mutton? I'm sure you've seen it dozens of times," and she assumed an odd position with her right leg sticking straight up in the air and somehow close to her head, almost like the contortionist that Peter had seen at the circus at Olympia who had twisted himself right around so that his head came down between his legs. He was sure that he could never do it.

Peter tried to imitate Jennie but only succeeded in winding himself into a worse knot. Jennie came to his rescue once more. "See here," she said, "let's try it by counts, one stage at a time. Once you've done it, you know, you'll never forget it. Now –

"One – rock on your tail." Peter rocked.

"Two – brace yourself with your left forepaw." Peter braced.

"Three – half sit, and bend your back." Peter managed that, and made himself into the letter C.

"Four – stretch out the left leg all the way. That will keep you from falling over the other side and provide a balance for the paw to push against." This too worked out exactly as Jennie described it when Peter tried it.

"Five – swing your right leg from the hip – you'll find it will go – with the foot pointing straight up into the air. Yes, like that, but *outside*, not inside the right forepaw." It went better this time. Peter got it almost up.

"Six – NOW you've got it. Hold yourself steady by bracing the right front forepaw. SO!"

Peter felt like shouting with joy. For there he was, actually sitting, leg of mutton, his hindquarter shooting up right past his cheek and the whole inside of his leg exposed. He felt that he was really doubled back on himself like the contortionist, and he wished that Nanny were there so that he could show her.

By twisting and turning a little, there was no part of him underneath that he could not reach, and he washed first one side and then, without any further instruction from Jennie, managed to reverse the position and get the left leg up, which drew forth an admiring, "Oh, you are clever!" from Jennie – "it took me just ages to learn to work the left side. It all depends whether you are left- or right-pawed, but you caught on to it immediately. Now there's only one thing more. The back of the neck, the ears and the face."

In a rush to earn more praise Peter went nearly

cross-eyed trying to get his tongue out and around to reach behind him and on top of him, and of course it wouldn't work. He cried – "Oh dear, THAT must be the most complicated of all."

"On the contrary," smiled Jennie, "it's quite the simplest. Wet the side of your front paw." Peter did so. "Now rub it around over your ears and the back of your neck."

Now it was Peter's turn to laugh at himself. "How stupid I am," he said. "That part is just the way I do it at home. Except I use a wash-rag, and Nanny stands there watching to make certain I go behind the ears."

"Well," said Jennie, "*I'm* watching you now…"

So Peter completed his bath by wetting one paw and then the other, on the side and in the middle of the pads, and washing first his ears, then both sides of his face, the back of his neck, his whiskers and even a little under his chin, and over his nose and eyes.

And now he found that having washed himself all over, from head to foot, the most wonderful feeling of comfort and relaxation had come over him. It was quite a different sensation from the time that Jennie had washed him and which had somehow taken him back to the days when he was very little and his mother was looking after him.

This time he felt a kind of glow in his skin and a sense of well-being in his muscles as though every one of them had been properly used and stretched. In the light from the last of the shaft of the sun that was just passing from the window of the storehouse he could see how his white fur glistened from the treatment he had given it, as smooth as silk and as soft.

Peter felt a delicious drowsiness. His eyes began to close, and as from a distance he heard Jennie say: "It's good to take a nap after washing. I always do. You've earned it. I'll join you, and after we've slept a little, perhaps I'll tell you my story as I promised."

Just before he dropped off to sleep, Peter felt her curl up against him, her back touching his, warm and secure, and the next moment he was off in sweet and dreamless slumber.

When he awoke, Jennie Baldrin was stretching and yawning at his side, and he joined her, imitating her movements, first putting out his forepaws as far as they would go and stretching backwards from there and then arching her back in a high inverted 'U'.

"There," Jennie said when she had done. "How do you feel now?"

"Ever so much better," Peter replied, and he really felt like a new boy, or rather cat. Then he continued, for he had not forgotten what she had promised – "Now won't you please tell me about you? Please, Jennie, I should so love to hear it…"

The tabby could not resist a small purr at Peter's sincerity, but immediately after she became serious. "Dear me," she said, "I didn't think I'd *ever* be telling of this to anyone as long as I lived. Still – since you really wish it, so be it."

And she began.

CHAPTER SIX

Jennie

"MY NAME," SAID the tabby, "as I told you, is Jennie. Jennie Baldrin. We are partly Scottish, you know—" she added with considerable satisfaction. "My mother was born in Glasgow, and so was I."

"I say 'partly' Scottish, because way back we came from the continent. Africa, I mean, and then across into Spain. Several of our branch of the family were ships' cats aboard vessels of the Spanish Armada. My mother's ancestor was wrecked on the coast of Scotland, which is how we came to settle down there. Interesting, isn't it?"

"Oh yes," replied Peter. "I've read about how Drake defeated the Spanish Armada and a storm came up and wrecked all the galleons. But I didn't know about there having been any cats…"

"Indeed," said Jennie Baldrin. "Well, there were – dozens of them. Actually we go much further back than that, Kaffir cats, you know, from Africa – Nubia, Abyssinia – places I'm sure you've heard about. Someone named Julius Caesar is supposed to have brought us to Britain in 55 to 54 B.C. But that wasn't *our* branch of the family. *We* were in Egypt two thousand years before that when, as you've no doubt read, cats were sacred. A lot of people try to be or act sacred, but we actually were, with temples and altars, and priests to look after us. I suppose you have noticed how small my head is. Egyptian strain. And then of course *this*."

And here Jennie rolled over on to her flank and held up her paws so that Peter could inspect the undersides of them. "Why, they're quite black," Peter said, referring to the pads. He then looked at his own and remarked, "Mine are all pink."

"Naturally," Jennie said, quite pleased. "Wherever you come across black pads – that's it, the Egyptian strain again. Have you ever seen the relief from the tomb of Amon-Ra in the British Museum, the one with the sacred cat on it? They say I look quite like her."

"I've been to the British Museum with Nanny," Peter said, "but I don't think I ever—"

"Ah well, never mind," Jennie went on. "It isn't really important, especially today when it is what you are that counts, though I must say it is a comfort to know *who* you are, particularly at times when everything appears to be dead set against you. If you know something about your forebears, who they were and what they did, you are not quite so likely to give up, especially if you know that once they were actually sacred and people came around asking *them* for favours. Still…" and here Jennie Baldrin paused and gave four quick washes to the end of her tail.

Peter was afraid she might not go on, so he coaxed – "Yes, and after you were born…"

"Oh," said Jennie, leaving off her washing and resuming her narrative, "we came to London from Glasgow on the train in a basket, my mother and brothers and sisters and I. We travelled at night. I didn't get to see much because I was in the basket all of the time, and anyway, my eyes weren't open yet because I was very young. That's my earliest recollection.

"We were a family of five kittens, two males and three females, and we went to live in the cellar of a boarding house in Bloomsbury. My mother was owned by a printer who had been working in Glasgow and came back to London. It was his mother who managed the boarding house in Bloomsbury. I don't know if I'm making myself clear…"

"Oh yes," said Peter, "quite!"

"Our mother was wise and good. She fed, washed, cuffed and taught us as much as she thought necessary. She was proud of our family and our strain, and said that wherever we were, *our* dignity and ancestry would bring honour to whoever might be looking after us. She most emphatically did not believe it was beneath her to be living in a boarding house or belong to a printer. Do you?"

Peter was somewhat taken aback by the unexpected question, but replied that he did not, particularly if the people were kind.

"Exactly," said Jennie, and appeared to be relieved. "Our mother said that some of us might go no higher than to be a grocer's cat, or belong to a chimney sweep or a charwoman, while others might come to live in a wealthy home in Mayfair, or even a palace. The important thing was that *they* were all people and we were who *we* were, and if there was love and respect between us, no one could ask for anything better.

"One day, when I was seven months old, it happened to me. Some people came to our house and took me away with them. I was adopted.

"How fortunate I was, or at least I thought so at the time. I went to live with a family in a house near Kensington High Street, a father, mother and little girl. And there I grew up and stayed for three years with never a cloud in the sky."

Peter asked, "What was the little girl like?"

Jennie paused while a tear moistened her eye again, but this time she did not trouble to conceal it with a wash. "She was a dear," Jennie replied. Her voice had taken on the tender tone of remembering someone who had been good and beautiful, and her glistening eyes were gazing backwards into the past. "She had long, wavy brown hair and such a sweet face. Her voice was soft and never harsh on my ears. Her name was Elizabeth, but she was called Buff, and she was ten years old. I loved her so much that just thinking about it was enough to set me to purring.

"We weren't rich, but we were quite well off. I had my own basket without a cushion in it and was allowed to sleep in Buff's room. The Pennys, for that was their last name, saw to it that I had some of the meat from their ration, and I had fish every other day and all the milk I could drink. When Buff came home from school in the afternoon I would be waiting for her at the door to jump up into her arms and rub my cheek against hers and then lie across her shoulders and she would carry me around as though she were wearing a fur."

Peter felt sad as he listened to her story, for exactly as she was telling it was how he would have wished to have had it in his own home – a sweet and friendly puss to be there when he returned, who would leap up on to his shoulder and rub against him and purr when he stroked her and be his very own.

Jennie sighed now as she told about the good times. The first thing in the morning when the maid came in to part the curtains, the little cat would leap up on to the bed, calling and purring to say good morning and begging Buff to play the pounce game which they both loved. This was the one in which the child would move the fingers of one hand under the blankets while Jennie would watch the mysterious and tantalising stirrings beneath the covers and finally rear up and land on the spot, always careful not to use her claws, and Buff would scream with laughter and excitement. What a wonderful way to start the day.

"Oh, and Christmas and New Years," Jennie continued, "packages arrived tied up in tissue paper and I was allowed to get into boxes that had been emptied, and the whole house smelled of good things to eat. On my own birthday, which, if you would like to remember it, is on April 22nd,

I always had new toys and presents, and Buff gave a party for me. Of course I was spoiled and pampered, but I adored it. Who wouldn't have done so?

"Those were the three happiest years of my life. I was with Buff or her parents every minute that they were home, and I loved them with all my heart. I even learned to understand a little of their language, although it is very difficult, harsh and unmusical. I've forgotten most of it now, but then, between the words that I recognised and their expressions or tone of voice, I always knew whether they were pleased or displeased and what they wanted of me.

"One day, early in May, just about two years ago, I noticed that everyone seemed to be very busy and distracted and occupied with themselves and that *something* strange was going on in the house."

"Oh dear," said Peter, beginning to be quite upset, "I was afraid something would happen. It was just too perfect..."

Jennie nodded. "Yes. It seems it's always that way. I went around peering into their faces, trying to make out what might be going to happen. And then one morning, trunks, bags, valises, holdalls, canvas sacks, suddenly appeared from the attic, boxes and crates, and barrels full of straw and sawdust were brought into the house, and men in rough clothes, aprons and peaked caps came in to pack them, and of course after that I knew. They were going to move. But whether it was to be to a house in another part of the city, a place in the country, or abroad, I had no means of knowing or finding out.

"Until you've been a cat yourself, Peter, and have gone through it, you will never understand what it means to sit by, day in and day out, while everything which is familiar and to which you are attached, furniture, and things on mantelpieces and tables, disappear into crates and boxes for shipping, and *not know*."

"Not know what?" asked Peter.

"Whether or not you are going to be taken along."

"Oh, but of course you get taken along!" Peter burst out, thinking how he would act under the same circumstances if he had ever had a cat as sweet and good-natured as Jennie Baldrin. "Why, nobody would think of going away and leaving you behind, even—"

He stopped in mid-sentence because Jennie had turned away abruptly and was washing furiously. There was a kind of desperation in her movements that touched Peter's heart and told him more plainly than words that she was suffering. He cried: "Oh, poor Jennie Baldrin! I'm so sorry. It can't be true. Nobody could be so cruel. Tell me what happened."

Jennie left off her washing. Her eyes were quite misty and she looked leaner and bonier than ever. She said "Forgive me, Peter. I think perhaps I'd better stop for a little. It hasn't been easy, remembering back and living over those beautiful days. Come. Take a walk with me and we'll poke about a bit to familiarise you with this place so that you'll know the ins and out of it, as well as the secret entrance, and then I can tell you the rest of the story of what happened to me that fatal May."

Peter was terribly disappointed at the interruption, but he did not wish Jennie to know this, he felt so sympathetic because of the tragedy in her life, even though he could not imagine how people as good and kind as the Pennys seemed to be could go off and leave her behind. But he kept his counsel, and when Jennie jumped down from the bed, he followed her. He was feeling much stronger now and had no difficulty keeping up with Jennie as she squeezed through the slats at the end of the bin and turned left up the corridor.

They prowled down a long, dark corridor, on either side of which were storage bins such as they had just left. They turned into several passageways, went down a flight of stairs, and came around a corner into a place where the room was illuminated by an electric bulb that hung from a wire overhead. It was an enormous enclosure where the ceiling was three times the height of their own and it was filled from top to bottom in the strangest manner, not only with all kinds of things but also with places.

There was a kind of glittering palace, and right next to it some wild stretches of the Scottish Highlands with huge rocks and boulders piled up and menacing trees throwing dark arms to the sky. Then there was somehow a view of the blue sea with some distant mountains, a trellised garden, a cottage with a thatched roof, a row of Arabian nomad tents, a gloomy piece of jungle all overhung with creepers and vines, a railway station, a piece of Greek temple…

Peter cried, "Why, I know what it is. It's theatrical scenery, like they use in the Christmas Pantomime. I suppose this is where they store it."

"Is that what it is?" said Jennie Baldrin. "I didn't know, but I thought it might interest you. I often come here when I feel the need of a change. Let us go over there and sit on that rock in the Highlands, because it reminds me of where we came from, at least the way my mother used to describe it."

Of course they couldn't actually sit on the rock, since it was only painted on canvas in an extraordinarily lifelike manner, but when they had squatted down and curled their tails around them right *next* to the rock, it was really, Peter felt, almost like being in that part of Scotland about which his Nanny too had so often told him.

When he and Jennie had settled, Peter said, "Jennie dear… Do you think perhaps you might go on now…?"

Jennie closed her eyes for a moment as though to help herself return once more to those memories that were so painful to her. Then she opened them again, sighed, and took up her narrative:

"It was a large house, you know," she said, "and it seemed to take perfect ages to get everything packed and sealed and ready to be moved.

"I walked around and into and over everything and smelled and fretted and tried to feel – you know how we can sometimes acquire bits and pieces of information and knowledge just through the ends of our whiskers—" (Peter didn't, but he also didn't wish to interrupt at this point, so he did not reply and Jennie went on) – "but it was useless. I couldn't make out the slightest hint where everything was going to, or even when, though I knew it must be soon, because for several days the family had not been sleeping there, since all the beds were taken down and crated. Mrs Penny and also Buff would come back during the day and pack, and of course feed me.

"In the evening they would take my basket upstairs to the top-floor sewing-room under the eaves of the roof and leave me there with a saucer of milk and one of water for overnight. The sewing-room was quite bare. I didn't even have any of my toys. I shouldn't have minded that if only I hadn't been so worried and upset by not knowing. Of course, I imagined that very likely the Pennys were stopping with friends or at a hotel where perhaps they couldn't have me until the new house should be ready wherever it was. But then, on the other hand, how could I be sure they weren't going far away somewhere over the sea where I could not go along?"

Peter knew all about moving. In military circles people were always packing up their belongings and starting off for India, or Australia, or Africa. And he thought too that he understood the anxiety Jennie must have felt. For he remembered enduring nights of terror and sudden panic himself when the thought had come to him from nowhere at all, as it were, "What if Mummy were not to come back to me ever? Supposing I wake up in the morning and she isn't there?" And then he had lain fearful and wide awake in the darkness, listening and straining with his ears and all his senses for the sound of her key in the front door and her footsteps in the corridor going past his room. And not until this had come to pass, and more often than not it was well after midnight, would he be able to fall into a restless and troubled sleep.

Jennie's voice brought him back from these memories. "One morning," she was saying sadly, "they did not come back; nor did they ever. I never saw them again, my dear, beloved Buff, or Mrs Penny, or Mr Penny. They had gone away and cold-bloodedly abandoned me."

Peter gave a cry of sympathy. "Oh, poor Jennie Baldrin!" But then he added: "I can't believe it. Something must have happened to them…"

"I only wish I could think so," Jennie declared, "but when you grow older – I mean, after you have been a cat for a while, you will come to understand that people are *always* doing that. They keep us while we are convenient to them, and not too much trouble, and then, when through no fault of ours it becomes *inconvenient*, they walk out and leave us to starve."

"Oh, Jennie," Peter cried again, quite horrified at such cruelty, "I would never go away and leave you…"

"*You* wouldn't, perhaps," Jennie said, "but people do, and THEY did. I remember that morning. I couldn't believe it at first when the time came and they were not there. I watched at the window. I listened at the door. Time passed. Then I started to shout, hoping perhaps that somehow they had managed to slip into the house without my hearing them.

"I cried myself hoarse. I threw myself against the door. I tried desperately to open it, but it was one of those slippery doorknobs instead of a latch I might have worked. Morning turned into afternoon and afternoon into evening. I hardly slept at all, but kept pacing the floor of the empty sewing-room the whole night hoping against hope that they would come the next day.

"On the morrow something much more terrifying occurred. *They* didn't come, but the moving-men did. From the window I could see their van drawn up in front of the house. All day long they went in and out of the house, removing the furniture, crates, boxes and barrels. By late afternoon everything was loaded and tied on behind with ropes. Then they climbed into the front seat and drove away. And that night there wasn't any milk or water left, and I had nothing to eat or drink, nor the next, nor the one after that."

"Poor, poor Jennie!" Peter said. "Weren't you awfully hungry?"

"The pain wasn't in my stomach, Peter," Jennie replied, "it was in my heart. I only wished to die of longing, misery, loneliness and sadness. More than anything, I wanted my Buff to be holding me in her arms close to her and giving me the little squeezes she used to because she loved me.

"And then suddenly to my horror I found myself hating her. I wanted to bite, scratch, claw and kill her for having abandoned me. Yes, I learned to hate, Peter, and that is worse than being sick, or starved, or thirsty, or in pain. It replaced all the love I had felt for Buff. I had no hope of ever getting out of that room alive, but I swore that if I did I would never again trust a human being, or give them love or live with them.

"And then one morning, when I was nearly dead, release came. I heard someone at the front door and then footsteps. I knew it wasn't *their* footsteps, and yet I hoped that somehow I was mistaken and they *had* come, and I was all ready to welcome them and purr and even try to reach Buff's shoulder to show her I had forgiven her. Oh, I would have put my paws to her face and kissed and kissed her if she had only come back and not forgotten me."

Peter said, "I do wish she had, Jennie…"

"It wasn't, of course," Jennie continued. "It was just people, two women, very likely come to look at the house. One of them made sympathetic sounds and picked me up. But I was weak and dizzy from starvation and nearly out of my mind with worry, and didn't know what I was doing. I bit her. She dropped me, and I was so frightened I found the strength to run out of the door and down the stairs. Or rather I fell more than ran down them and didn't stop until I got to the bottom and out the front door. That was the beginning…"

"Of what?" Peter asked.

"Of being independent of human beings, of never again asking for a favour, of spitting and growling whenever one tried to reach down and stroke me or pick me up, of never again entering a house to live with them."

Peter wanted to show her how sorry he was it had all turned out so badly, but he could not think of anything to say, because if it was really true that her family had abandoned her so heartlessly he felt very much ashamed that they were human beings. Instead he arose, went over to her, and bestowed a few licks on the side of her cheek.

Jennie gave him a winning smile and purred for a moment.

"That was sweet," she said, "but I like the life of a stray now, really. It's a rough one, and sometimes it isn't easy, but at least no one can hurt me any more. I mean inside, where you can't get at it and it never heals up. There isn't much that is open to cats that I haven't seen or done in the past two years. I found this place months ago. It's wonderful, because people hardly ever visit here. Come along, and I'll show you my secret entrance..."

They left the Highland scenery, walked by the Pyramids and the Sphinx, skirted the rooftop of a penthouse in New York, wound their way in and out of a drawing-room in Mayfair and a castle on the Rhine and retraced their steps down he long, dark, musty corridors.

But just before they turned the corner to enter that part of the warehouse where Jennie's home was, she stopped, gave a low growl, and Peter saw her tail fluff up to twice its size. He halted behind her and heard voices, footsteps, scrapings and bumpings, and was all for running around the corner to see what it was, when Jennie whispered – "Get down, Peter! If they see us, we're in for it. It's our home! They're moving it out. Looks like your friend Napoleon has come for his bed."

Peter felt it might embarrass her if he were to reveal that Napoleon had been dead for more than a hundred years, and anyway, it did not make much difference; more to the point, it was no longer there, and everything else in the bin was also being moved out either to a sale or an exhibition.

"Pity," said Jennie. "It was a nice home. I'd grown rather fond of it, particularly your friend's bed. Ah well, one can always find another somewhere else."

"There must be dozens of storage bins we passed where we might be cosy," Peter said.

"Won't do. Not in here," Jennie said decisively. "Once people show up, you've had it, and if you are wise you will clear out. When the movers get those things into the light they'll find evidence of our having lived there. Your hairs and mine. And the mouse business. Then there'll be a hue and cry and a hunt for us all through here – lights up and dust swirling, and men poking about with torches and sticks. No, trust me, Peter, I know. As soon as they have finished we'll use my emergency exit. There's still plenty of daylight left to look about for a new place to stay the night. Keep out of sight until I give the word."

Peter did as she bade him, for he very well appreciated that Jennie was more experienced and must know what she was talking about.

And then, what with all the dust about, the washing and the talking and not having had anything to drink after all that running through London, Peter fell prey to a most dreadful thirst and it suddenly seemed to him that he would perish if he did not soon feel something cool and moist going down his throat.

CHAPTER SEVEN

Always Pause on the Threshold

"I'M AWFULLY THIRSTY, Jennie," Peter whispered.

They had been crouching there around the bend of the warehouse corridor for the better part of an hour waiting for the men to finish the work of carrying out the furniture from the storage bin.

Jennie flattened herself and peered around the corner. "Soon," she said. "There are only a few pieces left."

"How I wish I had a tall, cool glass of milk," Peter said.

Jennie turned her head and looked at him. "Dish of milk, you mean. You wouldn't be able to drink it out of a glass. And as for milk – do you know how long it is since I have seen or tasted milk? In our kind of life, I mean cut off from humans, there isn't any milk. If you're thirsty you find some rainwater or some slops in the gutter or in a pail left out, or you can go down the stone steps to the river landings when they are deserted at night, if you don't mind your water a little oily and brackish."

Peter was not at all pleased with the prospect and he had not yet got used to the fact that he was no longer a boy, with a home and family, but a white cat with no home at all and no one to befriend him but another scrawny stray.

He was so desperately thirsty and the picture drawn by Jennie so gloomy and unpleasant that he could not help bursting into tears and crying, "But I'm *used* to milk! I like it and Nanny gives me some every day…"

"Sshhh!" cautioned Jennie, "they'll hear you." Then she added, "There's nobody goes about setting out dishes of milk for strays. You'll get used to not having it eventually."

But Peter didn't think so, and continued to cry softly to himself while Jennie Baldrin watched him with growing concern and bewilderment. She seemed to be trying to make up her mind about something which apparently she did not very much wish to do. But finally, when it appeared that she could bear his unhappiness no longer, she whispered to him, "Come, now… don't take on so! I know a place where I think I can get you a dish of milk. We'll go there."

The thought caused Peter to stop crying and brighten up immediately. "Yes?" he said. "Where?"

"There's an old watchman lives in a shack down by the tea docks," Jennie told him. "He's lonely, likes cats, and is always good for a titbit, especially for me. He's been after me to come and live with him for months. Of course, I wouldn't dream of it."

"But," said Peter, not wishing to argue himself out of milk but only desiring to understand clearly the terms under which they were to have it, "that *is* taking from people, isn't it?"

"It's taking, but not *giving* anything," Jennie said, with that strange, unhappy intenseness that came over her whenever she discussed anything to do with humans. "We'll *have it* and then walk out on him."

"Would that be right?" Peter asked. It slipped out almost before he was aware of it, for he very much wanted the milk and he equally did not wish to offend Jennie. But it was just that he had been taught certain ways of behaviour, or felt them to be so by instinct, and this seemed a poor way of repaying a kindness. Clearly he had somewhat put Jennie out, for she stiffened slightly and with the nearest thing to a cold look she had bestowed upon him since they had met, said, "You can't have it both ways, Peter. If you want to live my kind of life, and I can't see where you have very much choice at the moment—"

"But of course I do!" Peter hastened to explain, "it's just that I'm not yet quite familiar with the different way cats feel from the way people feel. And I will do as you say, and I do want to learn…"

From her expression, Jennie did not appear to be too pleased with this speech either, but before she could remark upon it there came a loud call from the movers: "That's the lot, then," and another voice replied, "Righty-ho!" Jennie peered around the corner and said, "They've finished. We'll wait a few minutes to make sure they don't come back, an then we'll start."

When they were certain that the aisle was quite deserted again, they set off, Jennie leading, past the empty bin and down the corridor in the direction the men had taken, but before they had gone very far Jennie branched off to the right on a new tack until she came to a bin close to the outside wall of the warehouse, filled with horrible, new, modern kind of furniture, chrome-bound leather and overstuffed plush. She led Peter to the back where there was a good-sized hole in the baseboard. It looked dark and forbidding inside.

"Don't be afraid," Jennie said. "Just follow me. We go to the right and then to the left, but it gets light very quickly."

She slipped in with Peter after her, and it soon grew pitch black. Peter now discovered that he was feeling through the ends of his whiskers, rather than seeing where Jennie was, and he had no difficulty in following her, particularly inasmuch as it soon became light enough to see that they were in a tunnel through which a large iron pipe more than a foot in diameter was running. Then Peter saw where the light was coming from. There was a hole in the pipe where it had rusted through a few feet from where it gave exit to the street.

Apparently the pipe was used as some kind of air-intake, or had something to do with the ventilation of the warehouse, for it had once had a grating over the end of it, but the fastenings of that had long since rusted and it had fallen away, and there was nothing to bar their way out.

Peter was so pleased and excited at the prospect of seeing the sun and being out of doors again that he hurried past Jennie and would have rushed out into the street had not the alarm in her warning cry checked him just before he emerged from the opening.

"Peter! Wait!" she cried. "Not like that! Cats never, *never* rush out from places. Don't you know about Pausing on the Threshold, or Lingering on the Sill? But then, of course, you wouldn't. Oh dear, I don't mean always to be telling you what to do and what not to do, but this is really Important. It's almost Lesson Number 2. You never hurry out of any place, and particularly not outdoors."

Peter saw that Jennie had quite recovered her good nature and apparently had forgotten that she had been upset with him. He was curious to find out the reasons for her warning. He said, "I don't quite understand, Jennie. You mean I'm not to stop before coming in, but I am whenever I go out?"

"Of course. What else?" replied Jennie, sitting down quite calmly in the mouth of the exit and showing not the slightest disposition to go through it and into the street. "You know what's inside because you come from there. You don't know what's outside because you haven't been there. That's common ordinary sense for anyone, I should think."

"Yes, but what is there outside to be afraid of, really?" enquired Peter. "I mean, after all, if you know where you live and the street and houses and all which don't change—"

"Oh, my goodness," said Jennie, "I couldn't try to tell you them all. To begin with – dogs, people, moving vehicles, the weather and changes in temperature, the condition of the street, is it wet or dry, clean or dirty, what has been left lying about, what is parked at the kerb, and whether anybody is coming along, on which side of the street and in how much of a hurry.

"And it isn't that you're actually afraid. It's just that you want to *know*. And you ought to know, if you have your wits about you, everything your eyes, your ears, your nose, and the ends of your whiskers can tell you. And so you stop, look, listen and *feel*. We have a saying, 'Heaven is overcrowded with kittens who rushed out of doors without first stopping and *receiving* a little'.

"There might be another cat in the vicinity, bent on mischief, or looking for a fight. You'd certainly want to know about that before you stepped out into something you weren't prepared for. Then you'd want to know all about the weather, not only what it's like at the moment, but what it's going to be doing later, say an hour from then. If it's going to come on to rain or thunder, you wouldn't want to be too far from home. Your whiskers and your skin tell you that.

"And then, anyway," Jennie concluded, "it's a good idea on general principles not to rush into things. When you go out there are very few places to go to that won't be there just the same five minutes later, and the chances of your getting there will be ever so much better. Come here and squat down beside me and we'll just have a look."

Peter did as she suggested and lay down directly in the opening with his paws tucked under him, and felt quite natural doing it, and suddenly he was glad that Jennie had stopped him and that he hadn't gone charging out into goodness knows what.

Feet went by at intervals. By observation he got to know something about the size of the shoes, which were mostly the heavy boots belonging to workmen, their speed, and how near they came to the wall of the warehouse. The wheeled traffic was of the heavy type – huge horse-drawn drays, and motor-lorries that rumbled past ominously loud, and the horses' feet, huge things with big, shaggy fetlocks, were another danger. Far in the distance, Peter heard Big Ben strike four. The sound would not have reached him as a human being, perhaps, but travelled all the distance from the Houses of Parliament to his cat's ears and informed him of the time.

Now he used his nostrils and sniffed the scents that came to his nose and tried to understand what they told him. There was a strong smell of tea and a queer odour that he could not identify, he just knew he didn't like it. He recognized dry goods, machinery, musk and spices, and horses and burned petrol, exhaust gases, tar and soft coal smoke, the kind that comes from railway engines.

Jennie had got up now and was standing on the edge of the opening with only her head out, whiskers extended forward, quivering a little, and making small wrinkly movements with her nose. After a moment or so of this she turned to Peter quite relaxed and said, "All clear. We can go now. No cats around. There's a dog been by, but only a mangy cur probably scared of his own shadow. There's a tea boat just docked. That's good. The Watchman won't really have any responsibilities until she's unloaded. Rain's all cleared away. Probably won't rain for at least another forty-eight hours. Goods train just gone down into the docks area. That's fine. Means the gates'll be open, and besides, we can use the wagons for cover."

"Goodness!" Peter marvelled, "I don't see how you can tell all that from just one tiny sniff around. Do you suppose I'll ever—?"

"Of course you will," Jennie laughed, and with a bit of a purr added, "It's just a matter of getting used to it and looking at things the way a cat would. It's really nothing," and here she gave herself two or three self-conscious licks, for, truth to tell, she was just a trifle vain and nothing delighted her so much as to appear clever in Peter's eyes, which was only feline.

"Well, I don't understand—" Peter began, saying just the right thing and giving her the lead which she was quick to take up.

"It's really quite simple," she explained. "For instance, you can smell the tea. Well, that wasn't around last time I was outside. Means a tea boat has come in and they've opened the hatches. No cats about – I don't get any signals on my receiver, at least not hostile ones. The dog that went by, well, goodness knows, you can smell *him*. If he had any class or self-respect that might lead him to chase cats, he'd be clean, and a clean dog smells different. This one was filthy, and that's why I say he's nothing to worry about.

He'll be slinking along down back alleys and glad to be left alone. And as for the goods train that went by, after you get to know the neighbourhood it'll be easy for you too. You see, the smoke smell comes from the left, down where the docks are, so of course it went that way. And you know it was a goods train, because you can smell everything that was in the wagons. There, you see how easy it is?"

Peter again said the right thing, for he was learning how to please Jennie. "I think you're *enormously* clever," he told her. Her purr almost drowned out the sound of a passing horse-drawn dray. Then she cried to him gaily, "Come along, Peter! We're off!" and the two friends went out into the cobbled street.

CHAPTER EIGHT

Hoodwinking of an
Old Gentleman

THE PAIR WENT off down the busy commercial street towards their destination not at a walk, lope, trot, or even a run, but a series of short, swift charges, a kind of point-to-point dash, and again Peter learned something about the life and ways of a homeless city cat that has no friends and must fend for itself.

For, as Jennie explained and he could very well see, in a city that was stony, hostile and full of all kinds of moving vehicles, rushing people, bicycles, delivery hand-trucks, carts, lorries, wagons, hardly heeding one another, much less anything that might be so close to the ground as a cat, it would never do to be caught simply carelessly walking along or even running.

"You never leave one place of shelter," was the way Jennie had explained it to him, "until you have the next one ahead of you picked out where you are going to go in case of trouble of any sort. And then the best thing to do is to make a dash for it and not linger between them. Of course, when you're in your own neighbourhood you know all sorts of spots to get to in a hurry, and you can afford to be more relaxed. But when going through strange territory, always play for safety."

And so they made their way from point to point and cover to cover in little short rushes that Peter found most exciting and exhilarating until they reached the gateway to the dockyard where everything was exactly as Jennie had said it would be. The great iron gates to the yards stood open, a goods train had been through, indeed the last of the trucks and the brake van actually were not yet inside the gate, though the train had stopped, so long was it. And here too they no longer needed to indulge in the short rushes, for the goods wagons, vans, tankers, box and refrigerator wagons gave them excellent cover and they were able to trot along beneath them in perfect safety and at a rapid pace.

The shack was far down at the very end of the docks, but on the land side of the sheds, and consisted of a little wooden house of but one room with a door leading into it, two windows, one on either side, of which several panes were broken and stuffed with rags, and a crooked stove-pipe that emerged from the tin roof instead of a chimney.

In spite of its drab surrounding amidst coils of rope and cable, rusting steel rails and oddments of wood, weatherbeaten and sagging as it was, the shack looked cheerful and even homelike, because on either side of the door, on the ground, were two long green boxes with earth in them, and in the boxes bright red geraniums were growing. From the open doorway as Peter and Jennie approached came the appetising smell of frying liver.

"He's in and cooking his tea," said Jennie. "The first thing to do is let him know we are here," and forthwith she emitted a plaintive and heartbreaking "Meeeeeeeow!"

In a moment an old man dressed in shabby clothes and with a stained and untidy moustache stood framed in the doorway with a saucepan in one hand.

"'Ullo!" he said, "if it isn't Tabby Puss come back to pay a visit to old Bill Grims! And brought a pal with 'er this time. Here then, puss, puss, puss!"

He had, Peter noticed, snow-white hair that hung down almost to his shoulders it was so long uncut, and fierce, bushy white eyebrows that framed a pair of the mildest blue eyes that Peter had ever seen, eyes that had in them a look of great kindliness and at the same time sadness. His cheeks, bristled with white stubble, were apple-red from the warmth of the shack, his hands gnarled, knotted and quite dirty.

Peter thought: "How very odd. He's old, yes, quite – and yet what he really looks like most is a little boy. He really doesn't seem to be much older than I am, at least that's the way he feels to me. I think I am going to like him."

The watchman's expression was so friendly as he put away the skillet and leaned down and said: "There now, you are a fine fellow! Come over 'ere and let's 'ave a look at you," that Peter wanted to go to him right away, even if his clothes and hands were dirty, but Jennie cautioned him:

"No, no, Peter! Let me handle this. If you give in right away you don't get any milk," and with that she sent up another plaintive series of miaows, a tone which even to Peter's ears was filled with the most false and evident pathos.

But apparently it struck the proper and necessary chord in the heart of old Mr Grims, for he said at once: "Reckon as 'ow the two of you could do with a bit of milk, eh? Don't you go 'way, and I'll fetch some right away," and he turned back into the inside of the shack.

"Aha!" said Jennie with a triumphant look on her face. "You see? I heard the word 'milk'. I didn't understand the rest."

"I did," said Peter. "He said we weren't to go, he was going to fetch some immediately."

Jennie stared at Peter as though she couldn't believe her ears. "Peter! You mean you can understand *every*thing he says?"

"But of course I can. Why not? He spoke in plain English. If he spoke in French or German I'm sure I shouldn't know a word, though Daddy says next year I'm to begin to learn French…"

"Well, I never!" Jennie said, and sat down and blinked several times. "This wants thinking over. I never would have believed it. Then you really *are* a little boy…"

"But I told you I was," Peter insisted.

"Of course you did," Jennie admitted, "and I believed you, though not entirely. But now here's the proof for once and all. For if you were entirely a cat you wouldn't understand *all* of his language, and I must say—"

But what Jennie felt compelled to say at that point was lost, due to the fact that Mr Grims returned to the door with a large flat saucer in one hand, a bottle of milk in the other.

"Here we are, then," he said, and called to them – "Come pusses. Nice fresh milk…" And he poured a generous helping into the saucer and held it up.

Peter's throat was so parched that he could hardly refrain from jumping for it, and he craned and stretched his neck and too uttered plaintive miaows.

Jennie said: "See if you can get him to give it to us outdoors. I'd rather not go inside if I can help it."

They both cruised back and forth in front of the door, their tails straight up in the air, reaching and crying. But Mr Grims said, "Come in if you want it, pusses. I'm just about to 'ave me tea."

Peter translated for Jennie, "He says we're to come inside if we want it."

She sighed and gave up. "Ah well… come along then," and treading cautiously over the sill and giving a sniff or two, she led the way with Peter following.

At once Mr Grims closed the door behind them and set the saucer of milk on the floor where Peter with a little glad cry that was half a purr, hurled himself upon it, buried his face in it, and tried to suck it up. The next moment he was sneezing, coughing and choking with milk up his nose and into his eyes and his lungs full of it.

"Oh, oh, eh!" cried Mr Grims as Peter backed away from the dish, "easy does it…"

Jennie said, "Oh dear!" and struggled not to laugh. "I didn't want to say anything, but I was afraid something like that would happen. Poor Peter... of course you can't drink milk that way. Horses can suck, but we have to *lap* it up."

"Ugh-ick-kaCHOO!" Peter coughed and sneezed the last of the milk from his lungs and nose, and with the tears still running from his eyes from the effort, begged, "Show be how to do id, please, Jeddie! I dever tried..."

Jennie squatted down at the side of the side of the saucer, her head just over it and lowered to the level of the milk. Then her little pink tongue emerged and vanished with incredible speed. The level of the milk in the saucer began to fall.

Mr Grims of course misunderstood completely what was happening and laughed, "Ho, ho, ho! 'Ad to 'ave a bit of a lesson in manners from your girl friend, eh, Whitey? 'Appens to the best of us. Now it's your turn."

But when Peter tried to get a drink of milk from the saucer he had no better luck. This time all the liquid splashed on to the floor next to the saucer and not a drop could Peter get into his parched mouth. He was almost in despair when Jennie, who had been watching and studying him closely, cried:

"Oh! Now I know! You must curl your tongue *under* when you lap. We don't curl it up and around, but down, around and under."

"But it doesn't make any sense," Peter protested. "Curling

it up makes it like a spoon, except it all runs out on to the floor. Turning it down under it would never hold anything. And besides, I'm sure I couldn't possibly do it, or learn. Our tongues just don't go that way."

"Yours don't, but cats' do," Jennie replied, "and whatever you once were, you are most certainly a cat now, so try it. Think of your tongue curling under, and see what happens."

So Peter went at it again, and thought hard of curling his tongue downwards, and almost at once, to his great surprise, it was bending in that direction quite as though he had been drinking milk in that fashion all his life, and the cool, sweet drops were splashing into his mouth and running down his throat. He drank and drank as though he would never get enough, but suddenly, in the midst of drinking, he remembered what Jennie had said about cats not being greedy and sharing what they had with others, and felt a little ashamed, and so, with his thirst still not completely quenched, he backed away from the dish and said politely to Jennie: "Please, won't you have some more…?"

Jennie rewarded him with her most winning smile, saying, "How sweet of you, Peter! I don't mind if I do," and therewith she returned to the dish and applied herself to it, giving Peter a chance to look around and see where he was.

The shack was most simply furnished with a wooden bed at the far end on which were some rumpled blankets, a few shelves containing some bare necessities. An unpainted and battered table was placed against one wall, with a small wireless set and an alarm clock with the glass broken out of its face standing on it. There was one rickety wooden chair with most of the slats out of the back. Right in the centre was a fat, pot-bellied stove, connected to a rusty pipe that went up through the roof. There was a fire in it now, a dented tea-kettle was singing on it over to one side, and the rest of the space on top of it was being used by Mr Grims to finish the job of cooking his slice of liver that he was planning to have with his tea.

All of the furnishings in the place, Peter noticed, were poor and shabby and worn out, and yet the room looked as gay and cheerful as a palace, for everywhere there was a place or a ledge, shelf or level spot to put it, stood a flowerpot with growing flowers in it – geraniums of every kind and variety, from pure snow white to darkest glowing crimson, some the colour of apple-blossoms, pink and white, and others all shades of pink verging on salmon, puce-coloured ones, and every variation of red from brick to blood to sunset. And the scent of them filled the shack and was stronger even than the odour of frying liver.

And while waiting for Jennie to finish the rest of her share of the milk, Peter wondered about Mr Grims, who he had been and what kind of a life he had led, what had happened to him that he was compelled to spend the end of it as a watchman in a mean little shack, and what had become of his family. It was a game Peter liked to play, trying to guess what people were by looking at them – but he could not make up his mind about Mr Grims except that he was very old and lonely and seemed to have nobody at all, for there were no pictures of any kind up on the wall.

Peter also remembered what Jennie had said, that Mr Grims had offered her a home and had been trying to persuade her to come and live with him for months, and suddenly, he did not know why, his heart felt heavy and intolerably sad. He set to washing himself violently down his back to see if it would make him feel any better, as Jennie had said it would. He found that it did somewhat, but not entirely.

"Cleanin' up, eh?" said Mr Grims in his friendly voice. "Maybe you'd be wanting to wait a bit with that…" He moved over to the shelf, got the bread and cut himself several slices, poured the tea, and transferred the liver from the skillet to one of his cracked plates. "It ain't often I have company for tea. I might be able to spare a bit o' liver for me pals. Share and share alike is my motto." And with that he took a knife, divided the piece of liver exactly in two, and commenced to cut up one of the halves into very small pieces.

"He's going to give us *liver*," Peter announced to Jennie with considerable excitement. Previously, when he had been living at home and he had been made by Nanny to eat liver to make sure he was getting enough vitamins, he hadn't liked it particularly, but now the smell, the look of it, and particularly the preparations sent him into a perfect fever of expectation and delight.

Jennie had a pleased and satisfied smirk on her countenance as she too cruised back and forth near the table where the cutting was going on, as though to say: "You see, I told you this would be a little bit of all right."

At last, the portions were ready. Mr Grims divided them into two even heaps, one on either side of a plate, and set the dish down on the floor. Peter and Jennie at once squatted down comfortably on either side and fell to eating without further ceremony.

On his part, Mr Grims poured himself a cup of tea, smeared a slice of bread with margarine, and sitting down to the table with knife and fork commenced to eat what was left of his liver with cheerful gusto and a running commentary of conversation addressed partly to no one in particular and partly at his two visitors.

Said he, spearing a piece of the liver and conveying it to his mouth, "It ain't much, but what I say is – you're welcome to what I've got. It ain't often we get to see a bit o' fresh meat like this now, and I'll wager you both are wondering 'ow I've come by it." He wagged his head and said, "Ah, well, you'll find old Bill Grims still 'as a friend or two.

"Mr Tewkes the butcher says to me: "Ere you are, Mr Grims, a fine fresh bit of English lamb's liver I've set by for you, for I says to myself, it's not much meat you gets to see on your ration book.'

"I says to him: 'Right you are, and I only wish there was something I could do for you some day.'

"Then he says to me: 'Well, now that you mention it, Mr Grims, there is a little something. I've a nephew very anxious to get into the docks to have a word with the foreman about a job, and I says to him, "Mr Grims the watchman can give you a 'and there—" eh, Mr Grims?'

"And I says to him: '*Quid pro quo*, meaning one good turn deserves another! *Quid pro quo*, Mr Tewkes, and thank you very much.' And 'ere we all are sitting down to liver for tea like the King himself in Buckingham Palace.

"It's quiet living here, but comfortable, pusses, with nobody coming to disturb you for weeks on end if there isn't a call for cargo to be shifted or a ship to unload or clear. Not that it don't get a bit lonely at times, but then the three of us would find plenty to say to one another, I reckon.

"Merry as grigs we three'd be in here, that is providin' as 'ow you liked flowers. But then I've never seen a puss as didn't like flowers, always sniffin' and smellin' around them and steppin' so nice and dainty with their feet so as not to 'urt them."

Here he arose and went over to the shelf from which he took down a jampot. He scraped down into the bottom of it with a knife, but scratch and try as he would, not a single smidgen of jam came forth there from on the end of the knife, showing that the pot was quite empty.

"Ah well," said Mr Grims, still in utmost good humour, "it comes and it goes. But never fear that *you* two wouldn't be well looked after. Ol' Bill Grims would see to that. Cereal in the morning with a bit off the top o' the milk ration.

And sometimes when a ship comes in from the Argentine, a bit o' real beef right off the 'oof as it were. The run o' the docks and storage 'ouses with me, and WOT parcels, crates, bales and packages to hinvestigate! I don't know where they all don't come from. Hindia, China, South Africa and NOO York…"

He glanced appraisingly about the tiny room and continued: "Now I'd shift me bed into *that* corner, so you'd have the other one on a pile of something soft and then none of us would interfere with the other comin' and goin', that is, pusses, providin' you're of a mind to stop and stay a while. It ain't much, but it would be 'ome for all of us, and welcome you'd be. And that goes for you too, Whitey, as long as you're a friend o' *hers*."

Feasting on the nourishing and delicious liver, satisfyingly full of milk, warm and comfortable, Peter felt there was nothing he would have liked better than to stay on with Mr Grims and be looked after by him. He didn't mind his being dirty and everything being poor and cracked and shabby, in fact he rather liked it because there wasn't any danger of hurting anything. At home he was always having to be careful of this article of furniture, or that piece of bric-à-brac…

"What has he been saying?" Jennie enquired of him, her meal finished, as she began licking her right paw and then carefully rubbing it over her whiskers and the side of her mouth and face.

Peter told her the gist of Mr Grims's conversation as

best as he could remember, but with emphasis on the fact that they were invited to remain there and make their home with him. Jennie interrupted her washing long enough to remark – "You see. Just as I told you. I didn't like it at all when he shut the door on us…"

"But he's so nice and kind…" Peter remonstrated.

"They all are – at first," Jennie replied. "Believe me, Peter, I know, You must trust me. We must watch for an opportunity. When it comes, do exactly as I say. Now then, get on with your washing, just as though we were quite content to stay here."

Peter would not have dreamed of disobeying Jennie, for he already owed so much to her wisdom and kindness and generosity, including his life, and so he too set about cleaning his face and whiskers while Mr Grims said cheerily, "That's what I like to see, pusses, settling down nice and 'omey and 'avin a bit of a clean-up."

He gathered all the dishes together and placed them in a bucket and went outside with them. "Water an' conveniences not laid on," he explained to them, "but the tap ain't far and it's no trouble. We'll all have a wash-up." He closed the door behind him very carefully and was only gone a few moments when he was back with the bucket full of water which he set upon the stove. But this time the latch of the door did not quite click. Peter did not notice it, but Jennie did. She edged over to him and said: "Get ready."

Peter was just about to whisper, "Get ready for what?"

when it happened. A breeze of wind from outside stirred the door and opened it just a foot.

"Now!" cried Jennie. "Follow me!" and was off like an arrow through the crack, her tail standing out straight and streamlined, and ears flattened back.

Peter was so startled that before he knew what he was doing he was up and after her, right on her tail, through the door and beyond, running as though for dear life.

Behind him he heard Mr Grims calling – "'Ere now! No, no! Don't go, pusses. 'Ere, come back! Next time you shall 'ave *all* the liver. Puss! Whitey! Come back!"

Hard as he was running to keep up with Jennie, Peter yet managed to turn his head round and look back over his shoulder. Mr Grims was standing in the doorway of his shack with the boxes of red geraniums on either side, waving his hands in a helpless manner, and looking very bowed and old and lonely with his white hair and drooping moustache and shoulders.

"Ah, there, pusses," he called once more, "don't go away, please—"

Then Jennie ducked around behind a huge pile of oil drums, with Peter after her, and Mr Grims was lost from sight; and soon after, as they continued to run, passing from the drums to piles of green timber and then stacks of ingots of copper and tin, and finally into a perfect wilderness of piled-up steel rails where nobody could ever find anyone who didn't wish to be found, he passed also from their hearing. And not until then did Jennie pull up to rest with a "Well done, Peter!"

But somehow Peter couldn't managed to feel that they, or even he, had done well at all.

CHAPTER NINE

The Stowaways

"WASN'T IT A lark?" Jennie laughed. "I'll never forget the expression on his face. He looked so foolish when we ran off. Weren't you amused?"

"No," said Peter, "I wasn't."

They were sitting on a stringpiece down by the Thames-side near the London Docks, hard by Wapping Wall, watching three snub-nosed tugboats shoving, hauling and straining a long grey-and-white Esso tanker into position against the side of its pier. To his surprise he found that his tail, of which up to that moment he had not been particularly conscious, in spite of the fact that he had never had such an appendage before and it wanted some getting used to, was lashing back and forth, squirming and twitching and writhing like something separate and alive that did not belong to him at all.

Jennie noticed it at the same time he did, probably because she was just a little shocked at his brusque tone in reply to her question, for she said, "Oh dear, Peter, your tail! I'm afraid you're angry with me. Have I done anything wrong?"

"No," Peter replied. "At least I don't suppose you meant to. I'm sorry about my tail, but it's something that seems to be going on in spite of me. It's just that I feel such a rotter."

"But why, Peter? After all—"

"After all," Peter repeated, "he did give us half his rations when he was probably hungry himself. And he didn't look foolish or funny when we ran off, he looked disappointed and lonely and miserable."

"But, Peter," Jennie protested, "don't you see, he wanted something from us. That's why he gave us the milk and the liver. He was trying to bribe us to come and live with him in that dirty, stuffy little house. You wouldn't let yourself be bribed, would you?" she concluded, with what almost amounted to self-righteousness.

"It wasn't a bribe," Peter said with some indignation. "He gave it to us because he liked us. Couldn't you hear the way he spoke to us? And I think it was mean of us to run away from him as soon as the door opened a little bit."

A queer glitter came into Jennie Baldrin's eye, her ears began to flatten back on the top of her head and her tail to twitch ominously. "I think it was mean of HIM to shut the door on us. That should have given away to you what he was up to, if nothing else."

Peter said stubbornly, "Perhaps he shut the door on account of his flowers. He couldn't have been wicked and meant us any harm and kept so many flowers."

Jennie gave a low growl. "All people are wicked and I don't wish to have anything to do with them. I told you that when we first met, and why. And I still feel the same way."

"Then why do you continue to have anything to do with me?" Peter asked. "I'm a person, and—"

"You are not!" Jennie cried, "you're an ordinary white cat and not a very nice one at that, after all I've done to – Oh dear, Peter, do you realise we're having our first disagreement? And over a human being! You see what happens when they come into your life?"

Peter did realise that he was quarrelling with Jennie, and it made him feel ashamed because she had been so good to him and cared for him when he had been weak and injured, and so he said: "Dear Jennie Baldrin, I'm sorry. I didn't mean to be angry with you. You've been so kind and gentle to me. And if it upsets you to think or talk about people or Mr Grims, we won't do it any more."

Jennie's eyes softened, her tail quieted, and she said: "Peter, you are a dear, and I'm sorry I flattened my ears at you." She turned her head away and fell to washing vigorously, and in a moment Peter felt compelled to join her.

After they had washed themselves out of the embarrassment caused by the mutual show of emotion, Peter noticed that Jennie was staring at him with a most curious expression on her soft white face, almost like, well, if he had been a boy instead of a cat, he would have said almost like a cat that had swallowed a mouse. She seemed to be hatching up an idea that gave her a great deal of pleasure and excitement.

"Peter," she began, just as a large steamer with a buff-and-green smokestack came around the bend of the river and gave a deep-throated hoot. "You *are* so awfully clever. Can you read writing as well as understand everything people say?"

"Why, of course," replied Peter, "I should jolly well think so. I've been going to school for two years. I can read nearly everything, I mean if the words aren't too long and mysterious."

"Oh, Peter, show me! Read something for me. What does it say on the boat, for instance – the little one just pushing…"

"*Maude F. O'Reilly*, Thames Towing Co. Limited, Limehouse," Peter read without hesitation.

"And the one that's being pushed?"

"*Esso Queen*, Standard Oil Company, Bayonne, N.J."

"And the one out in the river, just going by…?"

"*Ryndam*, Amsterdam. But I don't know what that one means…"

Jennie gave a great sigh, and the look she turned upon Peter was positively doting. "Oh," she said, "you couldn't possibly be making all of those up out of your head, could you?"

"Certainly not," Peter replied in some wonder. "You asked me to read them to you, and I did. If you don't believe—"

"Oh, but I do, Peter, I do…" said Jennie in a voice that sounded absolutely thrilled, "I just almost didn't dare. Oh, I am lucky. Don't you see what it means?"

Peter tried to, but it was obvious to Jennie from his baffled expression that he didn't, so she told him. "It means that we are free. There is no place we cannot go or nothing we cannot do that we want to…"

But Peter still didn't quite understand.

The sun was now a red ball sinking down over the West of London and making a lurid crimson background for the forest of masts and funnels of the ships in the London Docks behind them, and the dark turrets and walls of the Tower of London rising up from Tower Hill in the distance. And as it dropped low in the sky and prepared to vanish behind the spires and chimneys of the city, a chill wind sprang up from the river, ruffling Peter's fur and reminding him that as yet they had not found a place to stay for the night where they would be warm and safe.

He started to ask Jennie, "It will be dark soon. Where will we go for the night…?" but she wasn't listening to him. She had a rapt expression on her face and a faraway look in her eyes. And then she said to him in a most momentous tone of voice:

"Peter… how would you like to go off on a little trip with me?"

At once Peter was interested, nay more, captivated, for he loved going places and was happiest when he was travelling.

"A trip? Oh, I'd love it! Where to? When?"

"Now. At once. Tonight, I mean, or whenever it goes. But we can look for it tonight. To Scotland. I'd love to go back and visit Glasgow, the city where I was born. And all the relatives I have at Balloch and Garelochhead and Balmaha. Oh, Peter, Peter, wouldn't it be the most fun…"

Peter's eyes were now quite as wide with excitement as were Jennie's as he listened to the names of the places that sounded so far off and so fascinating, for Nanny had often told him all about Glasgow, and he cried, "But, Jennie, how *can* we? We haven't any money, or tickets…"

"Oh, that part, that's simple," said Jennie. "We'll take a job and work our way north to Glasgow…"

"A job," Peter repeated, bewildered. "But what can we do?"

"Plenty," Jennie replied. "We'll find a ship bound for Glasgow and sign on as ship's cats – after they discover that we're aboard. It's easy."

It was now Peter's turn to look with wonder and admiration at his companion. "Jennie!" he said, "do you mean to say you've done it already, you've been away to sea?"

"Oh, yes, several times," she replied, falling into that careless nonchalance that she could not seem to help adopting whenever Peter admired her, "but the trouble was I could never tell where I was going. I wanted very much to go to Egypt to visit the tombs of my ancestors, and instead I landed up in Oslo. Did *I* ever get tired of eating dried fish! And once I went all the way to New Orleans and back. I thought that one would never end. Twenty-eight days at sea. *Such* a bore... But now that I know you can read the names of ships and where they are going..."

A sudden thought struck Peter. "But, Jennie," he said, "being on ships – isn't that being with people, after all, I mean, you know what you said about not caring to—"

"Not at all," Jennie replied coolly. "It's quite different. You're working for your living, and believe me, you work. Anything you get you earn, keeping down the mice and rats, forecasting the weather, locating leaks and bad smells, and bringing good luck and whatnot you're called upon to do. It's all on a strictly business basis. The sailors and mates and masters have their work to do, and precious little time over it leaves them to try to get sentimental with you. And you have yours, and that keeps you occupied, and there's an end to it. The food isn't too bad, and what's important, it's regular – no worries about it, and plenty of it. You get your sea legs after a day or so, and outside of a certain monotony if you stay out of sight of land too long, it isn't a bad life. What say, friend?" And the look that she threw him was both eager and pleading as well as challenging.

"Right-ho!" Peter cried. "I'm for going."

"Bravo, Peter!" Jennie called, giving a little croon of delight. "I knew you would. We'll search these docks back here in the basin first. Your job will be to read off the names. I'll pick the one we want to go on."

They set off immediately from Wapping Wall to the London Docks. At each ship they passed berthed in the Old or New Basin and the seemingly endless Dock area, Peter would gaze up at the wondrous, alluring names lettered in gold beneath the taffrail, with their home ports, and read them off to Jennie.

"*Raimona* – Lisbon," he read.

"Lisbon is *full* of cats – my type," Jennie commented.

"*Vilhialmar* – Helsinki…"

"No more dried fish, thank you," Jennie remarked, a little acidly.

"*Isis* – Alexandria…"

Jennie went all dreamy, and even appeared to hesitate for a moment as though on the verge of changing her mind, but then said, "Some day, perhaps, but not now. When we come back, maybe. Alexandria, Cairo, then up the River Nile. Bubastis is where I want to get to. We really were sacred there…"

Ship after ship they inspected whose home ports were dotted all over the globe from Suez to Calcutta, from Singapore to Colon, and from Bangor, Maine, to Jamaica, West Indies, and Tampico, Mexico. And then, right at the end of the largest basin, almost at the entrance to St Catherine's Docks, they came upon a little one squatting low and lumpy alongside its berth, and its letters weren't in gold, but plain white, and that so smudged and dirty from smoke and grime that Peter could hardly make them out and had to squint up a second time through the growing darkness, but when he did read it his heart gave a leap of excitement.

"Jennie! It says: '*Countess of Greenock* – Glasgow'!"

"Lumme!" Jennie whooped, a little inelegantly. "That's our ship. There's your new home for the next few weeks or so, Peter."

Peter's enthusiasm cooled somewhat as he looked her over, for she was far from a thing of beauty. Her hull was black and rusted red in spots, squat and ugly, with a stubby bow from which rose a short mast with an enormous cargo boom that was engaged at the very moment lifting crates and packing-cases and huge nets filled with barrels and drums from the dockside and lowering them into her interior.

She had an island bridge amidships with a wheelhouse a-top in several different shades of brown, that reminded Peter of a large slice of chocolate layer cake. Another mast and busy boom stuck up behind this, and then back of the second cargo hold rose the brief cabin section with quarters, two lifeboats fastened on either side, and to cap it a long, thin, dirty smokestack in part buff topped with black. Thick smoke was pouring from this funnel, and from it there came a soft-coal smell so raw, acrid and pungent that Peter sneezed violently several times.

"Bless you," Jennie said, and then added with feeling: "It's going to be a job to keep ourselves clean aboard her. But of course you know what it means when she's smoking like that. Probably getting up steam to sail tonight. We're just in time. You see they're loading as fast as they can."

Jennie studied the situation for a moment and then observed: "Looks to me like they're loading general cargo. Which means plenty of work for us, especially since there'll be foodstuffs. Well, Peter, are you ready to go aboard? We might as well, while they're busy, and pick ourselves a spot to stow away until they cast off."

Peter could hardly keep his teeth from chattering from pure excitement. But he said to Jennie, "What if when they find us they are angry and decide to throw us overboard?" For he remembered reading that it went hard very often with stowaways found aboard ship after sailing.

"What?" said Jennie, a little scornfully, "sailors? Throw us overboard? You forget that *we* are cats and *they* are superstitious. Now then! We shan't want to risk getting stepped on where they're loading. There ought to be a third gangway aft to the officers' quarters." The mere sight of the vessel had been sufficient to turn Jennie's speech quite nautical. She continued: "If I know anything about the discipline aboard, the way this tramp seems to be kept, there won't be any watch on it. The crew is probably mostly ashore having a last fling. Come along, we'll have a look."

They crept around the darkened portion of the pier to the stern of the *Countess of Greenock*, where, sure enough, a small gangway led up from the dock to the head of a narrow companionway on the lower deck. And as Jennie had prophesied, there was no sailor on watch duty at either end, in fact there wasn't so much as a soul about.

"No time like the present," said Jennie cheerfully, having inspected the set-up thoroughly. She took a few more cautious sniffs all around, and then, without further ado, trotted up the gangplank with Peter following her close behind.

CHAPTER TEN

Price of Two Tickets to Glasgow

ONCE ABOARD, JENNIE'S experience and knowledge of ships stood her in good stead. She called for the point-to-point method of procedure again, for she was particularly anxious not to encounter any humans before the ship had cast off, and while she herself could melt and blend with the shadows in corners and behind things, she was worried over the conspicuousness of Peter's snow-white coat. But she followed her nose and her instincts as well as her memory of the other steamships on which she had served, and soon was leading Peter down a narrow companionway that led to a small dining saloon and thence to the galley.

Tea was long since over, all of the crew and officers were on deck engaged with the cargo and preparations for leaving, and Jennie counted on finding that part of the ship deserted. She was right. The galley fires were out and there was no immediate sign of cook or sculleryman. Also no doors were shut anywhere, which gave Jennie further indication as to what kind of a craft it was, and she led him from the galley through the pantry to the small storeroom where the immediate supplies were kept. At the end of this room was a doorway, and a narrow iron staircase that descended to another passageway, on one side of which was the refrigeration room and on the other a large dry-stores enclosure where the ship's supplies in bulk were kept – sacks of flour and beans and dried peas, tins of fruit and vegetables, boxes of biscuits, tea, coffee, etc.

The slatted door to this also stood wide open. It was dark, but an electric light burning far down the passageway shed sufficient light so that with their acute vision they soon accustomed themselves and could see their way about the boxes and cartons and barrels as well as though it were broad daylight.

And it was there in the storeroom, well concealed behind a case of tinned tomatoes, that Peter saw and missed his first mouse, revealing what might have been a fatal weakness in their plans. It had never dawned on him, and Jennie too had quite neglected to think about it and take into consideration that for all his looking like and appearing to be, and learning to behave like a cat, Peter had not the faintest idea how to go about the difficult and important business of catching a mouse.

Indeed, it was only through the lucky break that in the last moment more cargo arrived and the *Countess of Greenock* did not sail that night, nor the next night either, that they were able to remedy this deficiency at least partly, for superstition or no, a cat that proved itself wholly unable to catch marauding rodents might have received short shrift aboard such a craft.

The awkward discovery came when Jennie called his attention to the little scratching, nibbling sort of noise from the other side of the storeroom, whispering – "Ssh! Mouse! There he is over by the biscuit box. Let's see you get him."

Peter concentrated, staring through the gloom, and there indeed he was, just edging around the corner of the large tin marked Huntley & Palmer Ltd, Reading, a long, greyish chap with a greedy face, impertinent whiskers, and beady black eyes.

Peter was so anxious to show off to Jennie what he could do as a cat if given the chance, that he hardly even set himself to spring, or paused to measure the distance, the obstacles, and the possible avenues of escape open to the mouse. Without a moment's thought or plan, he launched himself through the air in one terrific pounce, paws spread wide, jaws open to snatch him.

There was of course no mouse there when Peter landed.

And not only that, but his teeth clicked together on empty air, there was nothing beneath his paws and, in addition, having miscalculated the distance, or rather not calculated it at all, he gave himself a nasty knock on the head against the side of the tin box, all of which did not help the feeling that he had made a perfect fool of himself.

But while the mouse had saved itself momentarily, it also committed a fatal error by failing to dodge back behind the tin. Instead, gripped by panic, it emitted a squeak and went the other way, and the next instant, like a streak of furred lightning, Jennie had hurled herself through the air, her front paws, talons bared and extended, striking from side to side in a series of short, sharp, stunning hooks, even while she was in passage. The blows, as she landed, caught the mouse, knocking him first to one side, then back to the other, dazed and bewildered, then tossed him up in the air, batted him a couple before he came down, at which point Jennie seized him in her mouth and it was all over before Peter had even so much as recovered his balance as well as from his confusion.

"Oh dear," Jennie said, dropping the mouse. "I hadn't thought of that. Of course you wouldn't know how. Why should you? But we *shall* be in a pretty pickle if were caught here before you know something about it. And I don't know how much time we shall have. Still…"

Peter at last found his tongue and emitted a cry of anger and mortification. "Goodness," he said, "isn't there *anything* I can do? Does EVERYTHING have to be learned?"

"It's practice, really," Jennie explained. "Even *we* have to keep practising constantly. That, and while I hate to use the expression – 'know-how'. It's like everything else. You find there's a right way and a wrong way. The right way is to catch them with your paws, not your mouth, and of course the preparation is *everything*. Look here, I'll show you what I mean…"

Here she crouched down a few feet away from the dead mouse and then began a slow waggling of her hindquarters from side to side, gradually increasing the speed and shortening the distance of the waggle. "*That's* what you must try, to begin with," she explained. "We don't do that for fun, or because we're nervous, but to give ourselves motion. It's ever so much harder and less accurate to spring from a standing start than from a moving one. Try it now and see how much easier it is to take off than the other way."

Peter's rear-end waggle was awkward at first, but he soon began to find the rhythm of it – it was almost like the "One to get set, two to make ready and THREE to go" in foot-racing, except that this was even better because he found that what Jennie said was quite true and that the slight bit of motion did start him off the mark like an arrow.

Next he had to learn to move his paws so that, as he flew through the air and landed, they were striking left, right, with incredible speed, a feat that was much more difficult than it sounds since he could not use them to land on but had to bring up his hind part in time while lashing out with the front.

His second mouse he missed by a hair's breadth, owing to over-anxiousness, but Jennie praised his paw-work and spring, criticising only his judgement of distance and haste. "You rarely lose a mouse by waiting just a little longer," she explained, "because a mouse has a one-track mind and will keep on doing what it started out to do provided it isn't disturbed, and if it is disturbed it will just sit there and quake so that you have all the time in the world really…"

But his third mouse Peter caught and killed, one-two-three, just like that. Jennie said that she could not have done it better herself, and when Peter made her a present of it she accepted it graciously and with evident pleasure and ate it. But the others they saved because Jennie said that when they came to be discovered it would be a good thing to have some samples of their type of work about them.

And so for the rest, Peter practised and hunted busily, and Jennie advised him to keep the mouse alive and in the air as long as possible, not to torture it, but to gain in skill and accuracy, and train his muscles to react swiftly at the slightest movement.

It was the second night before they sailed that Peter awoke to an uncomfortable feeling. There was a new and unpleasant odour in the storeroom, one that tended to make him a little sick. And suddenly from a far corner he saw glowing two evil-looking red eyes. Before he could stir, he sensed through his whiskers that Jennie was awake too, and for the first time using this means of communication with him so that there should not be a sound, she warned: "Rat! It is serious, Peter, and very dangerous. This is something I cannot teach you or help you with. You'll just have to watch me and try to learn as best you can. And above all now, whatever happens, don't move a muscle, don't stir, and don't make a sound, even if you want to. Now remember. I'm off."

Through the shadowing gloom, Peter watched the stalk, his heart thumping in his chest, for this was different from the gay, almost lighthearted, hunt of mice. Jennie's entire approach and attitude was one of complete concentration, the carriage of her body, the expression of her head, flattened forward, the glitter in her eyes, and the slow, fluid, amazingly controlled movement of her body. There was a care, caution, and deadly earnestness about her that Peter had never seen before, and his own throat felt dry and his skin and moustache twitched nervously. But he did his best to hold himself rigid and motionless as she had told him, lest some slip of his might bring her into trouble.

The wicked red eyes were glowing like two hot coals now, and Peter's acute hearing could make out the nasty sniffling noises of the rat and the dry scrabbling of its toes on the storeroom floor. Jennie had gone quite flat now, and was crawling along the boards on her belly. She stopped and held herself long and rigid for a moment, her eyes intent upon her prey, measuring, measuring...

Then, inch by inch, she began to draw herself up into a little ball of fur-covered steel muscles for the spring. The rat was broadside to her. She took only two waggles, one to the left, one to the right, and then she was in the air, aimed at the flank of the rat.

But lightning-fast as she was, the rodent seemed to be even faster, for his head came around over his shoulder and his white teeth were bared in a wicked, slashing movement – and Peter wanted to shout to his friend: "Jennie, LOOK OUT!" but just in time he remembered her admonition under no circumstances to make a sound, and choked it down.

And then he saw what seemed to him to be a miracle, for launched as she was and in mid-air, Jennie saw the swift movement of the rat and, swifter herself, avoided the sharp, ripping teeth and making a turn in the air, a kind of half-twist such as Peter had seen the high divers do in the pool at Wembley one summer, she landed on the back of the rat and immediately sank her teeth in its spine, just below the head.

Then followed a dreadful moment of banging and slamming and scraping and squealing, and the sharp snick of teeth as the rat snapped viciously and fought to escape while Jennie hung on for dear life, her jaws clamping deeper and deeper, until there was a sharp click and the next moment the rat hung limp and paralysed and a few seconds later it was all over.

Jennie came away from it a little shaken and agitated, saying, "Phew! Filthy, sickening beasts! I *hate* rats – next to people… They're all unclean and diseased, and if you let them bite you anywhere, then *you* get sick, for their teeth are all poisoned, and sometimes you die from it. I'm always afraid of that…"

Peter said with deep sincerity, "Jennie, I think you are the bravest and most wonderful person – I mean cat – I ever saw. *Nobody* could have done that the way you did."

For once Jennie did not preen herself or parade before Peter, for she was worried now since it was she who had coaxed him into this adventure. She said: "That's just it, Peter. We can't practise and learn on the rats the way we did on the mice, because it's too dangerous. One mistake and, well – I don't want it to happen. I *can* show you the twist, because you have to know how to do it to avoid that slash of theirs, but the spring, the distance, the timing, and above all just the exact place to bite them behind the neck to get at their spines – well, you must do it one hundred per cent right when the time comes, and that's all there is. If you get them too high on the head they can kick loose or even shake you off. Some of the big fellows weigh almost as much as you do, and if you seize them too far down the back they can turn their heads and cut you."

"But how will I learn, then?" Peter asked.

"Let me handle them for the time being," she replied, "and watch me closely each time I kill one. You'll be learning something. Then if, and when, the moment comes when you have to do it yourself, you'll either do it right the first time and never forget it thereafter, or—" Jennie did not finish the sentence but instead went into the washing routine, and Peter felt a little cold chill run down his spine.

When they were finally discovered it was some seven hours after sailing, as the *Countess of Greenock* was thumping her slow, plodding way down the broad reaches of the Thames Estuary. When the cook, an oddly triangular-shaped Jamaican negro by the name of Mealie, came into the storeroom for some tinned corned beef, they had a bag of eight mice and three rats lined up in lieu of references and transportation. Three of the mice were Peter's, and he felt inordinately proud of them and wished there could have been some way whereby he might have had his name on them, like autographing a book perhaps – "Caught by Peter Brown, Storeroom, *Countess of Greenock*, April 15th 1949."

The negro grinned widely, increasing the triangular effect, for his face and head were narrower at the top than at the bottom, and he said: "By Jominy, dat good. Hit pays to hodvertise. I tell dat to Captain," and forthwith went up on to the bridge, taking Jennie's and Peter's samples with him. It was the kind of a ship where the cook did go up on to the bridge if he felt like having a word with the captain. There he told him the story of finding the two stowaways, and then added: "But by Jominy they pay possage already. Look you dat!" and unrolling his apron showed him the fruits of their industry.

The captain, whose name was Sourlies and who was that rare specimen, a fat Scotsman, looked and felt ill, and commanded Mealie in no uncertain language to throw the mess over the side and go back to his galley. It was the beginning of his time of deep unhappiness, anyway, for he hated the sea and everything connected with it and was reasonably contented only when in port, or near it, or proceeding up and down an estuary or river with plenty of land on both sides.

He carried this queer notion to the point of refusing even to dress the part of a ship's captain, and conducted the affairs of the *Countess of Greenock* wearing a tweed pepper-and-salt business suit with a gold watch-chain across his large expanse of stomach, and a mustard-coloured fedora hat, or trilby, with the brim turned up all round.

However, as Mealie was leaving, he did decree that inasmuch as the cats seemed to have got aboard and appeared inclined to work their passage they might remain, but to shift one of them to the fo'c'sle as the men had been complaining of the rats there.

But Mealie took his time going aft, and told his story and showed the bag to everyone he met, with the result that there arrived back in the storeroom quite a committee consisting of Mr Strachan, the first mate; Mr Carluke, the second; Chief Engineer McDunkeld; and the bo'sun, whose name appeared to be only Angus.

They held a meeting, the gist of which Peter tried to translate rapidly for Jennie's benefit, and before they knew it the two friends found themselves separated for the first time, with Jennie sent forward to live with the crew and Peter retained, chiefly through the insistence of Mr Strachan, in the officers' quarters.

Jennie had only time to say to Peter, "Don't worry. We'll find ways to get together. Do your best. And if you come across a rat, don't hesitate and don't play. Kill!"

Then the bo'sun picked her up by the scruff of the neck and carried her forward.

Chapter Eleven

The *Countess* and the Crew

WHEN PETER HAD been a boy at home, Nanny had often told him stories about the small steamers that used to tie up at Greenock and Gourock, the two port towns outside of Glasgow, where she used to live when she was a little girl. But never, Peter decided, could there have been such an odd ship with such a strange and ill-assorted crew as the *Countess of Greenock* and her motley band of officers, sailors and deckhands whom he now learned to know, as the *Countess* loafed lazily along the south and west coasts of England, thrusting her stubby, rust-eaten bow into port apparently at the slightest opportunity and even when there did not seem to be a legitimate reason for her doing so.

For nobody on board, as far as Peter could make out, seemed to make much sense. With the exception of the second engineer, who was absolutely not to be separated from the ancient and clanking machinery and somehow still managed to propel the *Countess* at jellyfish pace through the choppy waters of the Channel, each and every one appeared to have some peculiarity or hobby which interested him and took up more of his time than was devoted to the necessary duties connected with keeping the ship afloat and guiding it to its destination.

To begin with, there was the Captain, Mr Sourlies, and when, in their spare time during the afternoon, Peter and Jennie used to foregather in the cargo hold just abaft the island bridge, or keep a rendezvous astern to gossip and exchange notes on their work, adventures and the people they had met, they agreed that from everything they had seen and heard they had never encountered a queerer one than he.

His dislike of the sea and everything and everyone connected with it, Peter learned through listening to the officers and members of the crew discussing him, stemmed from the fact, according to Mr McDunkeld, the chief engineer, that Captain Sourlies came from a long line of seafarers. But when it came *his* turn to take up the profession, he had run away from home in Glasgow to a farm, for what he was really interested in was agriculture.

Mr Fairlie, the radio operator, to whom Mr McDunkeld told this story, said that he had often heard of farm boys running away to sea, but never in all his born days had he known of a sea-type running away to a farm. Peter then heard Mr McDunkeld say that as far as he knew it was true, and that Captain Sourlies's father had been very angry when he found him in the midst of a lot of cows and chickens and pigs, and brought him back, shipped him off to sea, and forced him to take a master's ticket. When his father had passed on, he had hung the final anchor around his son's neck by willing him the controlling interest in the *Countess of Greenock*. Captain Sourlies's Scottish thrift and business acumen would not permit him to entrust her to others, and so he, who so loved the land, was doomed to a life at sea.

By keeping the *Countess* in the coastwise trade, and causing her to call at as many ports, almost, as there were between London and Glasgow, he managed to avoid the sea as much as possible, as well as pick up a great deal of business. While *en route* between ports he was silent, gloomy, irritable and unhappy, and kept to himself in his cabin where he studied the subject of agriculture. He rarely appeared on the bridge. Any delay encountered at sea between ports, such as engine trouble, or fog, or headwinds, would see him show his head at the door for a moment to enquire into the cause thereof, and then, no matter what the reason, retire to his cabin in a huge and absolute tantrum which manifested itself in his breaking every bit of glassware or crockery that happened to be within reach at the time.

Peter and Jennie estimated that the captain weighed close on twenty-two stone, which would be over three hundred pounds. He had smallish eyes, somewhat deep-set and knowing, like a pig's, and a series of chins that rippled out from a small and petulant mouth, reminding Peter of the concentric rings that formed in a pond when you throw a stone into the water. But what astonished them both the most was that instead of the deep and thunderous rumble one would expect to have emerged from such an enormous

129

frame and cavernous chest, his voice when he spoke was high-pitched and cooing like a dove, and the angrier he became over anything, and most things when he was at sea made him angry, the higher and sweeter and more softly he cooed. He never appeared on the bridge or anywhere on deck without his mustard-coloured trilby hat, and in bad or wet weather he wore not oilskins and sou'westers as did the rest of the crew, but a tan mackintosh. He only cheered up and appeared for occasional meals aft when the *Countess* was running up river somewhere, or landlocked in an estuary.

Quite the opposite was Mr Strachan, the first mate, a tall, youngish fellow with red hair, narrow blue eyes, and a low forehead, who, as Jennie pointed out, was not very bright, but who loved the sea and considered everything that took place on or about it to be an adventure, great or small. This naturally was bound to bring him into conflict with the captain, and truth to tell, the two men did not get on too well. But since, at any rate at sea, Captain Sourlies left practically the entire operation and management of things to Mr Strachan, this did not matter too much.

Peter soon discovered that Mr Strachan, in addition to his profession, had two major interests in life. One was indulgence in the art of fence – and he faithfully attended the sessions of a fencing club when he was ashore both in Glasgow and London – and the other was a passion for telling not entirely credible yarns tinged with a 'believe-it-or-not' flavour, of miraculous things and adventures that had happened to him in his life at sea and various foreign ports.

When the listener expressed wonder or even polite doubt that such an occurrence could have taken place, Mr Strachan would present 'proof' of the incident by, for instance, exhibiting a burnt-out matchstick, or a small pebble, or a bit of paper, and saying "…ond this verra bit o' paper I'm showing ye here was in me pocket at the verra instant all this was hoppening to me." He was always busy collecting such odd bits and scraps to be used for this purpose, and he was quite upset with Mealie, the cook, for eventually obeying Captain Sourlies's orders and dropping the rats and mice that Peter and Jennie had caught over the side, as he felt that the corpses of the rodents would have furnished incontrovertible evidence of the story of the two cats who had stowed away aboard ship and when found had their passage money ready in this form.

Quite fascinating to Peter who, as a boy, had always had a fondness for reading stories and seeing pictures of swordplay, was Mr Strachan's fencing practice during the voyage. It took the form of attacking a dummy that Mr Box, the ship's carpenter, had made for him, and which he set up on the after cargo hatch when the weather was fine, and belaboured with a sword.

This dummy was known to one and all aboard the *Countess of Greenock* as 'Auld Sourlies', for whether the carpenter had intended so or not, he had somehow managed to make him in considerable resemblance to the stout captain both in face and in figure. Auld Sourlies, the dummy, that is, had a wooden arm, canvas-covered, with a powerful spring in the wrist to which was attached his sword, an epée with three needle-sharp little steel points. When Mr Strachan struck it preparatory to making an attack upon him it would waggle almost as though Auld Sourlies was vigorously defending himself.

And so when he was off duty, there would be Mr Strachan on the canvas-covered after-hatch, bare to the waist and sword in hand, shouting "Hah!" and "Heh!" at Auld Sourlies set up dumbly facing him, and "Oh, ye would, would ye? Alez, then take thot and thot and thot!" as he leaped in and out jabbing the point of his sword into the dummy's canvas body, while Peter and Jennie, when they also happened to be off duty at the same time, sat a little distance away and watched him, enthralled, their eyes bound to the flashing point and their heads moving as it moved, forwards and backwards, or side to side, almost like patrons at a tennis match.

Once, quite early in the voyage, when Mr Strachan made a particularly violent attack and lunge, he apparently missed parrying the dummy's riposte somehow, when the blade snapped back and Auld Sourlies's point then laid his arm open almost from wrist to elbow, wounding him grievously. All the crew and officers of the *Countess* promptly dropped whatever they happened to be doing at the moment and came to look, including Captain Sourlies who had the first-aid kit and put six stitches in Mr Strachan's arm. He did so, it seemed to Peter, with considerable satisfaction. In fact, it appeared to both Peter and Jennie that the captain was almost pleased with what had happened and was acting in a way as though it had been *he* who had done it to Mr Strachan instead of the dummy, as he swabbed and stitched the injured arm, murmuring that he hoped that this would be a lesson to Mr Strachan.

To the mate, however, it was another miraculous yarn to tell of himself being probably the only fencer in the world ever to be defeated and seriously wounded by a dummy, and what was more, there was the proof of it on his arm, which he would carry to his grave.

But Peter's real favourite among the officers was the second mate, little Mr Carluke, who looked somewhat like an inoffensive stoat, and who wrote Wild West and cowboy and Indian stories for the tuppenny dreadfuls and serial magazines in his spare time to eke out his income and prepare for the day when he would retire from the sea and devote his entire time to literature. He had never seen an Indian except in the pictures, or been west of the Scilly Isles, but he had read a great deal about cowboys and their ways and was given to acting out some of his dramas in the seclusion of his cabin between watches, before setting them down on paper.

He was fond of cats, and so Peter was able to spend many a pleasant and exciting hour sitting on the table where Mr Carluke was writing one of his tales. It was, he told Jennie later, almost as good as going to the cinema. For the little second mate would lay down his pen and quite suddenly and dramatically leap to his feet, clap both hands to his sides in the action of one extracting two horse pistols from their leather holsters, and then, pointing his forefingers with thumbs cocked like the hammers of a pair of six-shooters, he would say in a tense voice, "Dinna ye move, thar, Luke Short, ye no-good hoss thief, or I doot not I'll be lettin' some ventilation through ye with my twa double oction forty-five colibre gats, forbye!" Then he would go quickly back to his desk and write it all down exactly as he had said it, which Peter found quite miraculous. Or he would pick up a kitchen knife and go through the motions of lifting the scalp of an imaginary redskin, and even imitate the sound of the chase when the cavalry came to the rescue by slapping his hands briskly in rhythm against his legs, thup-athup, thup-athup, thup-athup.

Since Jennie's domain was the forecastle where during the night watches she constituted herself a very terror among the giant rats which inhabited it, to the delight and satisfaction of the members of the crew who had to live there, she was more familiar with the characters up for'ard and brought Peter tales she had managed to glean of some of the strange people in that part of the ship.

There was, she told him, a sailor who had once been a hermit and lived in a cave for ten years until one day he thought better of it, another who had operated a permanent-wave machine in a beauty parlour in Edinburgh until something had unhappily gone wrong with it and he had toasted a client's hair to a crisp, so that it had all fallen out and he had been discharged, and a third who used to give exhibitions at Brighton of staying under water for extraordinary lengths of time holding his breath.

Through practice and association, Jennie was becoming more conversant with human speech again, and her most remarkable story was of Angus the bo'sun and how he occupied his spare time when not on watch or engaged in other duties. What did Peter suppose he did?

Peter had seen Angus, an enormous giant of a man, whiskered like a Highlander, with arms like the branches of oak trees, horny hands with red, bony knuckles, and fingers as big and thick as blood-pudding sausages. When Peter said that he couldn't imagine what his hobby would be, she told him – "Embroidering." He embroidered beautiful flowers with coloured thread on a linen cloth stretched over a wooden hoop. They were really exquisite, for she had spent one entire morning watching him, and so lifelike one could almost smell them.

One of the new men on board had been so foolish as to sneer at Angus and mock him, whereupon Angus had stretched him unconscious on the deck with one blow, and thereafter there was no more laughter. When the fellow returned to consciousness, after several buckets of water, the men had told him that he had been foolish to ridicule Angus, not because of the blow he had received, but because he ought to have known that when the *Countess of Greenock* arrived in Glasgow, Angus took the embroidery to a certain place and received three pounds ten for it.

It was remarkable that in spite of the strange mixture of men, interests and hobbies, the crew of the *Countess of Greenock* and the officers, with the exception of the captain and the first mate, got along quite nicely with one another and somehow managed to perform their duties sufficiently well to get her from port to port along the coast without breaking down, running her aground, or getting lost too often. Jennie said that of all the ships she had travelled on she had never seen a more inept or inefficient bunch of sailors, and naturally with nearly everybody aboard having some kind of sideline or other interest, from the captain down, nobody had much time or inclination to keep the *Countess* either clean or shipshape. But since Captain Sourlies did not seem to care whether his ship looked like a pigsty, nobody else did either, and so they all lived quite happily and contentedly in this mess. Jennie found it rather distasteful, but Peter being part boy thought it a real lark to be some place you simply couldn't get dirty because it was already so, and he only bothered to keep himself clean because of not wishing to let Jennie down.

But outside of this, Jennie had few complaints to make, and Peter none at all. She had been quite right about the routine aboard the ship. Everyone attended either to his job or to his private affairs, whichever happened to interest him the most, and no one had either the time of the inclination to be loving or sentimental with the two cats. Mr Carluke would sometimes timidly rub Peter's head a little when he sat on his desk, but otherwise they were left quite to themselves.

It was not necessary for them to eat their kill, for twice a day, morning and evening, Mealie the Jamaican cook set out a pan of delicious food for them – cereal with tinned milk over it, or salt meat chopped up, or a bit off the frozen joint mixed up with some vegetables. They were protecting *his* stores from the depredations of mice and rats, and he was grateful and treated them with the respect due to regular crew members who were doing their job. In the morning when he came in to make the galley fire he would call down the companionway to Peter below: "Ho, you Whitey! How many you cotch los' night?" Then he would come and look down to where Peter would have the night's bag of mice neatly laid out at the foot of the ladder.

He would laugh and call down, "Ho, ho! You Whitey, you do good job. I give you and your gorl-friend good brokfost this morning. How you like to have a piece fry bacon?"

Peter and Jennie were on duty at night only, since by day the wary rodents kept out of sight, particularly after the news got around, which it did very quickly, that not one but two cats were on board. They then slept most of the morning after they had had breakfast and met in the late afternoon either in one of the cargo holds amidships, or when the weather was clear and sunny and the sea calm, on deck aft where they could breathe the fresh, invigorating salt air while the *Countess of Greenock*, pouring black smoke and cinders from her funnel, wallowed close enough to the emerald-green pastures and dark rocks of the English coast for them to see the purple haze of the vast bluebell patches, and, further south, the clifftops dotted with yellow primroses.

But they did not neglect their lessons and practice either, and in bad weather when it was blowing and raining, or when the *Countess* was held up by fog, they repaired to a clear space in the Number 2 cargo hold where Jennie resumed her labour of love to try to teach Peter all of the things he would need to know if he were to become a successful and self-supporting cat.

CHAPTER TWELVE

Overboard!

USING THE SMOOTH sides of a huge packing case as a practice ground, Peter learned the secret of the double jump-up, or second lift, or rather, after long hours of trial with Jennie coaching, it suddenly came to him. One moment he had been slipping, sliding and falling back as he essayed to scale the perpendicular sides, and the next he had achieved it, a lightning-like thrust with the hind legs, which somehow this time stuck to the sides of the case and gave him added impetus upwards, and thereafter he could always do it.

Jennie was most pleased with him, for, as she explained it, this particular trick of leaping up the side of a blank wall without so much as a crack or an irregularity to give a toe-hold, was peculiar to cats, and it was also one that could neither be wholly explained, demonstrated or taught. The best she was able to tell him was: "You *think* your way to the top, Peter. You just know you are going to be able to do it, and then you can."

Well, once the old *Countess* had taken a bit of a roll in the trough of a sea, and that helped Peter a little and gave him confidence. And the next time he felt certain he was going to be able to do it, and he did.

Jennie was endlessly patient in teaching Peter control of his body in the air, for she maintained that few things were of so much importance to cats. With her he studied the twist in mid-air from the spring so that once he had left the ground he could change his direction almost like flying, and Peter loved the sense of power and freedom that came to him when he turned himself in the air like an acrobat or a high diver, and this he practised more than anything. And he had to learn too, how to drop from any normal height and twist in falling so that he would always land on his feet, and soon, with Jennie's help he became so expert that he could roll off a case no more than a yard from the ground and still, turning like a flash, whip round so that his four paws touched the deck first and that without a sound.

But their free time was not all devoted to hard work and practice. There were quiet hours when they rested side by side on a hatch combing and Peter would ask Jennie questions, for instance, why she always preferred to perch on high things and look down, and she would explain about the deep instincts that survived from the days millions and millions of years ago when no doubt all cats were alike in size and shape and had to learn to protect themselves to survive. To escape the dangers that lurked on or near the ground from things that crawled, slithered, or trampled, they took to living high up in rocky caves, or perched along branches of trees where they could look down and see everything that approached them.

In the same manner, Jennie explained, cats liked to sleep in boxes, or bureau drawers, because they felt completely surrounded on all sides by high walls, as they were deep in their caves, and therefore felt relaxed and secure and able to sleep.

Or again, Peter would say: "Jennie, why, when you are pleased and happy and relaxed, do your claws work in and out in that queer way? And once back home, I mean when we lived in the warehouse, I noticed that you were moving your paws up and down, almost as though you were making the bed. I never do that, though I do purr when I am happy—"

Jennie was lying on her side on the canvas hatch cover when Peter asked that question, and she raised her head and gave him a most tender glance before she replied: "I know, Peter. And it is just another of those things that tell me that in spite of your shape and form you are really human, and perhaps always will be. But maybe I can explain it to you. Peter, say something sweet to me."

The only thing Peter could think of to say was: "Oh, Jennie, I wish that I could be all cat – so that I might be more like you…"

The most beatific smile stole over Jennie's face. Her throat throbbed with purring, and slowly her white paws began to work, the claws moving in and out as though she were kneading dough.

"You see?" she said to Peter. "It has to do with feeling happy. It goes all the way back to our being kittens and being nursed by our mothers. We cannot even see at first, but only feel, for when we are first born we are blind and our eyes open only after a few weeks. But we can feel our way to her breast and bury ourselves in her soft, sweet-smelling fur to find her milk, and when we are there we work our paws gently up and down to help the food we want so much to flow more freely. Then when it does, we feel it in our throats, warm and satisfying; it stops our hunger and our thirst, it soothes our fears and desires, and, oh, Peter, we are *so* blissful and contented at that moment, so secure and peaceful and… well, just happy. We never forget those moments with our mothers. They remain with us all the rest of our lives. And, later on, long after we are grown, when something makes us very happy, our paws and claws go in and out he same way, in memory of those early times of our first real happiness. And that is all I can tell you about it."

Peter found that after this recital he had need to wash himself energetically for a few moments, and then he went over to where Jennie was lying and washed her face too, giving her several caresses beneath her soft chin and along the side of her muzzle that conveyed more to her than words. She made a little soft, crooning sound in her throat, and her claws worked in and out, kneading the canvas hatch cover faster than ever.

But likewise, during the long days of the leisurely voyage, and particularly when they were imprisoned in Dartmouth

Harbour for two days by pea-soup fog, there was mock-fighting to teach Peter how to take care of himself should he ever find himself in any trouble, as well as all the feline sports and games for one or two that Jennie knew or remembered and could teach him, and they spent hours rolling about, growling and spitting, locking in play combat, waiting in ambush to surprise one another, playing hide-seek-and-jump-out, or chasing one another madly up and down the gangways and passages below deck, their pads ringing oddly on the iron floors of the ancient *Countess*, like tiny galloping horses.

And here again, Peter was to learn that not only were there methods and strict rules that governed play as well as the more serious encounters between cat and cat, but that he needed to study as well as practise them with Jennie in order to acquire by repetition the feeling of the rhythms that were a part of these games.

Thus, Jennie would coach him: "I make a move to attack you, maybe a pass at your tail, or a feint at one of your legs; raise your left paw and be ready to strike with it. That's it. That makes me think twice before coming in. No, no, Peter, don't take your eyes off me just because I've stopped. Be ready as long as I am tense. But you've got to *feel* it when I've changed my mind and relaxed a little. You can drop your left paw, but keep watching. There! *I've* looked away for a moment – now WASH! That stops everything. I can't do anything until you've finished except wash too, and that puts the next move up to you and it's your advantage."

Most difficult for him was the keeping of the upper hand by eye and body position and acquiring by experience the feeling of when it was safe to relax and turn away to rest, how to break up the other's plans by washing, luring and drawing the opponent on by pretending to look away and then timing his own attack to the split second when the other was off balance and unprepared for it, and yet not violate the rules, which often made no rhyme or reason to him at all.

None of these things Peter would have done instinctively as a boy and he had to learn them from Jennie by endless repetition, and often he marvelled at her patience as she drilled him over and over: "Crouch, Peter. Now sit up quickly and look away… WASH! Size up the situation out of the corner of your eye as you wash. I'm waiting to jump you as soon as you stop washing. Then turn and get ready. Here I come. Roll with it, on to your back. Hold me with your forepaws and kick with the hind legs. Harder… harder… No, stay there, Peter. I'm coming back for a second try. Chin down so I can't get at your throat. Kick. Now roll over and sit up, paw ready and threaten with it. If I blink my eyes and back away, WASH. Now pretend you are interested in something imaginary. That's it. If you make it real enough you can get me to look at it, and when I do, then you spring!"

Jennie had a system of scoring these bouts, so many points for buffets, so many for knockdowns and roll overs, for breakaways and washes, for chases and ambushes, for the amount of fur that flew by tufts to be counted later, for numbers of back-kicks delivered, for bluffs and walk-aways, feints and ducking, with bonuses for position and length of time in control, and game plus one hundred points called any time one manoeuvred into position to grip teeth on the throat of the other.

And gradually, almost imperceptibly at first, the scores drew nearer level, and soon Peter found himself winning regularly over Jennie in the training ring they had arranged among the crates and boxes in the forward hold. And when this proved to be the case and Peter won almost every time, none was prouder and happier over it than Jennie. "Soon," she said with satisfaction, "you'll be cat through and through."

And yet when the tragedy happened it was just as well that Peter was not all cat.

In a way it began when Peter caught his first rat. The *Countess of Greenock* was ploughing the Irish Sea 'twixt the Isle of Man and the Cumberland coast, close enough inshore that one could see the peaks of the Cumbrian mountains inland, shining in the sun. The ocean was flat, calm and glassy, and the only cloud in the sky was the one made by the black smoke poured forth by the *Countess* and which, owing to a following breeze over the surface, she carried along with her over her head like an untidy old charwoman shielding herself from the sun with an old black cotton umbrella. They were on the reach between Liverpool and Port Carlisle on the Scottish border, and Captain Sourlies was in a great hurry to make it before nightfall, which was why the *Countess* was under forced draught, emitting volumes of soft-coal smoke and shuddering from the vibrations of her hurrying engines.

Peter had an appointment with Jennie on the after-deck at six bells of the early afternoon watch, or three o'clock, for he had quickly learned to tell the ship's time from the strokes of the bell struck by the look-out on the bridge. This was always a kind of do-as-you-please time aboard the *Countess*, for then Captain Sourlies would be taking his afternoon nap in his cabin, Mr Carluke, torn from his latest literary composition, which he was calling *The Bandit of Golden Gulch*, was on duty on the bridge, and everybody else followed his hobby or loafed by the rail or snoozed in the sun. And since Mr Strachan, the first mate, still had a badly aching arm from the stitches taken in it, his dummy lurked in a corner in disgrace and the red-haired mate on this day was yarning with Mr Box, the carpenter, about an episode that had happened to him in Gibraltar during the war, and as proof produced an 1890 Queen Victoria copper penny that he had happened to be carrying on his person at the time of the adventure.

Jennie was already dozing in the soft spring sunshine, squatted down atop the stern rail. She liked to perch there because it was fairly high and gave her an overall view, and also to show her superiority, for everyone was always prophesying that some day she would be knocked or fall off from there into the sea. But of course there never was a cat more certain or surefooted than Jennie Baldrin.

Peter awoke promptly at ten minutes to three – he found that he could now awake at exactly any time he desired – and made a rough toilet with his tongue. He stretched and strolled casually from the lower storeroom which was his quarters and which it was also his job to keep clear of vermin. Up to that moment there had been only mice, which Peter had kept down quite handily.

He should have smelled the rat long before he saw it, but then, although his smell senses were feline and quite sharp, his mind was still human and he had been thinking that he must tell Jennie about a member of the black gang, a stoker who fed the furnace, who was such an admirer of Winston Churchill that he had a picture of him tattooed on his chest, cigar and all. And so he had not been alert. When he saw the rat, he was in a very bad position.

The beast was almost as large as a fox terrier and it was cornered in a small alcove made by some piled-up wooden cases of tinned baked beans from which several boxes had been removed from the centre. Also it was daylight, Peter wasn't stalking, and the rat saw Peter at the same time that Peter saw him, and uttered an ugly squeal of rage and bared long yellow teeth, teeth that Peter knew were so unclean that a single scratch from them might well poison him beyond help. And for the first time he really understood what people meant by the expression 'fight like a cornered rat', or rather he was about to understand. For in spite of the fact that Jennie had warned him never to go after a rat except when it was out in the open, he meant to attack this one and prove himself.

He was surprised to find that now in this moment of danger he was not thinking of lessons he had learned, or what he had seen or heard or what Jennie had said, but that his mind seemed to be extraordinarily calm and clear and that, almost as though it had always been there and ready and waiting, his plan unfolded itself in his mind. It was only much later he found out that this was the result of discipline, study, patience and practice that he had put behind him at Jennie's behest.

His spring, seemingly launched directly at the foe, appeared to be sheer folly, and the rat rose up on his hind legs to meet him head on, slashing at him viciously. But not for nothing had Peter learned and practised the secret of continuing up on a smooth wall from a single leap from the floor. A split-second faster than the rat, his fore and hind legs touched the slippery sides of one of the piles of cases for an instant and propelled him high into the air so that the flashing incisors of the rodent like two hideously curved Yataghans whizzed between his legs, missing him by the proverbial hair's breadth.

The extra impetus upwards now gave Peter the speed and energy to twist not half but the whole way around in a complete reverse and drop on to the back of the rat, to sink his own teeth deep into its spine just behind the ears.

For one dreadful moment Peter felt that he might yet be beaten, for the rat gave such a mighty heave and surge, and lashed so desperately to and fro, that Peter was thumped and banged up against the sides of the boxes until he felt himself growing sick and dizzy and no longer certain whether he could hold on. And if once he let go, the big fellow would turn on him and cut him to ribbons.

In desperation he set his teeth with all his might, and bit – one, two, three times hard, and at the third felt the rat suddenly stiffen. The swaying and banging stopped. The rodent kicked twice with its hind legs and then was still. It never moved again. Peter unclamped his aching jaws and sat down quickly and did some washing. He was badly shaken and most emphatically needed to recover his composure.

Nevertheless it was exactly at six bells that he came trotting on to the after-deck carrying the rat in his mouth, or rather dragging it, because it was so large that when he held it in the middle, its head and tail hung down to the deck. It was so heavy that he could barely lift it. But of course he managed because he simply had to show it off to Jennie and anyone else who happened to be around.

It was Mr Box who saw him first and let out a yell – "Blimey, looka there! The white un's caught a bloomin' Helephant."

Mr Strachan also gave a shout, for Peter passed quite close to him and the rat dragged over his foot causing him to jump as though he had been stung. The cries brought several deckhands over on the run to see. They also woke up Jennie Baldrin.

She had not meant to fall so soundly asleep, but the peaceful sea and the warm afternoon sun had lulled her deeper than she had intended, and now the sudden cries sent alarms tingling down her spine. And when she opened her eyes they fell on Peter and his rat, and in the first confusion she was not certain whether the rat was carrying Peter or vice versa, whether it was alive or dead, whether Peter was still engaged in fighting it. The sound of running feet added to her confusion and she recoiled from the unknown and the uncertain and the thought of possible danger to Peter.

But there was no place to recoil to from her precarious perch on the ship's rail, and with an awful cry, her four paws widespread, and turning over once in the air, she fell into the sea and was swept away in the white salt froth of propeller wash.

"Cat overboard!" a deckhand cried, and then laughed.

"Goodbye, Pussy," said Mr Box. "Arskin' for it, she was, perched up there loike that."

Mr Strachan stared with his mouth open.

The sailor who had been a hermit said to Peter: "There goes yer pal, Whitey. Ye'll no see Coptain Sourlies tairnen his ship aboot to rrrrrrrescue a wee puss baldrin—"

But Peter was no longer there. There was only a white streak of fur as he dropped the rat, leaped to the rail, and from it, long and low, shot straight into the sea after Jennie.

CHAPTER THIRTEEN

Mr Strachan Furnishes the Proof

SPLASH! INTO THE water Peter went!

It was roiling and boiling and full of sizzle and foam, surges, lifts, thrusts and undertows from the powerful strokes of the *Countess's* propeller just beneath the surface. Also it was shockingly cold.

Peter felt himself caught in the grip of an irresistible whirlpool; he was pulled down, rolled over, thrust head over heels, then shot to the surface, and before he could gasp his lungs full of air, sucked down again into the green depths. With his chest near to bursting from want of air, he fought and struggled to rise, swimming with all four feet, and at last reached the surface sufficiently far behind in the wake of the ship to be no longer subject to the forces stirred up by her machinery. The whirlpool died away, the choking white foam vanished, and he was swimming at last on top of the chill, salt, green and glassy sea.

Off in the distance, perhaps fifty or sixty yards away, he saw a tiny pinpoint of an object moving in the water and tried to call out – "Jennie! Don't be afraid! Hold out. It's me, Peter. I'm coming!" – but succeeded in getting only a mouthful of salt water which tasted horrible, and thereafter he decided to keep his mouth closed and concentrate on reaching her side. But he thought he heard a faint answering cry from her, and finding that he had no difficulty in staying up now and holding his head out of the water by lifting his chin, he swam as rapidly as his four legs would take him in her direction.

What would happen when he reached her, he did not know, or at least he was not minded to think about, since it was certain that the sailor was quite right and the last thing Captain Sourlies would do was put the *Countess* about and stop her, losing precious time for no better purpose than to snatch two vagrant cats, who were aboard quite uninvited, at that, from a watery grave. But at least, whatever happened, they would be together, he and the kind and gentle little cat who had first saved his life and then been so devoted to him. They would be together to swim to the mainland that glittered so green and enticing in the distance, and if they could not reach it – well, then, at least they could comfort one another in their last moments and would not be separated.

Now Peter had halved the distance between Jennie and himself and to his dismay saw that she was barely making headway in his direction. Her little head, with the ears thrown back, sleek and wet, was hardly borne above the surface, and she was swimming but weakly. Even then he heard her call to him, though it was barely audible – "Peter, go back! You shouldn't have come. I can't hold out any longer. Goodbye, Peter dear—"

And with that, her head vanished beneath the water. It reappeared once more, and now Peter was close enough to see the despairing look in her eyes before she went down again – she was gone. He redoubled his efforts, making his paws fairly foam through the water, while his breastbone parted the sea in the shape of an arrow or an inverted 'V' on either side of him, in a frantic effort to reach her in time, but now he could no longer see her or where she had been. Indeed, he would have lost her for ever, had not just at that moment the tip of her tail appeared above the surface like a buoy marking the spot. The next instant, more human than cat, he dived beneath the water, his eyes wide open, settled his teeth gently in Jennie's skin at the back of her neck, and quickly pulled himself and her with him back to the surface again.

By swimming slowly now, that is, just moving his feet, he was able to keep his head as well as hers above the water, limp and apparently senseless as she was, but he knew that there was no longer any question of their reaching the mainland a good two or three miles away. Indeed, the immediate question was how long would his own strength hold out to enable him to keep them on top of the sea. For he just now realised that he had been severely strained by his fight with the giant rat, while the thumping and battering he had taken against the sides of the cases had bruised him and further drained his strength. For the first time he began to have serious doubts as to whether they could manage to save themselves, and he had a treacherous moment given over to wondering whether it would not be easier to give up and, side by side with Jennie Baldrin, to sink for ever beneath the waves, or whether it was worth the struggle to keep on swimming and try to test out the old adage that while there was life there was yet hope.

Up to that moment, Peter had not even looked after the *Countess of Greenock*, for the sight of the ship diminishing in the distance and cruelly abandoning them to their fate would have been too painful to be endured, but now with the knowledge that it was only a matter of minutes before his own strength, taxed by the added difficulty of holding up Jennie, must give out, he began to swim in a small circle and permitted himself one despairing look to see just how far away it was she had sailed since he had leaped from her deck into the sea.

To his utter surprise and joy he saw her floating, stock still and motionless except for the black column of smoke pouring straight skyward from her funnel, not more than a hundred yards away. Turned broadside, her hull rising like a wall from the smooth surface of the water, she looked larger than pictures he had seen of the *Queen Mary*, and twice as handsome. And what was ten times more beautiful was the sight of the lifeboat manned by eight straining sailors, commanded by Angus the bo'sun and with Mr Strachan perched in the bow, already halfway between the rusted sides of the *Countess* and himself and Jennie. True, as a display of oarsmanship it was shocking, for no two of the blades dipped, pulled or emerged from the water in the same time; the lifeboat rocked alarmingly on the dead-calm sea, threatening to pitch both Angus and Mr Strachan over the side at any moment, and it resembled nothing so much as an inebriated porcupine trying to stagger along the roof of a glasshouse conservatory. Nevertheless, it was making definite headway and giving a convincing demonstration that the miracle *had* happened. The *Countess of Greenock* had gone about, circled and stopped, put forth a boat, and they *were* about to be rescued.

A few moments later, urged on by the shouts of Angus and the directions given by Mr Strachan from the bow, the lifeboat drew alongside. Mr Strachan was armed with a long pole, to the end of which was attached a dip-net. Leaning over the side, he thrust it through the water beneath Peter and Jennie, and with a triumphant cry of "Hah! Got 'em!" swept both out of the sea and into the bottom of the lifeboat, where Peter moved feebly, trying to disentangle his paws from the mesh of the net and feeling like crying from sheer relief and gratitude, and Jennie Baldrin moved not at all.

"Ready all!" bawled Angus — "Feather your oars! Port row, Starboard hold! Now then, DIP and PULL."

All of the sailors put their oars in and out of the water exactly as they pleased, but somehow in spite of them the lifeboat managed to turn round after nearly upsetting in the process and forthwith set out upon its disorderly progress back to the waiting *Countess of Greenock*.

In the bow, Mr Strachan squatted, fondly gazing upon

Peter and the still limp and motionless Jennie, and murmured: "'Tis a meeracle and an exomple of the wonders of nature. They'll nae be able to deny me the proof o' this tale in Glasgie at the Crown and Thistle," and he began to rehearse – "Unable to stond the sicht o' his little sweetheart droonin' in the cruel sea, yon braw and bonnie white tomcat, overcooming its notural aveersion to water, indoolged in a grand and flying leap over the side to swim to the rrrrrrrescue o' his ain true love…"

Mr Box, the carpenter, who was rowing stroke oar, sniggered and said: "'E won't arf catch it from the old man when he gets back. Wait until old Sourlies wakes up from his nap and finds out that Strachan has stopped 'is ship, wasted time, coal and money, and missed 'im the tide. Ow, 'e won't arf smash all 'is dishes, 'e won't."

The sailor who had been a hermit said: "Aye, that he will, but 'twould have been bad luck to let the wee puss baldrin droon, and though I canna give Muster Strachan full marks for his motives and pairpose in effecting the rrrrrrrescue. Yet the resoolts are what count, though I am afeered that the breath o' life has gone out o' the wee one."

Peter was desperately afraid of the same thing, for Jennie lay there, soaked and limp like a wet dishcloth, and nothing whatsoever seemed to be stirring beneath her thin ribs.

Also it was apparent that Mr Box had been right and their reception at the *Countess of Greenock* was not to be a happy one. For waiting at the gangway which had been lowered just beside the falls to enable the crew to make their way back on board from the lifeboat before it was drawn up out of the water via the davits, and looking like an enormous swollen thundercloud that was carrying just about as much thunder and lightning in its midst as it could without letting go, was Captain Sourlies. His pepper-and-salt tweed suit buttoned tightly about him, his purple necktie stood out belligerently from the narrow celluloid band that encircled his throat like the collar on a St Bernard, and the mustard-coloured trilby hat was perched on top of his head in the exact centre. His little eyes were screwed up with rage, and his tiny mouth drawn together in the smallest possible 'o' that could be imagined. All of his chins were quivering.

His temper was not improved by the fine mess the crew made of getting the lifeboat alongside, nearly ramming the *Countess*, and breaking an oar in the process, but with the aid of much shouting from Angus it was finally accomplished.

Peter found himself picked up by Mr Strachan and held under one arm. Under the other the mate carried the unconscious form of Jennie, head down. A small stream of water ran out of her. Then he marched up the steps of the gangway and aboard the *Countess of Greenock* to face the Master.

Loaded though he was with pent-up ire, nevertheless, Captain Sourlies drew in a long, deep breath before he spoke. By all odds, the volume of angry sound that was about to pour forth ought to have rattled the funnel stays, collapsed the mizzen cargo boom, and blasted Mr Strachan clear to the Cumbrian peaks that formed the distant background to this drama of the sea.

Instead, there emerged a thin, treble-piping, a reedy, dulcet squeak – "Well, MUSTER Strachan! Would ye then care to ontertain me with your vairsion of oxactly why ye gave orders to halt my shup and ongage in rowing exercises over the sairface of the sea when Mr McDunkeld is nearly taking the boilers out of her in an effort to make tide…?"

Unfortunately, Mr Strachan elected to try out the yarn as he planned to tell it at his favourite pub, the Crown and Thistle in Stobcross Street in Glasgow, when he went on leave after arrival there. Acquainting Captain Sourlies with the events that had caused Jennie to fall overboard, he went into his speech beginning – "Unable to stond the sicht o' his little sweetheart droonin' in the cruel sea…" and which he concluded with – "Under the saircumstances it seemed only richt an' proper to heave to, stand by, lower away and go to the rrrrrrescue."

Captain Sourlies inhaled another forty cubic yards of air, and then cooed – "In holy St Andrew's name, Mr Strachan, WHAT FOR? For two mangy strays thot—"

Mr Strachan drew himself up – "The proof, sor, of one of the true meeracles of nature. Who would have believed thot yon puss would have forsaken the safety and comfort of this vessel to join his mate in the mairciless sea? *But here they both are*, and who will be able to dispute the proof?"

"Proof! PROOF!" turtle-doved Captain Sourlies, though by the amount of oxygen he took in and the empurplement of his features the sound at the very least should have split the *Countess* amidships – "PROOF! ye clobberhead! What proof have ye got but one dead cot and anither that is half dead? Ye big, red-headed gossoon, ye could exhibit those in the market square from now until Michaelmas and not an iota of proof would ye have for yer blosted fairy tale…"

Peter thought that his heart would break with grief at the captain's words that Jennie was dead. Tucked under Mr Strachan's arm, he saw the puzzled expression spread over the face of the mate as he tried to comprehend the captain's argument.

"But, sor," he protested, "what more proof could anyone want than thot I'm the mon, stonding before their verra eyes, that fished the two oot of the drink, and here are the verra pusses they will have just heard aboot—"

"Muster Strachan! MUSTER!" said Captain Sourlies, in the last extremity of indignation, anger and outrage, which caused his voice to fall away to a mere trill-like gurgle – "Ye will oblige me by carrying out my orders. Ye will retire to yer quarters, relieved of all duties as of this unhoppy moment. On the way ye will drop yon dead cot over the side, and for all of me, the ither one with it. Upon our arrival in Glasgie, ye will hond me yer papers ond prepare to sever all further connexion with this craft. Dismissed."

At the order to drop poor Jennie over the side, Peter managed to squirm out of Mr Strachan's arms on to the deck, prepared to fight to prevent this, unaware, of course, that Mr Strachan had no intention whatsoever of carrying out the captain's command. At that particular moment the mate was less distressed over the fact that he had been summarily dismissed from his job than over the doubt the captain had cast over the nature and validity of his proof of quite the most wonderful yarn through which he had ever lived or actually played a part.

Having given his orders, Captain Sourlies turned on his heel and marched to his cabin, from which thereupon issued the sound of smashing glass and crockery and which continued for a long time, four and three-quarter minutes, to be exact, for Mr Box timed it by the biscuit watch he carried in his trousers pocket attached to a leather thong. Since Mealie had not yet removed the luncheon dishes, nor for that matter the breakfast things either that day, he had rather more ammunition than usual, and he was likewise a good deal angrier than he had ever been before.

The engines of the *Countess of Greenock* rumbled, shuddered and pounded, the propeller thrashed, the column of dirty black smoke ascending straight up into the air flattened out and again became an umbrella. She thrust her blunt nose northward once more and resumed her wallowing progress towards her ultimate destination.

Mr Strachan, with Jennie still under his arm, started back aft to his quarters with Peter trotting at his heels, prepared to spring at the back of his neck and bite and paralyze him as he had done the rat at the first sign of dropping Jennie over the side. The mate, however, was sorely baffled, and needed time and quiet to think things out. In the meantime, he had no intention of disposing of the proof no matter what the captain had said, and anyway, since he had been discharged, what difference did it make what he did?

And so with Peter still at his heels he went inside his cabin, tossed the body of Jennie Baldrin on to a mat in one corner, and sat down at his desk to try to think. Here, however, he was overtaken by the thought of the injustice of it all, the contrariness of Captain Sourlies, and the fact that he had lost his job. And because he was young and such things are very serious at such a time, he put his head down upon his arm and gave himself up to the pleasures of being genuinely sad over the unhappy turn that events had taken.

But Peter truly mourned over his good, kind and dear friend, and the tears that fell from his eyes as he sat over her who had once been so lively and animated and full of the spirit of adventure and independence, and saw how small and still she now was, were no less salty than the sea water that matted her poor coat.

And Peter thought that as a last respect to his lost friend, he would wash her.

He began at her head and the tip of her nose, and washed and washed, and in every stroke there was love and regret and longing, and the beginning in the awful loneliness that comes when a loved one has gone away. Already he was missing and wanting and needing her more than he ever dreamed he could when she had been alive.

The salt on her fur stung his tongue, the ceaseless motion of his head added to the other efforts he had made that day brought on fatigue and weariness almost beyond endurance; he wanted to close his eyes and crawl away and sleep for ages, but he was caught up in the rhythm of the washing, a kind of perpetual motion, almost as though by continuing he could wash her back to life again.

Darkness fell, lights sprang up in the other cabins of the lumbering *Countess*, but Mr Strachan remained at his desk with his head buried in his arms, without moving, and Peter washed and washed.

He massaged her shoulders and neck, and the thin bony chest beneath which the stilled heart lay, her lean sides and long flanks, her soft white muzzle, the eyes and behind the ears, stroke after stroke, in a kind of hypnotic rhythm that he felt he could not have left off even had he wished to do so.

Wash, wash, wash. There was no sound in the darkened cabin but the even breathing of Mr Strachan and the rasping of Peter's tongue over Jennie's coat.

Until someone sneezed.

Peter thought his own heart would stop. For he was quite certain that it had not been his sneeze, and it was by no means a large enough one for Mr Strachan to be the author of it.

Wildly hoping, yet not really daring, Peter redoubled his efforts, rasping, scraping, massaging, working around under Jennie's shoulders and over the breast – from beneath which now came a small flutter. And then there were two more quite distinct sneezes, and Jennie in a faint voice called – "Peter... Are you there? Am I alive or dead?"

With a glad shout that rang through the cabin and caused Mr Strachan to raise his head from his arms with a start, Peter called – "Jennie! Jennie dear! You are alive! Oh, I'm so glad. Jennie, they all thought you were dead, but I *knew* you weren't, that you couldn't be."

At the noise Mr Strachan leaped up from his desk and switched on the cabin light, and there on the mat where he had dumped her lifeless form was Jennie, blinking in the light, sneezing a few more times to clear her lungs of the last remaining drops of the salt sea, and even managing to stagger weakly to her legs for a moment and give herself a few licks. And at her side was the big white cat still washing and ministering to her.

Making a queer kind of noise in his throat, Mr Strachan bent over Jennie, stroked her, and said, "For a' the siller in the National Bonk o' Scotland, I wouldna ha believed it. 'Tis the last and final meeracle and the grrrand finish to the yarn. Now will they nae believe the proof that's before their eyes?" and scooping Jennie up into his arms he ran out of the cabin with Peter after him.

Up the passageway, down the steps, across the after cargo hatch, up the iron steps, and on to the bridge ran Mr Strachan with Jennie clutched to his broad chest where she lay quietly, being yet too weak to struggle against such close contact with a human, and when he arrived there he shouted, "Coptain, Coptain Sourlies, look here, sor!" just as though nothing had ever happened between them.

And when the captain stepped out of his cabin, prepared

to quiver once more with rage, Mr Strachan solemnly showed him Jennie, now stretching and making small sounds of protest and craning her head around to try to see Peter who was right at his feet. And in the voice of one who is discussing Higher things, the mate said:

"What sae ye now that I nae ha proof? Raised from the dead she has been by the tender meenistrations of her mate, in my cobin before my verra eyes, and here's the proof, yawning and stretching before ye, and whoever else says it did not hoppen, there's the proof in the twa of them for him too…"

Strangely, Captain Sourlies no longer found it possible in his heart to be angry with Mr Strachan, since it was obvious that he was never going to be able to grasp the simple idea that an object was not and rarely could be proof of a happening long after the happening was over, but remembering how Jennie had looked hanging head down in the mate's grasp earlier, with the water running out of her, and how she appeared now with the sparkle back in her eyes, her nose pink once more, and her whiskers standing out stiff and straight, he suddenly felt better than he had in a long time, and besides, the lights of Port Carlisle were just ahead and they were going to make the tide after all.

And strangely, too, word had got around the ship that Jennie was not dead, but alive, and there was a kind of gathering of the men in the forward cargo well just beneath the chocolate layer-cake bridge, and when Mr Strachan came out and showed them Jennie there was a big cheer went up, and everybody suddenly grew lighthearted and began slapping his fellow on the back and shouting, "Well, well," and "'Tis woonderful," just as though something splendid had happened to them.

The sailor who had been a hermit called for three cheers and hip-hip-hooray for the white 'un, to which Mr Box said, "'Ear, 'ear," and they were given with a will, and Peter had never felt quite so proud and happy in all his life.

And the captain forgave Mr Strachan and said no more about turning in his papers and leaving the ship, and after the mate had ordered Mealie to open a tin of condensed milk and gave Jennie a big dish of it, he put her to bed in his cabin on his own bunk and resumed his duties on the bridge of the *Countess* with Peter happily purring at his feet. And that is where the Carlisle pilot found them when he came aboard to steer the ship into port.

CHAPTER FOURTEEN

Mr Strachan's Proof Leads to Difficulties

BY THE TIME the *Countess of Greenock* had been warped into her berth at the foot of Warroch Street in Glasgow, Jennie had quite recovered from her experience and was in fact, Peter thought, looking better than she ever had before. The sea air, the regular hours, the lack of worry as to where the next meal was to come from, had agreed with her.

She had filled out so that her ribs and flanks were no longer as lamentably lean and close together, her face was rounder and more full, which diminished the size of her ears somehow and gave her a more pleasing aspect, and of course what with the daily cleanings she bestowed upon herself, her coat was now in much better condition, softer even than velvet and with a fine sheen and glisten to it.

Had Peter been asked now, he would most certainly have called her beautiful, with her oriental eyes slightly slanted, the long, aristocratic dip of her head from ears to muzzle, the sweet pink of the delicate little triangle of her nose matching the translucent rose of her ears. While her head might appear too small to some, it fitted now in better proportion to her body, and when she stood straight, with her tail nicely curving away from her, she looked not only lovable but handsome and distinguished, with breeding evident in her long, graceful lines.

Jennie had prepared Peter and briefed him for their arrival in Glasgow as they sailed up the Firth of Clyde and turned the corner into the River Clyde, past the grimy red-brick towns of Gourock and Greenock scattered over the south bank, and the round green hills rising to the north. They were to lie low together until the *Countess* made fast and put out her gangways. Then, in the confusion attendant to unloading, they would seize the first moment when nobody was watching them or the gangplank to whisk ashore and run off. In a way, Peter was sorry at the anticipation of leaving the ship and those aboard her, but the prospect of seeing new places and encountering new and exciting adventures quite made up for any regrets, and as the river narrowed and they passed the great factories on its banks, and the famous shipyards and the big grey city drew near, he could hardly contain himself, and asked Jennie a dozen times when they should find the first opportunity to get ashore unnoticed.

Mr Strachan, however, had other ideas, for just before the *Countess* approached within shouting distance of the dockside, he came down from the bridge for a moment, seized both Peter and Jennie, and shut them up in his cabin and thus they were forced to view the fascinations of the entire landing operation, as performed with the usual inefficiency and raffish style by the crew, from the somewhat limited vantage point of the porthole.

However, they were able to see that no sooner had the gangplank been raised from the pier to the side of the *Countess* than Captain Sourlies was upon it and running down, making it sway, bounce and clatter with his weight and the speed of his descent. Once ashore, he immediately hailed a passing taxi, jumped into it, causing it to sag heavily on one side and proceed slantwise on two wheels, as it were, and drove off without another backward glance at the *Countess of Greenock* or anything or anyone aboard her.

"Now what do we do?" Peter fretted. "We shan't ever be able to get away if Mr Strachan keeps us locked up here all the time…"

But Jennie was unworried. She said: "He can't keep us for ever, and anyway, we shall be able to slip out sometime. I have yet to hear of a human that was able to keep a cat in a room when he didn't want to stay. And besides, I don't think he means to keep us here at all. He acts very much to me like somebody who has something on his mind. At any rate, we shall soon find out and watch our opportunity to escape. I am most anxious to get in touch with my relatives."

It was shortly after the stroke of four bells had announced six o'clock in the evening that Mr Strachan turned his duties over to Mr Carluke and came aft, letting himself into his cabin quickly so that there was no chance for either

Peter or Jennie to duck between his legs, and besides, since one would not have dreamed of going without the other they had to watch for the chance when both could slip away together.

He greeted them with: "Ah there, pusses. I ha' nae doot ye'll be ready for a bit o' shore leave an' as soon as I'll have me jacket an' kit we'll be off. We'll be stoppin' by for a moment at the Crown and Thustle for a pint o' bitter, after which it's hame we'll go while I introduce ye to the Mussis who'll be proud to know ye when I tell her the saircumstances in connexion."

Peter translated this piece of information quickly for Jennie's benefit and the little tiger tabby looked reflective but not too disturbed. "They *always* want to take you home – if they don't first want to kick you or throw things at you. Of course THAT won't do. We must get away as quickly as we can."

But it began to look as though the opportunity was not going to be easy to come by. Mr Strachan changed his jacket to one of a more shore-going cut with a belt at the back, set a blue cap on his red curls, picked up an old leather valise in his left hand, and tucking both Peter and Jennie together under his right arm he went out and down the gangplank, hailed a cruising hack, and ordering the proprietor to drive to a public house by the name of the Crown and Thistle on Stobcross Street, near Queen's Dock, North Basin, climbed in, holding the two cats firmly.

Jennie had been inside of a public house before, since

she had found them to be fertile places for a handout, particularly around closing time when the occupants might be counted upon to be mellow and in a mood to bestow largess of crumbs and scraps, but Peter had only looked in from the outside, and now, perched up with Jennie on the long, smooth mahogany bar of the Public Room of the Crown and Thistle, he found himself immensely intrigued with what he saw, heard and smelled. It was quite like what he had always imagined from looking in through the doors from the outside.

It was a largish, noisy, comfortable place, all done up in browns, with brown tables and chairs, panelling, and a long and gleaming mirror behind the bar reflecting rows and rows of bottles. The handles of the beer pumps looked like some of the levers from the machinery of the *Countess*, and round electric globes in clusters overhead shed a soft yellow light. The room was full of men clad in rough work clothes, some sea-, some shore-going, who occupied all of the tables as well as the space in front of the bar, and of course there was a darts game going on at the board at the far end.

Jennie wrinkled up her nose, but Peter found he liked the warm, cosy beer smell, man smell, clothing smell and off-stage cooking smell. So busy was the place that both a man and a woman, a buxom, elderly person with hairs growing in tufts and bunches from the strangest places on her face, served behind the bar. The man, who wore a corduroy waistcoat and had his sleeves rolled up, frowned at the presence of the two cats on the bar, but the woman thought they were ducky, and every time she passed close by she stopped to chuck them under the chin. The room was stylishly decorated with beautifully printed and coloured advertisements for beer, ale, stout and porter, and calendars and chromos of ships supplied by the big steamship companies. There had as yet been no opportunity for Jennie to give the signal for them to cut and run, since the door was shut to keep in the steamy, pleasant warmth, and there was too much danger of their being trampled underfoot if they tried to get out during the brief periods of its opening and closing.

Mr Strachan, with one pint of dark in his system and another at his elbow, was standing next to a little fellow, a factory-hand with a needle nose, in a peaked tweed cap, while beside him there was an enormous docker, his badge still pinned to his braces; also a commercial man, several sailors off a destroyer, and the usual roster of beer drinkers and nondescripts.

It was the little needle-nose man who eventually provided the opening for which Mr Strachan had been waiting. Nodding towards Peter and Jennie he said, "Huish, that's a fine pair o' puissies ye have there. I'll reckon ye are no little attoched to them…"

"Oh aye," said Mr Strachan, and then added in a slightly louder voice: "Would you say now, just standin' there lookin' at them, that there was onything verra extraordinary aboot the twa?"

This question naturally provoked the large docker and

the commercial man to turn and look too, as well as those sitting at the nearest tables. Challenged, the factory worker remarked, "Noo then, I wouldna like to say exoctly or draw comparisons twixt yin and th' ither, though it strikes me the white one might verra well be a superior specimen. What had ye in mind?"

"Would ye believe it?" asked Mr Strachan in a still louder voice which centred practically the attention of all except those who were watching the darts game upon him, "if I were to tell you that yon pair…" and without waiting for any further expressions from his audience launched full tilt into the tale of Peter and Jennie, that is, from his point of view and as he had seen it.

He told how they had been found stowed away in the storeroom of the *Countess of Greenock* with a supply of mice and rats laid by as an offering to pay their way, of the size of the rat that Peter had overcome and the subsequent disaster to Jennie, Peter's uncat-like and heroic act of going over the side to join her, the rescue by the lifeboat crew with Jennie given up for dead, and the final resurrection accomplished by Peter.

He told it quite well, it seemed to Peter, and listening to it he found himself rather enjoying the narrative plus being the centre of many pairs of interested eyes. There were a few details here and there he should have liked to have filled in, or elaborated upon somewhat, but in the main he felt that the mate was doing a good job and had done them justice. And if the truth be told, Jennie likewise

seemed far from averse herself to being the centre of
attention and even preened herself a little, washing, and
turning her head this way and that so that those in the rear
of the room who were now craning their necks could get
a better look, as Mr Strachan concluded his yarn with a
flourish: "...thus providing an exomple of unparalleled
fidelity, love and devotion far beyond the call of duty in
the onimal kingdom, and the proof of which ye see here
stonding on the bar before your verra eyes..."

The needle-nosed factory worker with the peaked cap
took a swallow of his beer, wiped the back of his hand
across his lips, and said just one word, which unfortunately
was "Tosh!"

"Eh?" said Mr Strachan. "I dinna believe I heered ye
correctly."

"Oh yus ye did," said Needle-nose, who really, Peter
decided, had a most unpleasant face and close-set distrustful
eyes. "I said 'Tosh', to which I will be glod to add 'Bosh'
and 'Fosh'. I will also say that I have never heered such a
pock of lies and fobrications in a' me life..."

Several of the bystanders sniggered, but one of them
said, "Ah've heered stranger things before and, like he says,
yon's the proof before ye..."

This support was all that Mr Strachan needed to restore
some of the confidence that Captain Sourlies had so badly
shaken, and he drew himself up to a good height with
"Bosh and tosh, is it? Sith an' if ye no can take the evidence
of yer ain eyes letting alone the fact that I was in commond

of the verra lifesaving craft that bore down upon them struggling for their lives in the sea…"

Needle-nose now turned and put his face, on which there rested a most unpleasant sneer, quite close to Jennie and Peter as though inspecting them minutely.

Jennie turned suddenly, squatted down on the bar with her head veered towards the door, and said very quietly: "Peter, I don't understand all they're saying, but I know the signs of how people behave – there is going to be a jolly little dust-up in here in just a minute. Whatever you do, don't leave the bar while they're fighting. Wait until the constables come and then follow me."

Needle-nose, having completed his investigation, turned his face to Mr Strachan again and said: "I have inspected your cots, and I no can find onything writ on them neither by hond nor in fine print to the effect that on such and such a day sairtain hoppenings took place. Ontil such time as such becomes legible, ye wull forgive me if I say – Tosh!"

Mr Strachan had had it. He was rubbed raw. The captain had badly upset him and his faith in himself, and now this nasty bit of work was proposing to ruin the best yarn he had ever told – with proof. "Ah weel," he said softly, with a kind of sigh, "perhops this will improve your veesion," and he carefully poured his untasted pint of dark over the head of Needle-nose.

The large docker next to him, with the badge, thereupon turned sadly upon Mr Strachan and said in a mildly reproving voice, "Now then. Ye shouldna ha' done that to little Jock who lacks the height of ye. Ye'll have some of your ain back then," and without further ado he poured *his* beer over Mr Strachan who at the same time received a punch in the stomach from Needle-nose.

The stranger who had originally taken Mr Strachan's part now reached for the docker, but in doing so jostled the two sailors, causing them to spill their grog. Mr Strachan, aiming a retaliatory blow at Jock, hit the commercial man instead, who fell into the nearest table showering the neighbouring one with the upset drinks.

And the next moment, to Peter's horror, everybody in the bar seemed to be fighting everybody else while the barman went up and down behind the bar with a bung-starter looking for heads to crack at, and the bar-woman screamed murder at the top of her lungs.

"Stand fast!" Jennie cautioned. "Don't let them push you off the bar, or they'll trample you to death. It won't be long now."

Faster and faster came the blows, the shouts, the cracking of chairs and tables knocked over and splintered, while Peter and Jennie leaped this way and that to avoid some of the swings aimed at no one in particular. Half the room was siding and fighting with Mr Strachan, the others had nominated themselves partisans of Needle-nose, and the gauge of battle turned first towards one, then the other. Somebody threw a bottle that went crashing into the street through the window. And then all of a sudden the door flew open and in marched the largest constable that Peter had ever seen, backed by a smaller one who stood in the open doorway.

"'Ullo, 'ullo, 'ullo, 'ullo," boomed the first constable. "What's a' this?"

His voice and words had a most amazing effect, just like in a fairy pantomime Peter had once seen when the wizard had spoken magic words and waved his wand and everybody had frozen stock still in whatever position or attitude they happened to be in, or whatever they were doing.

For as much as five seconds, nobody moved in the public bar. Some stood with arms drawn back, others half ducked, others still with their fingers intertwined in the hair of opponents, and the last thing Peter remembered was that Jock, the Needle-nosed one, had climbed halfway up Mr Strachan and was perched there like a monkey on a stick when Jennie said – "Now!"

In a flash they were both off the bar, on to the floor, and out the door and running together down the street as fast as they could.

CHAPTER FIFTEEN

The Killers

MORE AND MORE, Peter was aware of a change that seemed to have come over Jennie Baldrin. She did not appear to be her old, gay, talkative self any longer, but was given over to falling into moods and long silences, and several times he caught her apparently staring off into space quite lost in some inner contemplation. Once when he had offered her the traditional penny for her thoughts, she had not replied to him, and the sudden switching and twitching of her tail had warned him not to pursue the matter. Peter set it down to the shock of her experience when she had fallen overboard from the *Countess* and nearly drowned.

Not that her behaviour towards Peter had changed, except to become more loving and tender and somewhat dependent as more and more he learned the things that were necessary to be a free and masterless cat and less and less leaned on the memories of when he had been a boy. There was no doubt that she looked up to him ever since he had saved her life, and that she enjoyed doing so. Peter, in turn, had experienced some of the dangers of going off half-cock in this new and exciting life, and was always ready and willing to listen and to profit from his clever little companion who had learned so well how to take care of herself without the help of human beings.

If Peter was disappointed in their life in Glasgow, having expected goodness knows what of the city to whom its distance had lent enchantment, Jennie was not, for she had already found out that for the poor and underprivileged, the slums and backwaters and dock areas of one city are exactly like another, and this Peter was now too observing from experience.

It was one thing to arrive in a new city or place, or country, with your parents who would thereupon engage a victoria, fiacre, barouche or taxicab, and drive around to visit the points of interest: the parks with their fine statues reared to the memories of famous heroes and scientists, the main shopping streets with their glittering store fronts, the residential areas filled with beautiful villas and huge, ornate hotels, the museums, art galleries, exhibitions, churches and ruins, as well as the Strand or Corso or Mall where the band was playing. It was quite another to be alone and penniless, without food or shelter or a friend, in a strange city with somehow life to be preserved and a living to be won from it, particularly when, like Jennie, you were unwilling to pay the price of giving up your liberty in return for food, shelter and a home.

Under those circumstances you remained away from the more attractive centres of the city where a stray was most likely to collect abuse, kicks and blows, with the possibility even of a trip to the Pound and loss of life in the gas chamber, and confined yourself to those less favoured sections of the city where the inhabitants had enough to think upon to get along themselves without chivvying and worrying fellow unfortunates in the animal world.

To Peter, the docks along the Clydebank, the smells, the noise, the buildings, the hoists and derricks and tall cranes, the piles of ropes and cables, and the miles of railway trackage were very like those on the Thames in London, and the slums, warehouses and stern neighbourhoods in their vicinity quite alike.

Jennie taught him the art of working the cover off a dustbin to get at the scraps of food and disposed-of garbage remainders. It was done by standing up on the hind legs and pushing upwards with the nose under the rim of the can. The trick, as Jennie figured it out, was not to become discouraged if at the first attempt it could not be budged, but to try all around at various places on the circumference of the bin until sooner or later one found the weak spot where the cover was more loosely attached and would yield a trifle to the first shove. Once it began to go, it was only a question of patience and energy before it could be lifted off.

Peter soon became an adept at this, for he had had a good, sturdy little body as a boy and now was powerfully built as a cat, long and lean in the flank and strong and heavy in the shoulders. Too, in time, he came to be able to recognize a fellow vagrant at once by the tiny bald strip across the bridge of the nose where the hair was quite worn away from pushing up the iron rims of the lids.

Once the lid was off, a few sniffs were as good as a bill of fare to reveal the contents and its state of preservation, and they went at it with their paws or, if what appeared to be tempting and with a possibility of nourishment lay buried too deep, Jennie had worked out a refinement that lay open to the two cats working in concert in such a partnership as was shared between herself and Peter. It was just that the two leaped up and clung both to the same side of the bin as close together as they could, and usually their combined weight was enough to tip it over with a terrific crash and clatter, spilling its contents on to the ground.

Too, they learned to haunt the butcher's shop, the fishmonger and the greengrocer, as well as the alleys behind restaurants and hotels, when the big vans from the wholesale houses came to make their deliveries, for the chance to snatch at scraps that might fall off or be dropped between lorry and store, and make off with it for a meal which invariably they shared equally. For they ate not only bits of meat and fish when they could get it, or chewed-up old bits of bone, but also any pieces of fruits or vegetables, biscuit, bread, stale oatmeal, anything and everything, in short, that could be chewed, swallowed and digested.

And here again, Peter was discovering that it was one thing to be fastidious about your food and complain because Nanny had not cut all the fat off his lamb chop, or refuse to eat his spinach because there was a bit of grit in it, or dawdle over a banana sliced thinly on to cereal with plenty of sugar and milk, and indeed quite another never to have enough in your stomach and not know when or where your next meal was to come from. Of course, being a cat, his palate was quite different from what it had been when he was a human being, but as Jennie pointed out, the average pampered house cat turned loose in a city to fend for itself would soon starve to death if it did not learn to subsist on anything and everything.

They ate old carrots and onions, bits and pieces of melon rind, raw cauliflower and old bread crusts, cooked turnips and cabbage stumps, mysterious leavings from cocktail parties, cake crumbs from tea, bits of haddock skin and heads and tails of smoked herrings, beef gristle and lamb bones that had been boiled until they were white; they licked out the inside of corned-beef tins to get at the fat, and learned to go down to the quayside where the foreign ships from Sweden and Norway, Finland and Spain and Portugal, dumped their more interesting garbage overboard, and fight the screaming and enraged gulls for some of the bits and pieces that floated alongside the stone jetty steps and which they could fish up out of the water with their paws.

But, as in London, it proved to be a hard, rough, hazardous life, albeit an adventurous one, and rarely tempered by any softness or luxury. Compared to it, as they ranged up and down the Clyde, along the Broomielaw, Anderson and Custom House Quay, and then across the big steel-and-iron

Glasgow Bridge to the southern part of the city, life aboard the *Countess of Greenock* had been palatial. Glasgow was a manufacturing city, and the smoke and grime drifted down and got into their fur and skin and it was difficult to keep clean, besides which it rained a great deal and they were hard put to find places to keep dry.

Nevertheless, Jennie seemed to find this quite a normal way to live and did not complain or seem to mind except for those moody silences already referred to and the something which seemed to be occupying her mind.

Nor had the quest for her family prospered particularly or seemed likely to, until at last they came across a grey, scarred-up Maltese tabby who appeared to be a distant relative.

There had been one of those cold, penetrating, misting showers for which the Scots city is famous, and Peter and Jennie sought out a dry place under one of the arches of a bridge over the Clyde when they were warned by a low, throaty growl and a disgruntled, petulant voice saying, "'Ware. You're trespassing!"

"Oh, I beg your pardon," said Jennie politely, "we did not mean to."

Peter, as usual when they had to do with another cat, held his tongue so as not to say something wrong, as he had promised Jennie. The speaker, he saw, was a somewhat weatherbeaten, darkish-grey Maltese with bright yellow eyes and the scars of battle on her ears and nose, and of course the well-known sign of the dustbin ridge. She was not particularly large or formidable-looking, and he and Jennie together might well have routed her, but Jennie always insisted upon the politeness and amenities of cats even though frequently they seemed to be superfluous. There was room enough for a hundred or ten times that many cats beneath the span, but because the grey had got there first, by all the rules the territory belonged to her, particularly if she chose to make an issue of it. It all seemed very foolish to Peter, but he knew that Jennie would have insisted upon the same rights had she been there first and that this was a part of the lore of being a cat.

"We will, of course, be leaving at once," Jennie said. "I was just looking for some relatives of mine. My name is Jennie Baldrin and this is my friend Peter. The Baldrin is on my father's side, of course. Pure Scot for generations, and Highland at that. On mother's side we're almost a hundred per cent Kaffir. But then you'll have recognized that, naturally. The usual route, you know. Central Africa, Egypt, Morocco, Spain and then that Armada business."

The grey did not seem to be too much impressed. She said: "Well, *we* came by way of the Bosphorus originally, but long before the Turks laid siege. We were in Malta already when the Knights of St John came. Our family got to Scotland with one of Nelson's captains after he took the Island. There's a remote connexion between us, probably on the Baldrin side. Where did you say you were from?"

"Well," Jennie replied, "we're up from London on a visit, but my mother came from Mull. And of course you know the Baldrins were all Glasgow cats…"

The Maltese stiffened perceptibly. "London, eh? What have they in London that we haven't twice better here?"

Peter could not resist chiming in – "Well, for one thing, it's ever so much larger, and—"

"Size isn't everything," the Maltese said curtly and added: "I'll wager you have no shipyards the match of ours. We have no need of any London cats to come up here and lord it over us…"

"But I wasn't meaning to lord—" Peter began to protest when Jennie interrupted him to say: "Of course, Glasgow is most beautiful and I'm glad I was born here. Do you know where any others of the family are?"

The Maltese looked down the side of her nose. "Can't say I bother much. They're all over the place and many of them are no better than they should be. There's a branch supposed to have gone to Edinburgh, but of course WE don't have any dealings with anybody on the East Coast. Provincial. Why did you clear out of here? Wasn't good enough for you, I suppose."

"Oh, no," Jennie replied. "I was taken in a basket. And then, of course, being brought up there one gets used to things being… well, different. But one does like to come back—"

"…and put on airs," concluded the Maltese unpleasantly. "But they say that's what the family is coming to. *Our* side of it always found Glasgow good enough for them…"

Jennie said, "Well, I guess we'd better be going…"

"Never mind," said the Maltese, but not at all graciously.

"You may bide a while. I was just going myself. At any rate, you haven't lost your manners in London, which is something, though I can't say as much for your friend. Good day to you," and she arose and left.

It was just in time, for Jennie's tail was lashing and waving violently...

"Oh!" she cried, "what a thoroughly odious person. If *that's* what my relatives are like, I shan't be wanting any more of them. And did you hear her – 'What's London got that we haven't twice better?' And she dared to talk about someone being provincial. Of course she isn't really Scottish at all, with all that Italian blood in her. The Scottish are kind and hospitable, once they get to know you..."

The words 'kind' and 'hospitable' suddenly made Peter feel very sad. For, truth to tell, he was missing the friendly companionship of the weird crew of the *Countess of Greenock*, and even though he was learning to look after himself and had Jennie constantly by his side for company, he knew that there was something lacking and that cats were not meant to live as they were living.

And besides, it was cold, wet and drizzly, and in spite of their being beneath the arch of the huge bridge where the rain could not get at them for the moment, the wind was blowing the damp in from the water and they had had bad luck and had not eaten for the last twelve hours. Peter began to think not of home and his mother and father and Nanny, oddly enough, but of what it would be like to belong to someone who had a nice cosy place by the fireside for him, who would rub his head and stroke his back and scratch him under the chin, feed him regularly and let him sleep on a cushion, someone who would love him and whom he could love.

"Jennie! I wish… Oh I wish we *belonged* to somebody…" he words came out in spite of himself and knowing how Jennie felt about people and having anything to do with them. But oddly enough she did not become angry with him, but only gave him a long and searching look. She opened her mouth as though about to speak, and then, apparently thinking better of it, closed it again without uttering a sound.

Encouraged, Peter was just about to say, "Jennie, don't you think you might try just once more—" when without a moment of warning, baying, barking and slavering, three dogs burst upon them from out of the gloom around the stone and steel abutment of the suspension bridge, and were almost upon them before they could move.

There was a snap of teeth and a shrill scream from Jennie: "Peter! Run! They're killers…" and he saw her flash upwards, a giant pit bull at her heels, and the next moment, gripped by absolute terror and panic he saw the other two bearing down upon him. Long after, he could remember only the horrible burly effect of them made by their massive chests and the small, long, snake-like heads with the cropped ears and slanted eyes, now blazing with the quarry in sight. Their jaws were open, tongues lolling, white sabre teeth shining, and the sound of their feet and toenails scrabbling and pounding on the stone was horrid. And then he was off, running for his very life, around the stone abutment in which was set the tall steel south tower of the suspension bridge.

What had become of Jennie he did not know, nor in his panic could he so much as even think, but he knew her warning to be a supreme effort on her part to save him. For if the dogs once caught them, they would destroy them as cleanly and as quickly as he and Jennie had killed their rats and mice. A snap, a wrench, a toss and it would be all over.

Never was there a sound as horrible as the hoarse, throaty growl, a murderous cry if ever there was one, and it was coming nearer as with each stride the long-legged, powerful brutes gained on Peter. There was a snick and something touched one of his hind feet, yet still managed to miss a hold. He felt their horrible breath as they closed in.

And thereafter Peter could remember nothing but going up, up, up, straight up into the air. His feet, urged on by panic, touched stone and steel, first rough then slippery and knobbed, slanted and crossed and riveted, a network of iron as it were, rising to the clouds, and as fast as his paws touched they were up and away, giving him new impetus, even higher and higher so that he did not seem to be climbing, but rather flying up and ever upwards.

The fog and the rain shrouded him in so that he could see neither where he had come from nor the next few yards higher, yet he kept on, driven by the fear that would not permit him to stop until gradually he became aware of the fact that the terrible growling and barking was no longer in his ears, not the sound of the pursuing feet, nor, for that matter, any sound whatsoever but the distant hooting of boats somewhere, and far, far in the distance, the roar of traffic.

Only then did he dare to slow down and to listen. For safety's sake he gave a couple of more spasmodic leaps still higher and then came to rest at last, but trembling from head to foot. There was no more pursuit, no dogs, nothing of anything.

He seemed to be wedged into a kind of an angle of several short lengths of riveted steel that came zigzagging up out of the swirling mists and vanished into the thicker fog above. There was a penetrating wind all about him too that seemed to pluck at him. Peter realised that he did not have the faintest idea where on earth or heaven, or between the two perhaps, that he was − or how he had got there. He wedged himself more closely into the angle of the steel and clung there with all four feet.

CHAPTER SIXTEEN

Lost in the Clouds

TIME WENT BY, how much, Peter could not tell. In the distance he heard at last a clock striking six, and then another and another, almost as though for some reason he could suddenly hear all the clocks in the world announcing the hour. But whether it was in the evening or in the morning he had no way of telling, for the shock of the sudden attack and escape had frightened him completely out of his wits.

However, now they were beginning to return to him. Whatever the hour, the gloom of darkness, fog and rain was still impenetrable and he was aware that there was nothing for him to do but remain perched where he was until he should be able to determine where it was he had got to in his frantic rush of panic.

At that moment he heard a faint call, a dear and well-remembered voice coming from out of the darkness, apparently a little below him. He shouted – "Jennie! Jennie, where are you? Are you all right?"

She replied at once, and although Peter could not see her, he could hear the relief trembling in her voice. "Peter!

Oh, I am so glad, I could cry. I was frightened to death they had caught you. Are you sure you aren't hurt?"

"Not at all," he replied, "except that I got terribly scared. But where are you? And for that matter, where am I? I want to come to you."

There was a moment of silence and then Jennie's voice came through the fog, quite tense. "Don't stir, Peter. We're up in the towers of the suspension bridge. Way up high, I think."

"Up in the tower," Peter repeated in amazement. "Why, I don't remember anything but just running – yes, for a moment I did seem to be flying... I say, how exciting..."

"Peter..." Jennie's voice was a little plaintive now. "Can you forgive me for leaving you that way? I couldn't help it. It's the one time when cats just don't think." And then before he could reply, she continued: "It's all my fault – being so upset over that foolish Maltese, with all her talk about Turks and Knights of St John and Lord Nelson. Of course, she doesn't come from the Island of Malta at all. Trying to pull the wool over my eyes with her grand ways. They just call those short-haired greys Maltese. And then the way she talked about you. But even so, I should have smelled those dogs long before they got close enough to surprise us, and we could have taken steps, except that I haven't been myself these past days at all. Oh, Peter, I'm so sorry for all the trouble I've brought to you."

"Trouble..." Peter repeated in amazement. "But, Jennie, you haven't..."

"Peter," she cried, her voice full of despair this time, "you don't *know* what I've done. Everything is my fault."

Peter didn't know, and what was more, couldn't even think what she meant, except that something was troubling her about which she had not yet told him. When she did not speak to him further, he thought it best to remain quiet himself, and he settled down on the narrow, slanting piece of steel and clung there, cramped, cold and shivering.

An hour or so later, the rain stopped, a breeze sprang up, and the fog about Peter began to swirl and thin, drifting in wisps, shredding, permitting him almost to see and then closing in again, only at last to be pierced by the yellow rays of the mounting sun. Then the blue sky appeared overhead, the last patches of mist were dissolved and he could see everything. Jennie had been quite right. They were up in the towers of the Clarke Street Suspension Bridge.

They were high up too, almost at the top, with Jennie a few yards lower than he, stretched out on one of the upward-slanting girders of the twin neighbouring tower that paralleled the one he was on. Below them, like a map, lay all Glasgow, threaded by the grey ribbon of the Clyde and marked with the ugly patches of the Central and St Enoch's stations with their lines of railway tracks emerging from them like strands of spaghetti from a package.

Here, Peter thought, was the perfect bird's-eye, or to be more modern, aeroplane-pilot's-eye view of the great grey city. To the east lay the pleasant emerald gem of Glasgow

Green, to the west the broadening river, the docks and the shipping, among which he could even make out the shabby but loved lines of the *Countess of Greenock*, and he saw that there was black smoke pouring from her thin funnel which meant that she must be getting ready to sail. On and on his eyes travelled, like glancing over a page in a geography book. There were blue mountains and lakes in the misty north, and he was certain that he could see storied Ben Lomond rising among them.

To his surprise he found that the height made him neither dizzy nor frightened, and he could enjoy the view and the surroundings as long as he did not try to move. It was when he did so, as he wished to descend at least to Jennie's level, that he found himself in difficulties. He discovered that he could go neither up nor down.

Peter called over to his friend: "Jennie – I'm all right. But how do we get down from here? I'm sure the dogs have left by now. If you go first, I'll try to follow you." He thought perhaps if he saw the way she did it he might be able to take heart, or copy her the way he had in so many other things.

It was some time before she replied, and in the ensuing silence he could see her looking up at him with an odd kind of despair in her eyes. Finally she called to him: "Peter, I'm sorry, but I can't. It's something that happens to cats sometimes. We get up on to high places and lose our way and can't get down – even from trees or telegraph poles where we might manage to get a grip with our claws. But this horrible, slippery steel – ugh! I just can't think of it. I'm terrified. Don't bother about me, Peter. Try to get down."

"I wouldn't leave you even if I could, Jennie," Peter said, "but I can't. I understand what you mean. I'm the same way. I couldn't move an inch. What will happen to us?"

Jennie looked quite grim, and averted her eyes. "We're for it, Peter. We stay up here until we starve to death or fall off and are dashed to pieces below. Oh, I wish I were dead already, I'm so miserable. I don't care about myself, but when I think of what I have done to you, my poor Peter…"

Peter found that his immediate concern was less with the dangerous situation in which they found themselves, than with Jennie. For assuredly this was not the old, brave, self-possessed friend he had known who had a solution to every difficulty and the right answer to every question. Obviously, something was troubling her deeply and robbing her of her courage and ability to think and act in emergencies. He could not imagine what it was, but since it was so, it was his place then to assume the burden of leadership and at least try to support her as she had him so often. He said:

"Oh, come. At least we're still alive, and we have each other and that's all that matters."

His immediate reward was a faint smile and a small, soft purr. Jennie said wanly, "I love you for that, Peter."

"And besides," Peter continued stoutly, "sooner or later someone is bound to see us marooned up here and come to fetch us down."

Jennie made a little sound of despair in her throat. "Oh! People! My Peter, you don't *know* them as—"

"But I do," Peter insisted. "At least I know one is always seeing pictures in the papers of people gathered round and firemen climbing ladders to fetch cats down out of trees—"

"Trees, perhaps," Jennie said, "but they'd never bother about us way up here..."

"Well," said Peter, even though he did not feel at all certain that anyone would trouble to help them even if they were seen, "I'm for trying at least to attract somebody's attention," and inhaling his lungs full of air he emitted a long, mournful siren howl in which from time to time Jennie joined him even though she did not believe it would do much good.

And indeed, it appeared as though her pessimism was justified. Far below, the busy city came to life. Traffic began to flow through the streets, from which arose a kind of muted and distant roar that drifted up to the two fixed to their precarious perches and tending to drown out the cries by which they sought to draw attention to themselves. On the suspension bridge, footwalkers crossed in a steady stream between Portland Street and St Enoch's. People walked along the embankment and in the busy sidestreets. But no eyes turned upwards towards the sky and the top of the towers. Not any time that whole long day.

And all through that next night, Peter called down words of courage to Jennie and comforted her to try to keep her spirits up. But by the following morning both he and Jennie were perceptibly weaker. Their voices were nearly gone from shouting, and Peter felt that his grip on his girder was not as strong and secure as it had been. Nevertheless, he refused to give up, and said to Jennie: "Look here – we must make some kind of an attempt. *I'll* go first and you watch what I do and follow me."

But Jennie moaned, "No! no! I can't, I can't, I can't. I'd rather have the dogs get me. I can't bear coming down from high places. I won't even try…"

Peter knew then that there was nothing to do but stay there until the end. He closed his eyes, determined to rest and conserve his strength for as long as he could.

He must have fallen asleep, for it was many hours later that he was suddenly awakened by a confused shouting and cries from below, and the sound of engines and sirens and the clanging of bells. There was a crowd gathered on the south bank of the river on the square giving entrance to the bridge, people swarming like ants about trucks and wagons glistening with brass and gear and machinery, and new apparatus kept arriving, fire engines dashing along Portland Place, and police cars and equipment lorries from the light and telephone and bridge maintenance companies.

"Jennie! Jennie!" Peter called. "Look down. Look below you and see what is happening."

She did and her reply came floating back to him faintly: "What is it? There must have been some kind of an accident on the bridge. What difference does it make?"

And now that she looked more carefully she could indeed

see that all the white faces in the dark mass of the huge crowd that had gathered were turned upwards, that fingers were pointing up at them and men running about and policemen trying to clear a space about the bridge abutment from which rose the twin steel towers; ladders were being raised and apparatus hauled into place.

"There, you *see!*" Peter crowed. "It's all for us. Oh, I say, but we *are* important! Look, they have quite everybody come out to try and rescue us..."

Jennie stirred on her girder and the look that she sent up to him was absolutely worshipful. "Oh, Peter," she said, "you *are* wonderful. It's all your doing. If it hadn't been for you we both should have perished here, and all because of me..."

Peter enjoyed being admired by Jennie, though he did feel that she was allowing him rather too much territory, since he had done nothing but say, or hope, that they might eventually be rescued. However, before he could reply there was a rush and a roar and a small aeroplane dived at them out of the sky, and just as it seemed about to crash into them, wheeled upwards again over and away, revealing a young man leaning out of the fuselage pointing a box at them. The next moment it was gone.

Jennie gave a small scream. "Oh! What was that?"

"Taking our pictures for the papers, no doubt," Peter explained, thrilled to death.

"Oh dear," Jennie said, "and me a perfect fright, just when one ought to look one's best. Do you suppose he'll come back?" And as far as she could, without disturbing her balance, she commnenced to wash.

But Peter was far too excited and fascinated by the rescue operations to devote even a moment to this function at such a time.

First, the electric light and telephone wagons tried it, but their towers weren't nearly tall enough to reach Peter and Jennie, even when they were cranked as high as they would go.

The maintenance wagons were moved away with a good deal of noise and shouting, and the fire laddies had a go next. They raised their tallest rescue ladder as well as the water tower and sent up two firemen, the sun glinting handsomely on their brass helmets and belt buckles, as well as a large, red-faced police constable in a blue uniform.

But firemen and constable both remained stuck a good twenty feet below Peter and Jennie, for their equipment did not reach either, and Jennie was just about to despair when Peter, who really was having the time of his life, pointed out that now in the centre of the throng still further preparations were going forward.

This time it was two of the bridge maintenance men who had fitted themselves out with their climbing shoes, grappling-hooks, safety webs, sliding belts, gloves, helmets, sacks and ropes. Ready at last, each simultaneously placed his foot in one of the girders of the twin steel pillars and, as though at a given signal, started their ascent together to the accompaniment of a faint cheer.

First one would be leading in what developed into a race upwards, and then the other. Soon the sporting members in the crowd began to shout encouragement and lay bets at the same time: "Go to it, Bill! Ye've got him, Tam! A little more leg there, Tammas lad! Odds on Bill reaches the white 'un afore Tam climbs to the little puss. Three to two Tam's first down with hisn'. Bravo, Tam! Well climbed, Bill! Hooray!"

"We're saved!" Peter called down joyously to Jennie. "This time they're going to make it."

"Oh dear, oh dear," Jennie lamented. "I just know I'm going to bite and scratch when he comes, and I won't mean to. That's the kind of thing that gives cats a bad name, and we can't help it. I'm nothing but a bundle of nerves and hysteria right now, and I suppose that wretched aeroplane will be along to take the picture just at the moment I have my hooks entangled in Tam's hair. No, no, NO! Let go! I WON'T COME! MMMMFFF!"

This last was a kind of strangled protest and muffled cry as Tammas appeared on the girder alongside her, snapped on his safety belt to free his hands, plucked her, spitting, growling, clawing and fighting, from her perch and popped her into his bag.

Peter was just about to cry out to her – "Be brave, Jennie!" when Bill had *him* by the scruff of the neck, into the sack he went, and down they started.

It was a horrible sensation inside the sack, dark and stifling, coupled with the awful motion of the descent, but

Peter was more worried how poor Jennie must be taking it than by any discomfort he himself was experiencing. However, it was soon over and the increasing volume of ringing cheers made it obvious they were approaching the ground, and then at last, amidst shouts and cries of congratulation, he was let out of the bag to see Jennie quivering in Tam's grasp while he was held by Bill. Policemen, firemen and citizens crowded around, the men grinning and the women cooing, "Oh, the pretties. Isn't the little one sweet? Up there all the night, the poor things. Wonder who they belong to…"

Peter would have been delighted to have been the centre of such attention if he had not been so concerned about Jennie who, even now that she was safe and sound, continued to reveal the most miserable and unhappy expression upon her countenance, even as photographers arrived to take more pictures and a reporter interviewed both Tam and Bill, asking them what it felt like to be up there hundreds of feet above the heads of everyone risking their lives for the sake of two stray cats. Tam said: "Ah didn' feel nowt but 'er digging of 'er claws into me 'ide," while Bill declared modestly, "Aw, it was naethin'."

But the adventure was drawing to a close. For the firemen had packed up their ladders and lowered the water tower, the utilities maintenance wagons had cranked down their platforms, and now with a great grinding and roaring and chuffing of motors, clanging of bells, and muttering of sirens, the apparatus and vans and lorries and squad cars all started pulling away, backing, turning and starting up with a good deal of advice from the spectators.

Tam and Bill, once the pictures had all been taken, dropped Jennie and Peter to the ground where they crouched close to the stone abutment to keep from being trampled on, climbed aboard *their* equipment truck and drove away. And as fast as the crowd had gathered, now it began as quickly to melt. With all the excitement over, people returned to their business. Now and then one would stop to reach over and pat Peter on the head, or give Jennie a chuck under the chin, and say: "Feeling better now, eh, puss?" or "Pretty lucky they got you down from there, old man…" and then on they would go. Now that the suspense was over and they were safely down, no one thought to offer them something to eat, a drink, or shelter, and in a few minutes all the thousands of people had vanished, and except for the occasional passers-by bound for the bridge and who, being latecomers did not even know what had happened and therefore paid no attention to the two cats squatting on the walk beneath the shelter of the arch, Peter and Jennie were left quite to themselves.

"Goodness," said Peter, "but that *was* exciting…"

But from Jennie there issued only a long, deep sigh. She was still far from a happy little bundle of fur crouched down hard by the great stone abutment where two nights before their terrifying experience had begun. Peter looked at her curiously. "Jennie," he said, "aren't you *glad* that it all turned out so well and we were rescued and everything?"

Jennie bent her large, liquid eyes upon him and Peter noticed that they seemed to be almost on the verge of tears again and that she had rarely looked so desperately appealing.

"Oh, Peter," she moaned, "I've never been so miserable or unhappy in all my life. I've made such an awful *mess* of things…"

"Jennie dear!" Peter went over to her and sat down next to her and right close so that his flank touched hers in a comforting way. "What is wrong? Won't you tell me? Something has been upsetting and worrying you for so long."

She gave herself two quick licks to get a grip on herself and crowded close to him. "I don't know what I should do without you, Peter. You have been such a comfort to me. It's true. I have something dreadfully important to tell you about changing my mind, but I feel like such a fool. That's why I haven't told you before. But now I've been thinking about it for days, and after everything that happened I can't hold it back any longer…"

"Yes, Jennie," Peter coaxed sympathetically, wondering what on earth it could be. "What is it…"

"You promise you won't be angry with me?"

"I promise, Jennie."

"Peter," Jennie said, "I want to go back and live with Mr Grims," and then pushing quite close to him began to cry softly.

CHAPTER SEVENTEEN

Jennie Makes a Confession

PETER LOOKED AT Jennie as though he could hardly believe his ears.

"Jennie! Do you *really* mean it? We *could* go and live with Mr Grims? Oh, I'd love to."

Jennie stopped crying and put her head down close to Peter's side where it was half hidden from him so that he could not see how upset and ashamed she was.

"Oh, Peter," Jennie said in a low, soft voice – "then you're not angry with me?"

"Angry with you, Jennie? But of course not. I liked Mr Grims enormously, he was so cheerful and jolly and kind, and all the flowers in his little house and the way the tea-kettle sang on the stove and his offering to share everything he had with us. And besides, he seemed to be so awfully lonely—"

"Peter – don't," Jennie wailed, interrupting him, "I can't bear it. It's been on my conscience ever since we left him. It was a dreadful thing I did. Old people are always so very much more alone than anyone else in the world. I'll never forget the way he looked, standing there in the doorway, kind of lost and bent, calling to us and begging us to come back. It nearly broke my heart…"

"But, Jennie," Peter said, "you were angry with me when I said the same thing after we ran away. You remember I said I felt like a rotter…"

"My Peter, of course I was," Jennie said, still hiding her head, "because you were right and I knew you were. I was being mean and nasty and infeline and hard, and just hateful. And you were being sweet and kind and natural and wanting to do what was right, and of course it made me look and feel all the more horrid. That was why I made you come away with me to Glasgow…"

Peter felt quite confused now, and said: "But I thought you said you wanted to see your relatives and where you were born and—"

Jennie's head came up with a toss and she said, "Oh, bother my relatives. You saw what that one was like we happened to meet. And I suppose I have literally thousands of them up here who don't care any more about me than I do about them. But I thought if we went off on a little trip together it would take your mind off Mr Grims and what I had done and – oh dear, I guess what I really thought is that it would take *my* mind off it. I was running away from having been a perfect pig."

She leaned a little closer to Peter and continued with her confession. "And, of course, I couldn't get away at all. Wherever I was and wherever I went, down in the storeroom with you, up in the forecastle in the dark, waiting for a rat,

I'd see him again and the expression on his face when he was begging for us to come back, and even during the biggest noises I would keep hearing his voice and remembering how I had behaved and repaid his hospitality. And then I tried to tell myself the reason I acted that way was because of what Buff had done to me. Then I would hear *you* saying that she couldn't have done that to me, that something must have happened, that it wasn't her fault, and I would have the most awful feeling that perhaps you were right and I had been wrong all the time and maybe she had come back there looking for me sometime, perhaps the next day even, and how she would have cried when she didn't find me…"

Peter felt sorry for Jennie, but in a way he was relieved too, for this was beginning to be like the old Jennie again, who loved to talk and talk and explain, and besides, he was terribly happy about her wanting to go back to Mr Grims.

"And then," Jennie continued, having drawn a deep, full breath and taken one desultory lick at her side, "when I fell overboard I thought that it was the punishment being visited upon me for all my sins and that I deserved to be made an end of, and so when I found myself in the water I didn't much care any more and didn't really try very hard to keep up because I knew the ship would never turn around and come back to pick me up. Then YOU came to me and it was too much to bear, because I knew that I was to be the cause of your end too. After that I didn't remember anything more until I found myself in Mr Strachan's cabin and you were washing me. But then and there I resolved to go back and live with Mr Grims and try to make him happy and keep him company because I knew that until I did I would never have another peaceful moment."

"I know," Peter said. "I thought about him a lot myself."

"And then I was ashamed in front of you, Peter," Jennie said, "so very ashamed that I didn't know when or where or how to begin and tell you about wanting to go back. When we got marooned up there I kept thinking if we ever got down alive I *would* tell you at once and then perhaps I would stop leading you into such awful trouble and dangers—"

Peter interrupted – "Yes, but we always get out of them."

"Some time we won't," Jennie said grimly. "The humans have made up a sort of supposedly funny saying that a cat has nine lives, which is, of course, utter nonsense. You are entitled to just so many narrow escapes in your life and then the next time you are going to catch it. I don't want there to be any next time. If we can find some way to get back to London, soon..."

"Jennie!" Peter cried excitedly, "why not now – right away, if it isn't too late?"

"What do you mean, Peter...?"

"Why, the *Countess of Greenock*. I could see her when we were up on the tower. She was still there this morning with a lot of black smoke coming out of her smokestack, the way it was the day we went aboard her in London. She'll be going back again. Maybe if we hurry we won't be too late and can catch her before she sails."

Jennie gave a great sigh and pressed close to Peter for a moment. "Oh dear," she said, "It's so good to have a male about who *knows* what to do." Then she leaped to her feet. "Come on, Peter, let's run. She might be casting off any second."

Away they went then, tossing rules and ordinary feline discretions to the winds, not bothering to take cover, or employ the point-to-point system, but bounding, leaping, flying over obstacles with not only the speed and agility of cats, but with that extra something that is lent to the limbs and the feet when a great weight has been lifted from the spirit.

Under the railway and George V bridges they charged, past the steamboat wharf where passengers were queueing for trips to Greenock and Gourock and Inverary and Ardrishaig, down the busy Broomielaw, with ships loading freight and cargo for all sorts of interesting places, but not an instant did they linger now for they knew that when the black smoke belched from her funnel the *Countess* might depart any second.

On to the Quay they flew, along the Clyde, Cheapside and Piccadilly, and, sure enough, there a hundred yards ahead of them was the *Countess of Greenock* pouring forth her soft-coal cloud which ceased for a moment and was replaced by a squirt of white steam that curled around her stack like a feather, and they heard her hooter go.

"Oh," cried Peter, "she's leaving. Faster, faster, Jennie. All you've got." And they both flattened their ears back, let their tails streamline straight out behind them and fairly ate up the yards, a white blur and a dark brown one. How they ran!

And at that, they would have been too late if the crew of the *Countess* had not managed to get the gangplank stuck in the last moment when they came to unfasten it from the side of the little freighter preparatory to having it drawn back down on to the dock.

Mr Box, the carpenter, had had to be summoned with his tools, his hammers and chisels and sledges, saws and wrenches and drills and augers, ratchets and levers, and he grew red in the face and beat at it and prised, hoisted and pushed with a series of "Blimeys" and "Lummies" and "Coos", and could do absolutely nothing with it. For a moment it looked as though the *Countess* was either bound to the pier by the gangplank for the rest of her life, or would have to sail with it sticking out of her side.

At this point Mr Box wholly lost his temper and arising from his knees where he had been poking, sawing, chiselling and prising, he aimed a violent and vicious kick at the offending gangway which landed squarely on it and caused it to come loose quite easily, showing that that was what it had wanted all along, though the damage to Mr Box's boot and toe was later assessed as considerable.

"There you are, lads!" he shouted to the navvies waiting down on the dock. "Haul away."

And haul away they did at the precise moment that Peter and Jennie came whipping on to the pier and up the gangway. There was already a gap of several yards between the end of the gangway and the side of the ship, but at the speed that Peter and Jennie were travelling it was as nothing and they flew across the space like a couple of furred birds and landed kerplump on Mr Box's chest, knocking him flat on his back, since he was off balance anyway at the time due to hopping around on one foot.

"Blimey!" groaned Mr Box – "oh blimey. THEY'RE back!"

And back indeed they were on the iron deck of the dear, messy, smelly *Countess*. Everything was just the same as when they had left it, and in a way it was just like home. From the cabin of Captain Sourlies came the tinkle, crash and clatter of breaking glass and crockery. Mr Strachan was on the bridge, in charge, his blue cap set well back on his brick-red curls so that it was not at all difficult to see the still visible remains of what must have been the father of all black eyes. From the galley aft came drifting the mournful strains of Mealie's voice as he rendered in song a lament upon leaving. Mr Carluke was just emerging from his cabin, the fingers of his right hand pointed and cocked like a pistol, and his left swinging and manipulating an imaginary lariat.

And the crew, under Angus, who was roaring up by the steam winch for'ard, was making a beautiful, beautiful mess of the departure, casting off the wrong ropes and cables, making other wrong ones fast, turning things off when they ought to be turning them on, tripping over chains, coming near to letting the anchor go, permitting the *Countess* to get her stern caught in the tide so that she almost sideswiped an excursion boat bound for the Isle of Man, causing *her* captain to say a few words, and thus with the hooter hooting, black smoke pouring from her, and close to complete chaos reigning on board, she managed to cast off, back out into the Clyde, and eventually set a course down the river and towards the open sea once more.

Peter and Jennie did not linger but went right on aft to see Mealie, who welcomed them with a shout, after which he punched a hole in a fresh can of evaporated milk, cut some cold lamb off a joint in the larder, and invited them to dine with a "By Jomminy, you just cotch 'im up in time, hey? By Jomminy, you hungry, good and some. You bring possage money again, hey?" and he roared with laughter. "How many rots and mouses for one ticket? I think you hokay. By Jomminy, you want more lomb? How much can you hold? I give you what you got…" and he proceeded to cut them some more, and eventually, still laughing, turned the bone over to them which Peter and Jennie each at one end gnawed contentedly in the first good meal they had had since they had quit the ship.

The return trip to London was without incident and was spent mostly in eating, sleeping, resting and sunning, since there was little work to do. Word had got about in Glasgow as to the reign of terror that had been in effect aboard the *Countess*, no doubt spread by some lone survivor, and the rat and mouse population left her strictly alone, those ashore scheduled for a trip aboard her cancelling out and giving her a wide berth.

Mr Strachan, who apparently was having guilty feelings with regard to his actions towards Peter and Jennie and what had taken place, treated them rather diffidently and appeared to be avoiding them almost as though he were afraid that someone might find out from the two where, how and why he had acquired the black eye, but Mr Carluke became very friendly to both, scratching under their chins and rubbing their heads, and Peter and Jennie used to spend hours in his cabin watching him prepare a new work for Pipshaw's Western Rider Stories, something he was calling *Rootin Tootin Roger of Rabbit Gulch*. Roger shot his enemies with a pistol over his shoulder by looking into a mirror, thus taking them completely by surprise. Peter explained all this carefully to Jennie as Mr Carluke acted it out in front of his shaving-mirror, and she was just as impressed as Peter.

It seemed almost no time at all before they were rounding the North Foreland with Broadstairs and Margate plainly visible to starboard, picked up Mouse Lighthouse off the port bow, which, of course, because of its name held an especial fascination for Peter and Jennie, who stared and stared as it blinked on and off, and soon were steaming into the mouth of the Thames and then up the broad river itself. Only this time Peter and Jennie took no chances, and when three hours from their destination they went off and hid together down below the coal bunkers, close to the propeller shaft, where *nobody* could find them.

They remained there long after the *Countess* docked in

London, and at five o'clock in the afternoon, when no one was about aft, they sneaked ashore via the gangway where, as usual, there was no watch, and found themselves once more upon terra firma. Trembling with excitement and anticipation they set out to return over the way they had come from the lonely geranium-scented shack of Mr Grims…

Chapter Eighteen

Mr Grims Sleeps

FOR, ALL THE way home on the *Countess of Greenock*, Peter and Jennie had been talking about how pleased and surprised Mr Grims would be when he saw that they had returned and learned that they had come to stay with him for good.

The pair had discussed just how it might happen, and Jennie said it would be nice if they could get back around tea the way it had been the first visit and he would surely invite them in again, only this time when he left the door open, or had to go out, they would stay, and perhaps rub up against him, or settle down in a corner all curled up to show him that they were now his cats.

Peter thought that it might be even more fun if Mr Grims were away from his shack on the round of his docks and goods storage spaces and they might be able to get inside, either through the door left unlatched, or possibly through a window. But at any rate, as he imagined it for Jennie, they would be there, perhaps one sitting in each window by a pot of geraniums when he opened the door.

And he told Jennie how, when Mr Grims came in from out of doors, his eyes would not yet be accustomed to the change of light and very likely he would not see them at all at first if they kept very still, and then they would both miaouw a shout of "Surprise! Surprise!" as had happened once to Peter at one of his birthdays when there had been a surprise party given him.

Jennie liked this idea too enormously, particularly when Peter took pains to describe the pleased and happy expression that Mr Grims would have on his face when at last he realised what had happened to him. Then they fell to talking and planning what life would be like when they had settled down and belonged wholly to Mr Grims.

Because he was a boy, Peter dwelt more on the wonderful fun they would have exploring Mr Grims's domain over which he held undisputed sway at night, the hundreds of different kinds of bales, boxes, sacks, packages, crates, cartons and bulk cargoes there would be to explore, shipments from the Orient done up in parcels of plaited straw, heavy with the mysterious fragrance of the East; huge piles of nuts from Brazil in which to play and slide, and sacks of coffee; piles of tobacco that would make them sneeze, and teas that would intoxicate them. Female-like, Jennie was more concerned with the domestic arrangements and how to make Mr Grims comfortable at home and accustom themselves to his method of living. For there was more to being someone's cat, Jennie revealed, than just accepting meals and being about the house occasionally, or coming up with a mouse or two when it suited one. Jennie explained that they must get used to *his* hours of rising and going to bed, and work and leisure, and adjust their own so that they would be at hand whenever he wanted them; they would have to study whether he liked them most on his bed, or on his lap, or at his feet, or curled up near the stove, or perhaps in the windows, and whether he cared more to fondle them and scratch their heads or preferred it when they came and rubbed up against his legs, or jumped into his lap and pushed against him. There were many things to be learned, and adjustments to be made, Jennie said, so that they could all live in harmony.

Now the realization of these pleasant plans and dreams seemed to lie just ahead of them as they hurried along the docks and through the back streets, with Peter almost as skilled as Jennie now in negotiating the busy streets and the heavy and congested traffic.

And here, seeing Jennie so eagerly straining on to reach their destination, Peter felt a sudden fear and premonition come over him. What if Mr Grims should be no longer there? What if he had lost his job, perhaps, and had gone away and they were never able to find him? Or worse still, supposing something had happened to him and he had been taken off to a hospital? He was a very old man, Peter remembered, and a tumble or a knock, or an illness, might fall to his share at any time. In their talks and plan-makings aboard ship, he and Jennie had neither thought or nor discussed such an eventuality, and all Peter could think of was what a dreadful shock and disappointment it would be to Jennie were something to go amiss.

Something of this feeling seemed to have communicated itself to Jennie too, for although her feet were sore and tired from pounding along the rough cobbles and stone pavements she hurried forward now at even greater speed until at last, just after nightfall, they arrived at the iron gates of the docks, which were shut, indicating there was a quiescent period when no shipments or cargoes were arriving or being unloaded for distribution in the interior.

The locked gates presented no problem to Peter and Jennie since they were able to squeeze through the spaces of the ornamental grille-work at the bottom, and in a moment they found themselves on the other side and in the huge dock area itself. Except for a string of half a dozen goods wagons on a siding, it was quite empty, and the long ark-shaped sheds loomed like a mountain chain in the meagre light of a half-moon and the handful of early stars powdering the sky.

Jennie had already seen something that caused her to pause and give a little gasp of excitement. "Look, Peter, look!" she cried – "Down there, at the end."

Peter did look where Jennie indicated. Far, far away at the extreme end of the enclosure, the darkness was pierced by one tiny pinpoint of yellow light.

"That's it," Jennie said breathlessly. "It comes from the shack. That means he must be there. Oh, Peter, I'm so relieved."

But now that the goal towards which they had so strained was in plain sight, they did not rush forward to it, headlong and pell-mell, but for some reason that they could not fathom until long afterwards, walked forward slowly and soberly in the direction of the beckoning yellow light.

The illumination indeed came from the shack, as they saw when they had approached almost to the door a single, uncovered electric bulb hanging from the ceiling. And as they drew nigh they also heard loud voices emerging therefrom as though an argument of some kind were going on, but they could see no one, and otherwise to all intents and purposes the shack was exactly as they had left it. There were the two long boxes of red geraniums on either side of the door, and through the window they could even see some of the pots of pink, white, salmon and orange-coloured blooms. But except for the mysterious voices, none of which sounded like Mr Grims's, there was no sign of life about the place.

But the mystery of who was speaking inside was cleared up just as they approached the threshold, when the voices changed to a burst of music, a gay little musical comedy marching song.

Peter said, "It's the wireless. Perhaps he's gone away and left the light burning and the wireless turned on because he intended to come right back. Maybe we can surprise him after all, Jennie. Oh, I do hope the door is open…"

But Jennie in reply only uttered a low growl deep in her throat, and Peter turning to her saw that her tail was fluffed and that her hair was standing straight up at the back of her neck.

"Jennie!" he cried – "What's the matter...?"

"I... I don't know," she replied. "Oh, Peter, I just know I'm afraid..."

Peter said manfully, "Well, I'm not," though he was not too certain of it. "What is there to be afraid of? I'll go in first," and he went up to the door and leaned on it with his shoulder. The latch had just failed to catch, and now with the pressure it yielded with a loud click and with a gentle creaking the door swung ajar sufficiently for Peter to look inside.

The room was clean and neat and the table was bare, as though that night Mr Grims had not had anything to eat. Everywhere the geraniums in their pots were full, rich, ripe and blooming juicily, the leaves thick and velvety, and each blossom shedding fragrance so that the room was filled with the sweet, pungent and slightly peppery geranium scent.

Then the pupils of his eyes having adjusted to the brightness of the single light hanging overhead, Peter saw Mr Grims. He had gone to bed and lay there quite still, his worn, gnarled hands outside the covers, and apparently deeply asleep. And somehow, at the sight, Peter felt touched to his heart. Something very close to tears rose to his eyes, for he thought he had never seen anyone look so beautiful.

First, the thought came to his mind: "He looks like a saint," and then was replaced by a much more daring one – "Oh no. He looks like God." For the snow-white hair fell back from his brow and there was an extraordinary sweetness about the mouth and the gentle manner in which the closed eyelids lay over the eyes that Peter knew contained so much kindliness. The white moustaches now fell in two gentle lines about his lips, and with the thin arch of his nose and the pose of his head upon the pillow gave to his face the grave, tender mien of a patriarch, but filled at the same time with a sense of overpowering peace and majesty. From the clear, untroubled brow to the relaxed and resting hands, there was not a line of bitterness or protest at his fate. Something had come to touch Mr Grims with nobility.

Peter did not know how long he stared, for it seemed he could not take his eyes from him. Then the wireless, which had been playing away, stopped for a moment and brought him back. Peter turned to Jennie who was behind him and spoke in the low voice that one uses when a child is sleeping.

"Shhhhhhhh. He's asleep. We can still surprise him. When he wakes up, we'll be here for him to see…"

But Peter was wrong. Mr Grims was not asleep.

All through the night, with the burning eye of the electric light upon them, Jennie huddled miserably in a corner and wept for the old man who had been kind and befriended her and now would never know that she had come back to him. Peter sat by her and tried to comfort her with words, or an occasional sympathetic lick or two of washing, or just silently pressed his body close to hers. He could feel her trembling with sorrow and wished that there was more that he could do for her. In a way it seemed strange to him that Mr Grims should be so contented and serene and Jennie so shaken with misery.

The wireless played steadily on until midnight, when it shut down, only to come on again at very early in the morning and awaken Peter from sleep into which he had fallen in spite of himself. And with the dawn came voices and footsteps outside the door, and a moment later someone called –

"Oi there, Bill. Wotcher doin' with yer light on and yer wireless goin' at *this* hour. It's just the keys we're after."

It was one of the foremen accompanied by two of the dock workers, and seeing the door was open they started to come in when the foreman said – "'Ullo-'ullo! Steady there, boys. I don't like the looks of this at all. Here, Bill! Bill Grims! Are ye ill?"

One of the dock hands said, "If ye ask me, it looks loike the poor old chap's 'ad 'is last illness."

"Aye. And that's the truth ye've spoken."

All three removed their caps and came inside hesitantly and awkwardly, as if now that there was no longer any possible chance of their doing so they were afraid they might disturb Mr Grims. The foreman, with a grave look of sympathy and concern on his seamed and leathery face, studied the strange scene, the quiet figure on the bed, all the gay and gracious-coloured plants, the two cats, one tiger-striped brindle with small head, shining, liquid eyes and snow-white throat and mask, and the other a creamy tom with broad head and shoulders and not a single mark or blemish on him.

Then he snapped off the wireless set and at the same time extinguished the light so that nothing but the early dawn glow came in through the windows. "Aye," he said, "'tis so. And none but his two faithful pets here to ease the loneliness of his last hours and be at his side when the summons came."

The foreman's words gave Peter a wrench at his heart. He took some comfort that Jennie could not understand all the foreman had been saying and was glad likewise that he did not know that even that solace had been denied Mr Grims, and that when the call had come he had taken to his cot by himself and faced it alone.

The foreman gently drew the cover over Mr Grims's shoulders and head, and then went about the place performing the last offices of tidying up a little. One of the dockers bent down before he left and rubbed Peter's ears for a moment. "Aye, pusses, ye know, don't ye," he said. "Ye'll be in need of a new home now and someone else to feed and look after ye. Ah well… First there's to see that *he's* properly cared for and then we'll think of what's to be done for ye. Old Bill would have wanted his friends remembered…"

He and the two dockers went out quietly, leaving he door ajar.

Peter said to Jennie: "He's going to be looked after. I heard the foreman say so. You mustn't grieve so. We came as quickly as we could…"

But Jennie refused to be comforted. She said: "He shared his food and broke bread with us. He spoke to us sweetly and kindly and begged us to stay with him. And I laughed at him and made you run away. Peter, Peter… How can I ever forgive myself? Don't you see, if it hadn't been for me and the way I acted, if we *had* stayed, it could all have been different? He might even have had something to live for again, instead of falling ill and just lying down to die. And even so, we would have been here by his side, or maybe we could have run and got help for him. Oh, I wish *I* were dead…"

She fell silent again and Peter, squatting down beside her bethought himself of what to do. He felt that unless there was some way that he could distract her mind, she might well remain there mourning and brooding over something which could now no longer be helped, and perhaps even grieve and starve herself to death. He knew that neither he nor she would ever forget, that a thoughtless cruelty can be too late repented of, that life does not take cognizance of how one feels or what one would like to do to make up for past errors, but moves inexorably, and that the burden is more often 'too late, too late' rather than 'just in time…'" A good deed or a right action wanted much immediacy in its performance. He also knew that he must help Jennie at once.

He said finally, "Jennie… there is nothing further we can do here. I have a wish… I want to go home…"

"Home?" she said, as though the word had a strange and unfamiliar ring in her ears.

"To Cavendish Mews," Peter said, and then added – "Just to visit... Perhaps I could see Mummy and Daddy and Nanny, from the outside, for a moment. We might just walk by and look in..."

"Yes," said Jennie, in a dull, hurt voice, "you must go."

"But I can't go alone, Jennie. I don't dare. You must come with me. I need you. Don't you see? ...Just as you needed me to go to Glasgow, I need you to help me here. I'm not yet enough cat to get around London by myself. I'd get lost, I'm not sure I could even find my way, or get a meal, or secure a place to sleep at night. Jennie, please help me. I do so want to see them just once more..."

A change came over Jennie. Her lithe body lost the sick, slack, slumped crouch and pulled itself together again. As usual, when she was much moved, she sat up and gave her back a few licks. Then she said, "If you really think you need me, Peter..."

"Oh, but, Jennie, I do..."

"Then I'll go with you, whenever you say."

Peter jumped up and looked out of the window. Off in the distance, down by the goods wagons on the siding, he could see a group of people approaching, the foreman, the two dockers, a man carrying a black bag, and several others.

"I think we'd better go now," he said, "before they come back."

Without another word, Jennie arose and they slipped out of the door, but it was significant that this time it was Peter who led the way and Jennie who followed him. They quickly slipped around behind the shack, and then alternately running and walking down the water side of the docks and sheds, soon reached the iron gates of the pier, which now stood open, and went through them out into the street again.

CHAPTER NINETEEN

London Once More

IT WAS ONLY half true that Peter wanted to go home.

For boy and cat were becoming so intermingled that Peter was not at all certain any longer which he really was.

More than once during his voyage aboard the *Countess of Greenock* and the subsequent adventures, Peter had thought of his mother and father and Scotch Nanny and wondered how they were, if they were missing him, and whether they had any explanation for his mysterious disappearance. For certainly, none of them, not even Nanny, who had been right there at the time, could be expected to guess that he had changed suddenly from a boy into a snow-white tomcat under her very eyes almost, and had been pitched out into the street by her as a stray.

He thought it was probable that they would have notified the police, or perhaps, believing that he had run away, placed an advertisement in the 'Personal' columns of *The Times*, saying "Peter: Come home, all is forgiven – Mummy, Daddy and Nanny," or possibly it might have been more formally worded: "Will anyone who can give information as to the whereabouts of Master Peter Brown, vanished from Number

1A Cavendish Mews, London, WC2, kindly communicate with Colonel and Mrs Alastair Brown of that address. Reward!"

But in the main, when he thought of those at home he did not believe that he was much missed except by Nanny who, of course, had been busy with him almost from morning until night, leaving out the hours when he was at school, and now that he was gone would have nothing to do. His father was away from home so much of the time that except for their occasional evening romps he could hardly be expected to notice the difference. And as for his mother – Peter always felt sad and heavy-hearted when he thought about his mother, because she had been so beautiful and he had loved her so much. But it was the kind of sadness that is connected with a memory of something long ago that was. Looking back to what life had been like in those now but dimly recollected days, he felt certain that his mother had been a little unhappy herself at first when he was missed, but then, after all, she never seemed to have much time and now that he was gone perhaps it would not have taken her long to get used to it.

Really it was Jennie who had come more and more to mean family to him and upon whom he leaned for advice, help, companionship, trust and even affection. It was true, she talked a great deal and was not the most beautiful cat in the world, but there was an endearing and ingratiating warmth and grace about her that made Peter feel comfortable and happy when they slept coiled up close to one another, or when even he only looked at her sometimes and saw her sweet attitudes, kindly eyes, gamin-wise face and soft white throat.

The world was full of all kinds of beautiful cats, prize specimens whose pictures he had seen in the illustrated magazines during the times of the cat shows. Compared to them, Jennie was rather plain, but it was an appealing plainness he would not have exchanged for all the beauty in the world.

Nor was it his newly acquired cat-self that was seeking a return to Cavendish Mews in quest of a home, though to some extent the cat in him was now prey to curiosity as to how things were there without him and what everyone was doing. But he knew quite definitely that his mother and father were people who had little or no interest in animals, did not appear to have any need of them, and hence would be hardly likely to offer a haven to a pair of stray cats come wandering in off the streets, namely Jennie and himself.

Peter's suggestion that Jennie accompany him on a trip home to Cavendish Mews was perhaps more than anything born out of the memory that when he had been unhappy and upset about their treatment of Mr Grims at the time of the first encounter with him, *she* had managed to interest and distract him by proposing the journey to Scotland. When he saw her sunk in the depths of grief and guilt over the fate of the poor old man, Peter had plucked a leaf out of her book of experience in the hope that it would take her mind off the tragedy, and particularly what she considered her share in it. By instinct, he seemed to have known that nothing actually would have moved her from the spot but his expression of his need for her.

Whatever, it was clear after they had set out for Cavendish Mews that she was in a more cheerful frame of mind and anxious to help him achieve his objective.

It is not easy for cats to move about in a big city, particularly on long journeys, and Jennie could be of no assistance to Peter in finding his way back to Cavendish Mews, since she had never lived or even been there and hence could not use her homing instinct, a kind of automatic direction-finder which communicated itself through her sensitive whiskers and enabled her to travel unerringly to any place where she had once spent some time.

Peter at least had the unique – from a cat's point of view – ability to know what people around him were saying, as well as being able to read signs, such as for instance appeared on the front of omnibuses and in general terms announced where they were going. One then had but to keep going in that direction and eventually one would arrive at the same destination or vicinity. In his first panic at finding himself a cat and out in the street, Peter had fled far from his home with never any account taken of the twistings and turnings he had made. However, he was quite familiar with his own neighbourhood, and knew if he could once reach Oxford and Regent Streets he would find his way.

However, when it came to the lore of the city and how to preserve one's skin whole, eat, drink and sleep, Jennie as usual proved invaluable.

En route he learned from her all the important things they were to know about dogs and how to handle them, and that for instance he must beware of terriers of every kind, that the average street mongrel was to be despised. Dogs on leashes could be ignored even though they put up a terrific fuss and roared, threatened, growled and strained. They only did it because they *were* on the leash, which of course injured their dignity, and they had to put up a big show as to what they would do if they were free. They behaved exactly the same when sighting another dog, and the whole thing, according to Jennie, was nothing but a lot of bluff, and she for one never paid the slightest attention to them.

"Never run from a dog if you can control it," she admonished Peter, "because most of them are half blind, anyway, inclined to be hysterical, and will chase anything that moves. But if you don't run, and stand your ground, chances are he will go right by you and pretend he neither sees you nor smells you, particularly if he has tangled with one of us before. Dogs have long memories.

"Small dogs you can keep in their places by swatting them the way we do when we play-box, only you run your claws out and hit fast and hard, because most of them are scared of having their eyes scratched and they don't like their noses clawed either, because they are tender. Here for instance is one looking for trouble, and I'll show you what I mean."

They were walking through Settle Street, near Whitechapel, looking for a meal, when a fat, overfed Scottie ran barking from a doorway and made a good deal of attacking them, barking, yelping, leaping and charging in short rushes with an amount of snapping of its teeth, bullying and bravado.

Jennie calmly squatted down on the pavement, facing the foe with a kind of humiliating uninterest which he mistook for fear and abject cringing, and which gave him sufficient courage to close in within reach and risk a real bite with his teeth at Jennie's flank. Like lightning flashes her left paw shot out three times, while she leaned away from the attack just enough to let the Scottie miss her. The next moment, cut on the end of his nose and just below the right eye, he was legging it for the cover and safety of the doorway, screaming "Help, murder. Watch!!"

"Come on," Jennie said to Peter. "Now *we've* got to move out. You'll see why in a minute." Peter had long since learned not to question her, particularly when it was something that called for split-second timing, and he quickly ran after her out of range, just as the owner of the dog, a slatternly woman, evidently the proprietress of the dingy greengrocery, came out and threw a dishpan full of water after them, but missed, thanks to Jennie's wisdom and speedy action.

"I'm out of practice," Jennie said, with just a touch of her old-time showing-off for Peter, "I missed him with my third. Still… They'll run off screaming for help, and if you stay around you're likely to catch it, as you saw, though not from *them*… And you don't always have to do that. Quite often they've been brought up with cats, or are used to them, and are just curious or want to play, and come sniffing and snuffling and smelling around with their tails wagging, which as you know means that *they* are pleased and friendly and not angry or agitated or nervous over something as it does with us. Then you can either bear up under it and pretend not to notice it, or try to walk away or get up on top of something they can't reach. I, for one, just don't care for a wet, cold, drooly nose messing about in my fur, so I usually give them just a little tap with the paw, unloaded, as a reminder that we are after all quite totally different species and their way of playing isn't ours."

"But supposing it's a bigger dog," Peter said. "Like the ones in Glasgow…"

Jennie gave a little shudder. "Ugh!" she said. "Don't remind me of those. As I told you then, anytime you see a bull terrier, run, or better still, start climbing.

"But a great many of the others you can bluff and scare by swelling up and pretending to be bigger than you actually are. Let me show you. You should have been taught this long ago, because you can never tell when you are going to need it."

They were walking near Paternoster Row, in the wide-open spaces created by the bombs before St Paul's Cathedral, and Jennie went over a low coping and into some weeds and fire-flowers that were growing there. "Now," she said, "do just as I do. Take a deep breath, that's it, way in. Now blow, but hold your breath at the same time. Hard! There you go!"

And as she said, there indeed Peter went, swelling up to nearly twice his size, just as Jennie was, all puffed out into a kind of lopsided fur ball. He was sure that he was looking perfectly enormous and quite out of plumb, and he felt rather foolish. He said as much to Jennie, adding, "I think that's silly."

She answered, "Not at all. You don't realise it, but you really looked quite alarming. It's sort of preventive warfare and, on the contrary, makes a good deal of sense. If you can win a battle without having to fight it, or the enemy is so scared of you that he won't even start it, and goes away and there is no battle at all, that's better than anything. It doesn't do any harm, and it's always worth trying, even with other cats. For in spite of the fact that you know it's all wind and fur, it will still give you the creeps when someone does it to you."

Peter suddenly thought back on Dempsey and how truly terrifying the battle-scarred veteran of a thousand fights had looked when he had swelled up and gone all crooked and menacing on him.

"And anyway," Jennie concluded the lesson, "if it shouldn't happen to work, it's just as well to be filled up with air because then you are ready to let out a perfect rouser of a battle-cry, and very often that *does* work, provided you can get it out of your system before the other one does. A dog will usually back away from that and remember another engagement."

In the main, on this walk across a portion of London, Peter found cats to be very like people. Some were mean and small and pernickety, and insisted upon all their rights even when asked politely to share; others were broadminded and hospitable, with a cheery "Certainly, do come right in. There's plenty of room here," before Jennie had even so much as finished her gentle request for permission to remain. Some were snobs who refused to associate with them because they were strays, others had once been strays themselves, remembered their hardships, and were sympathetic; there were cantankerous cats always spoiling for a fight, and others who fought just for the fun of fighting and asserting their superiority, and many a good-natured cat belonging to a butcher, or a pub, or a snack-bar, or greengrocer, would steer them towards a meal, or share what they had, or give them a tip on where to get a bite.

Also Peter learned, not only from Jennie but from bitter experience, to be wary of children, and particularly those not old enough to understand cats, or even older ones with a streak of cruelty. And since one could not tell in advance what they would be like, or whether they would fondle or tease, one had no choice, if one was a London stray, but to act in the interest of one's own safety.

This sad piece of knowledge Peter acquired in a most distressful manner as they threaded their way past Petticoat

Lane, in Whitechapel, where a grubby little boy was playing in the gutter outside a fish and chip shop. He was about Peter's age, or at least the age Peter had been before the astonishing transformation had happened to him, and about his height, and he called to them as they hurried by, "Here, puss. Come here, Whitey…"

Before ever Jennie could warn him, or breathe a "Peter, be careful!" he went to him trustingly, because in a way the boy reminded him of himself and he remembered how much he had loved every cat he saw in the streets, and particularly the strays and wanderers. He went over and held up his head and face to be rubbed. The next moment the most sharp and agonising pain shot through his body from head to foot so that he thought he would die on the spot. He cried out half with hurt and half with fear, for he did not know yet what had happened to him.

Then he realised that the boy had twined his fingers firmly about his tail and was pulling. *Pulling HIS tail.* Nothing had ever hurt him so much or so excruciatingly.

"Nah then," laughed the boy nastily, "let's see yer get away…"

With a cry of horror and outrage, and digging his claws into the cracks in the pavement, Peter made a supreme effort and managed to break loose, certain that he had left his tail behind him in the hand of the boy, and only after he had run half a block did he determine that it was still streaming out behind and safely attached to him.

And here Peter discovered yet another thing about cats

that he had never known before. There was involved not only the pain of having his tail pulled, but the humiliation. Never had he felt so small, ashamed, outraged and dishonoured. And all in front of Jennie. He felt that he would not be able to look at her again. It was much worse than being stood in a corner when he had been a boy, or being spoken to harshly, or having his ear tweaked or knuckles cracked in front of company.

What served to make it endurable was that Jennie seemed to understand. She neither spoke to him sympathisingly, which at that moment Peter felt he would not have been able to bear, nor even so much as glanced at him, but simply trotted alongside minding her own business and pretending in a way that he was not there at all, which was a great help. Gradually the pain and the memory began to fade, and finally, after a long while, when Jennie turned to him and out of a clear sky said: "Do you know, I think it might rain tonight. What do *your* whiskers say?" he was able to thrust his moustache forward and wrinkle the skin on his back to the weather-forecasting position and reply:

"There might be a shower or two. We'd better hurry if we want to reach Cavendish Square before it starts. Oh, look there! There's the proper bus just going by now. We can't go wrong if we keep in the same direction."

It was a Number 7, and the sign on the front of it read "Oxford Street and Marble Arch".

"For Oxford Street crosses Regent Street, and then comes Prince's Street, and if we turn up Prince's Street, we can't help coming into Cavendish Square," Peter explained, "and then it's only a short step to the Mews and home."

Jennie echoed the word 'home' in so sad and wistful a voice that Peter looked at her sharply, but she said nothing more and proceeding quickly by little short rushes, from shop door to shop door, as it were, the two soon had passed from Holborn through New Oxford Street into Oxford Street, and across Regent Street to Prince's Street, where they turned up to the right for Cavendish Square.

CHAPTER TWENTY

The 'Élite' of Cavendish Square

NOW THAT THEY were at last in Cavendish Square, Peter was all afire to hasten on to the Mews. Here once more were all the familiar sights close to home that he knew so well, the small oval park surrounded by tall green shrubs, planted hedge-like so close together that they formed a palisade barring out all but cats and giving entrance actually only through the iron gate at the north.

Here, likewise inside the little gardens, were the nursemaids knitting by their prams, the children playing, safe from the traffic passing through the streets outside. Around the oval he recognised all the sleepy, dignified-looking houses on three sides of the square, elegant even to the one that had been fire-bombed and gutted and hid its wounds and empty spaces behind its untouched outer walls, doors and boarded-up windows, that all the more gave one the impression that it had shut its eyes and did not wish to be disturbed.

There, standing in front of it too, was Mr Wiggo, the Police Constable, tall and comfortable-looking in his round blue helmet, dark blue cape and clean white gloves; Mr

Legg, the Postman, was coming out of Number 29; the delivery wagon from the Co-Op was just turning the corner; it seemed to Peter that any moment he *must* see Scotch Nanny wearing her crisp, starched, blue-and-white Glengarry bonnet with the dark blue ribbons streaming from it, come marching into the square from the Mews, with perhaps even himself being held by the hand and dragging a bit maybe because he did not like being babied.

There it all was. Only a bit further and he would be seeing the home that he had left what seemed like such a long, long time ago. He said to Jennie, "Hurry, Jennie. Come along. We're almost there."

But much as she disliked having to do so, Jennie had to caution him and restrain his impatience, for this was after all new territory into which they were coming as strangers, and it behoved them to tread softly, make their manners, get acquainted, and above all answer questions politely and listen to what the residents had to say. Thereafter they would be free to come and go as they pleased provided they were accepted by the important members of the community. But to go rushing pell-mell through a district which obviously housed a large cat population, without pausing for amenities, could only lead them into trouble.

"It will only be a little longer, Peter," Jennie said. "But everybody would be most upset if we didn't stop and make ourselves known. Remember, we are strangers here. Come, walk quietly with me around the right side of the square and we'll see what they are saying. We'll tune in on them."

Peter did not wholly understand what Jennie meant by this until they passed the area-way of Number 2A where lived the janitor who was also the caretaker and keeper of the key for the tiny gardens. And there for the first time he encountered the wonders of feline communication by whisker antennae. It was like broadcasting. They thought something, and in a moment you knew what they were saying, or thinking of saying, at any rate, because it came in through your whiskers or the vibrissae or feeler hairs growing out from above your eyes. Then you thought the reply, and it went out to them. It operated only over short distances and one actually had to be close to the cat with whom one was communicating, but work it did.

For while the caretaker was not at home, his cat was, seated behind the window, and Peter was delighted to recognise the big black tom with the white patch on his chest and the enormous green eyes that he had seen so often when he lived near the Square. It was then he realised that the cat behind the window was broadcasting to them, for the window being closed he couldn't hear him, but he knew as plain as day that he had said: "Mr Black is the name. Blackie, for short. I rather run things around here. Are you strays, or home cats from another neighbourhood visiting?"

Peter felt Jennie reply politely, "Strays, sir."

"Hm!" The large round eyes were staring at them fixedly through the glass of the window-pane as Mr Black radioed the next question: "Just passing through, or were you thinking of stopping off?"

Peter could contain himself no longer, and quite forgetting Jennie's earlier admonition, sent out on his own wavelength – "Oh, but I live here. I mean, just north in the Mews. Don't you remember me? I'm Peter Brown from Number 1A… My father is Colonel Brown, and—"

Mr Black interrupted. He had a most suspicious look on his face. "Peter Brown, eh? Can't say I've ever seen you before in my life, and I rather know everybody around here. Never knew the Browns to keep a cat. They used to have a small boy, but he's gone away. Look here, my smart friend, if you're trying to crash this neighbourhood under false pretences, let me tell you—"

But here, fortunately, the quick-thinking Jennie intervened with, "Please, sir, it's what my friend *imagines*. That's his imagining game. He's always playing it…"

"Ah well," said Mr Black, "as long as that's all it is. We're not snobs in this neighbourhood, but we're rather full up on strays at the moment."

"We're just back from Glasgow," Jennie commented, rather irrelevantly it seemed to Peter, who had yet to learn how well she knew what she was about and that above all cats must be kept interested.

Mr Black *was* interested. "Glasgow. You don't say. I used to know some cats there. How did you come down?"

Peter had recovered from his mistake and felt that he could answer this. Proudly he sent forth: "We shipped out," using a phrase he had learned from listening to the sailors aboard the *Countess*. "*Countess of Greenock* – Glasgow – London…"

Mr Black looked impressed. "Well, well," he said. "Ship's cats. You two probably know your way about, then. I used to belong to a sailor once – well, a kind of sailor, perhaps more of a deck-hand person. He worked on the ferry that runs between Devonport and Torcross. Did you know that that operated on a cable that ran under the water from one shore to the other?"

Jennie indicated politely that she didn't, and that she had never heard of such an amazing thing!

"Well, it did," insisted Mr Black. "I don't suppose you would call that sailing, exactly, but it does give us something in common in a way, so I suppose it will be all right for you to stay. The bombed premises at Number 38 is where most everyone lives. You tell them I said it was all right for you to be there. And mind you, see that you obey the rules of the neighbourhood, or out you go, both of you. The principal one to remember is no tipping over of dustbins at night. The residents don't like it and complain to Mr Clegg. He's the man who does for me. He *owns* the park and the square and everything. And no fighting! That disturbs the residents too. If you must fight, go over to Wigmore Street or Manchester Square. There's fighting goes on there all the time. We try to keep our neighbourhood quiet and respectable. There are two spinsters who live down at Number 52 who are susceptible and will give you milk occasionally if you ask piteously enough. What did you say your names were?"

"Jennie Baldrin," Jennie replied. "I'm part Scottish, you know, and my friend's name *is* Peter, and—"

"Right you are," interrupted Mr Black. "Carry on then…" and he fell to washing vigorously.

"There now," Jennie said with quiet satisfaction as they went on slowly. "You see? Now we know we have a place to go, just in case. Greetings to you, my dears. Long life and good health to you both."

These last two remarks were addressed to the two greys with the ring tails and lyre markings on their heads, who sat spinning in the ground-floor window of Number 5 just as they always had when Peter lived in the neighbourhood, washing, blinking, purring and with their eyes following the people who came and went.

Their reply to Jennie's polite salutation as it came wafted through the window and was soft and sleepy and often it was difficult to tell which one was talking.

"I'm Chin."

"I'm Chilla."

"We're twins."

"We're actually Ukrainian."

"We're *never* allowed to go out of the house."

"Have you talked to Mr Black?"

Since this was the first question addressed to them and seemed to emanate from both, Peter took it upon himself to reply and said, "Yes, we have. He was very kind and said we might stay."

If a sniff can be broadcast, that was what seemed to come over to Peter and Jennie's whiskers next. "Hmph! Well! We always say we don't know what this neighbourhood is coming to. It was different when we moved in. Exclusive."

"Remember, no tipping over of dustbins…"

"Strays!!!"

"Long life and good health to you both!" Jennie murmured once more politely, as they passed out of sight, and then added – "Stupid snobs…!" From Number 5 came the vibrations of low and angry growling.

"Pedigree indeed," said Jennie. "I'd like too know how far back they go and what *their* ancestors looked like when mine were gods in Egypt. And where is the Ukraine, anyway?"

"I think it's in Russia," said Peter, who was not very sure, "or maybe Turkey."

"Russians!" Jennie said indignantly. "And they talk about what the neighbourhood is coming to…"

"Long life, good health and much comfort to you," Peter said as he had been taught, to the ginger cat with light green eyes, squatted behind the iron rail in front of Number 11, with its tail neatly wrapped around it. This he knew was the cat of Mrs Bobbit, the caretaker. He had seen it there often and had even stroked it. But now he went up and touched noses.

The ginger said, "Well spoken, youngster. It's nice to find *somebody* left with manners these days. *You've* been properly taught. Remember, there's nothing quite like manners to get you on in the world. I've been very cross this morning, and would as soon have knocked you ears over tail as not, until you spoke so softly. Wuzzy is the name. I suppose you've seen Mr Black?"

Jennie told their names. She was nearly bursting with pride at the praise Peter had earned from the ginger-coloured one.

Wuzzy said to Jennie – "Jennie Baldrin, eh? That's Scottish. But there's more to you from the look of you. Good breeding. Egyptian, probably – from your ears. I'm such a mixture *nobody* can say where it started. Come back and tell me all about you after you're settled…"

"Now THERE," said Jennie Baldrin firmly, "is one of the nicest cats I've EVER met. I must have a long talk with her," and she looked so pleased and gay and cheered that Peter was indeed glad that even for just a little he had managed to take her mind off poor Mr Grims.

As they went on, they were conscious of a soft call from someone above somewhere, giving them greetings, long life and milk with every meal. They looked up to see a tortoiseshell cat ensconced in the bay window of Number 18.

"Do stop a minute," she pleaded. "I'm so bored. You two look as though you've been places." ("Haven't we just," was Peter's thought to himself.) "My name's Hedwig. I've got everything in the world, and I'm very unhappy. I belong to a childless couple."

"Oh dear," Jennie sympathised. "That can be just too bad."

"It is," said Hedwig, "believe me. Carry me around all

day. On my back in their arms just like a baby. And cluck and coo and make noises that *I* can't make head or tail of. I've a basket with a blue ribbon, and pillows, and scratching-posts and toys, just drawers full of things. And I'm so sick of them all. I used to be pretty handy in an alley myself before *they* picked me up. If I can get out for a few minutes later I'll be over to the bombed house. I'm dying to hear how it is on the road."

"You see," Jennie remarked to Peter, as they went on towards the top of the square, "it isn't all cream and chopped liver…"

They continued and met a stunning, rose-coloured, pedigreed Persian who talked of nothing but show business and Blue Ribbons; a long-haired grey named Mr Silver who assured them that there was nothing like belonging to a bachelor for the very best kind of life; and three assorted tabbies who lived with the two spinsters said, if you didn't mind too much not being allowed up on things, there really was nothing like living with two old maid sisters because nothing ever changed or happened to frighten or worry one.

And in this manner it was that Peter, accompanied by Jennie Baldrin, went all the way around Cavendish Square and made the acquaintance of the friends and neighbours living there and was accepted by them as one of them, as Jennie had wished it, and having been so, he came at last to the street that led to the Mews.

Now, strangely enough, he was no longer in a hurry as

he had been before, but paused for a moment at the entrance to the narrow little pocket or blind alley, as it were, that was the Mews.

Yet for all of being a cat, and understanding them better than he had ever before, the thought that soon he would be able to see his mother and father made him very happy. He said to Jennie Baldrin, "We did it, Jennie. Here it is. And just down there is our house..."

Jennie's sadness had returned, for she had grown to love Peter very much. She said, "Yes, Peter. And perhaps just down there a little way is where you and I will have to part."

"Oh, Jennie!" said Peter. "Jennie, dear! Don't you know that whatever happens, I'll never leave you? Never, never, never!"

But Jennie was a better prophet than she knew. Except that it didn't at all turn out as she thought it would, that which awaited them at the tiny, narrow Mews...

CHAPTER TWENTY-ONE

Reunion in Cavendish Mews

AND, NOW THAT they were there at last, Peter found that he did not quite know what to do, or rather, that he really had no plan.

For this was not like a regular visit where you went up to the front door and rang the bell, and when someone came to answer, you sent in your card with a message scribbled on it – "Mr Peter Brown, late of Number 1A Cavendish Mews, solicits the honour of an interview with his mother and father, Colonel and Mrs Brown." Or you didn't even go bursting through the front door, granting that it was off the latch, shouting – "Mummy! Mummy! I'm home. I'm back again. Have you missed me?"

He couldn't even reach the doorknob, much less the bell. He had the shape and form of a large white cat and had lost the power to speak to human beings, though he could understand them, and even had he been able to talk to his mother and father or Nanny, who was afraid of cats to begin with, the idea of trying to persuade them that actually he was Peter to whom something very odd had happened, did not seem to him to be very sensible. He might have been able to explain it to someone of his own age without any difficulty, but a grown-up would be more likely to say: "Stuff and nonsense. Small boys don't turn into cats," and there would be an end of it.

But now that the moment had come he thought it might be nice if they just went and sat in front of the house for a while and looked. Perhaps his father was home and he could see him through the window on the ground floor if the curtain was not drawn, or his mother and Nanny might come in or out of the house and he would have the opportunity to observe that they were well and in good health, and above all to show his mother to Jennie Baldrin. He very much wanted Jennie to see how beautiful *his* mother was. And that is what he decided to do.

"It's there," he said, "the little one on the far side of the Mews." It was easy to point out to Jennie because it was such a small one, no more than two storeys high and rather huddled next to its neighbour, a much larger house of white granite that had been repaired recently, and into which some new people were to move just about the time whatever it was had happened to him to cause him to be changed into a cat.

Theirs was a pretty house, and had a beautiful black door framed in creamy wood, and on it his father had had fastened a shiny brass plate with his name on it – 'Col. A. Brown' because people were always having trouble finding the Mews, much less anyone who lived in it.

Yet now, even before they crossed the street, Peter could

see that there was something odd about the door, or rather different, yes, and something wrong with the sitting-room window too, giving on to the street, which always boasted of stiff, starched, lacy curtains through which one could just see the pie-crust table on which stood the small bronze statue of Mercury.

Peter saw now what was different. The brass plate was no longer on the door, nor were there any curtains in the window, or any furniture whatever in the room, for one could now look right in and see that it was empty. But in the corner of the window was a small white card with some black lettering on it, and what it said was that the premises were vacant and to let, and interested parties should address themselves to Tredgemore and Silkin in Sackville Street, or enquire of the superintendent. It was quite clear that the Browns had moved away and no longer lived at Number 1A Cavendish Mews, and as to where they had gone there was not one single, solitary clue.

Peter's first reaction was that he was not at all surprised. They always seemed to be moving from one place to another. He remembered that, and it had something to do with his father being in the Army and shifting his station.

His second emotion was one of bleak disappointment. It had not seemed so bad being a cat, particularly after Jennie had found him and taken him under her protection, and their adventures together he had enjoyed thoroughly. But suddenly he became aware that always in the background of his thoughts had been the comforting fact that no matter where he was, or what happened, his parents were there, living in the little flat in the Mews, and when he did think about them he could imagine just what it was they were doing. Above all it held out the promise that he could see them again any time he wished to go back, even though they could not recognize *him*.

And now they were gone.

Peter sat down in front of the black door and the empty window, and blinked his eyes hard to keep back the tears. Not even washing would have been a solace for the grief he felt. He had been so eager that his new accomplishments might be made manifest and that he would have been able to show his mother and father some of the things that he had learned to do, and let them know that this was no longer the same Peter who had to be held by the hand by Scotch Nanny when crossing the street. He could now go about London quite well, almost by himself. And he had taken a trip to a strange city on a steamship, been chased up a bridge by dogs, he could kill rats and mice, and earn his keep and the admiration of a man like Mr Strachan, the first mate, and altogether he had become a very important person.

He might have been able to control himself, but the quick-witted Jennie, even without being able to read, had guessed what had happened and tried to comfort him. "Oh, Peter," she said, brushing up close to him, "they've gone away and left you. I'm so sorry. It's just like… well, when my people went away and left me. It must be. I do understand.

Reminded thus of her own tragedy, Jennie felt on the point of weeping herself, but holding back with an effort she fell to washing his face firmly and lovingly with that sweetly gallant movement of her head which Peter found so touching, and of course this caused him at once to burst into tears.

Even so, he was sorry too for Jennie that she had been reminded of the great tragedy of her life, and so partly to try to recover his own composure, as well as to make known his sympathy for her, he reciprocated by washing *her* face at the same time she was washing his, with the result that now Jennie also lost control of her emotions. In a moment they were both sitting on the pavement in the Mews, lamenting piteously, seeking relief from their grief in loud, mournful song, and of course doing the one thing against which Mr Black had warned them, namely, making a noise and disturbing the residents, even though it was broad daylight and not yet two o'clock in the afternoon.

For upstairs on the second floor of the large white granite house next door, a window went up and somebody said, "Oh hush, kitties. Go away. You make me sad."

Thereupon a head appeared at the window, looking out and down upon the two unhappy cats, an extraordinarily pretty one belonging to a young girl whose long, wavy brown hair, tied with a red ribbon, tumbled down on either side of a fresh and sweet face featuring a tender mouth and soft, endearing brown eyes.

This was what was revealed to Peter as he gazed upwards

through his tears, but Jennie saw something else that made her recoil as though she had come face to face with a ghost. She stared at the apparition quite frozen into immobility for an instant with one paw upraised and the strangest expression on her face.

And simultaneously, the soft eyes of the girl went all round and alight with wonder, her mouth formed into an 'O' of surprise and momentary disbelief, and then she cried out – "Jennie! Jennie Baldrin! Oh, my darling! Oh wait! Wait! I'm coming to you…"

Then she was gone from the window, and both Peter and Jennie heard the sound of hurried footsteps running down the stairs inside, and before Peter had time to say more than – "Jennie, she knew your name, she called you by it," the door to the street burst open and through it ran the child all flushed and panting and gathered Jennie into her arms and was hugging and kissing her, holding and rocking and crying over her head and saying, "Jennie, my dear, dear, DEAR Jennie! Oh it *is* you. I've found you at last. Or was it you who found ME, you clever, clever cat. My darling, darling Jennie, you do know me, your own Buff, don't you dearest? Oh I must kiss you all over again…"

And there was no doubt that Jennie did know her, for in an instant and with a look of complete bliss and happiness on her face she had draped herself about Buff's shoulders like a long, live, limp fur-piece, and set up a purring louder than any aeroplane in the sky.

Now Buff shouted upstairs, as other windows in the

Mews began to open and people poked their heads out in curiosity at the noise – "Mummy, Mummy! Jennie's come back to me. She's found me. Mummy, come down and look. I'm sure it is Jennie."

Thereupon Buff's mother came downstairs, and she turned out to be a tall, sweet-faced woman who resembled Buff, and at the same time, Peter thought with a pang at his heart, resembled *his* mother too, so that for a moment he was not quite certain which was which, but she had no eyes for him whatsoever, as indeed neither did Buff, and now both fell to hugging and stroking and fondling Jennie, and talking together and to her, and to the nearest heads that were poked out of windows, marvelling, recounting, explaining the miracle of it all and how it had happened in the first place that they had come to lose Jennie three years ago.

But the thing was, of course, that Peter understood every word of what they were saying, and it made his heart swell with joy, because it did prove that they had not abandoned Jennie.

It seemed from what he could piece together that when they had moved away from their old home they had had to go to a hotel for a few nights, as the paint in the new place was not yet quite dry. The morning that they were to move in and had planned to come back and call for Jennie Baldrin, Buff had been taken violently ill and had been rushed to the hospital where for three days and three nights her life was despaired of. Doctors and nurses, her mother and father, had watched constantly at her bedside, and in the excitement Jennie was forgotten.

At last, when Buff had been pronounced out of danger and on the road to recovery, Mrs Penny had remembered Jennie, but more than five days had passed and when she hastened back to the old house it was to find Jennie gone.

Peter felt it was terribly important that Jennie should know this at once, and while all of the excitement and talking and crying was still going on he called up to Jennie, perched high and happily on Buff's shoulder, "Jennie! I've the *best* news for you. I've been listening to what they've been saying. They didn't go away and cruelly leave you behind. Buff was taken ill and had to go to a hospital..." and as quickly as he could he told her the whole story, and concluded – "I *knew* that people who really loved cats, and particularly you, couldn't be like that. Aren't you glad about it...?"

Strangely, although she smiled down at him quite happily and dreamily, Jennie did not appear to be impressed with the story or particularly elated over it, though no doubt she was pleased it had turned out that way, for she said only: "It doesn't really matter to me any more, Peter, what happened, or how, now that I have her back again and she loves me. You see, I could forgive her *anything*..."

This was a point of view so wholly feminine that Peter found it quite baffling and for a moment felt the forerunner of a real and awful pang of pain and loneliness which he quickly suppressed, for he wanted to entertain nothing but happiness that things had turned out so well for Jennie at last. But what Jennie said next was characteristic of her, and reassuring. She called down to him with that soft, crooning sound that was reserved only for their more intimate exchanges of thoughts – "Oh, Peter, we're all going to be so happy now. For I know they'll love you just as much."

But this was a dream that was soon shattered. For, as it turned out, Buff and her mother were hardly even aware of Peter's presence, and when at last the first excitement of greeting and crying over Jennie had begun to calm down, and all the heads that had popped out of windows in the Mews had drawn back inside again, Buff, with Jennie still draped lovingly about her shoulders and with one paw gently caressing her smooth cheek, turned and made her way inside Number 2 Cavendish Mews, the big granite house with the rich-looking vestibule where all of Jennie's troubles were to come to an end, and, quite naturally, Peter followed. But here Buff's mother, seeing a large white stray attempting to get through the door, bent down and gave him a gentle shove out into the street saying, not unkindly, "No, no, old chap. Sorry, not you. We can't have *every* cat inside. You run along home now…"

There was a slam and a click, and for a second time a door in Cavendish Mews was shut in Peter's face, leaving him standing alone and deserted on the outside.

It all happened so quickly that for a moment there was nothing he could do but stand there and look at the cold, blank, mahogany door, quite benumbed by what had taken place.

Except that this time he was not entirely deserted, for first he heard Jennie's wild cry from inside – "Peter! PETER!" and then he felt the waves of her thought broadcasting to him coming over so strongly as though she were standing next to him –

"Peter! Don't go away! I can't come now, but I'll manage things somehow. Don't worry. Go to the bombed house at Number 38 and wait for me. I'll come as quickly as I can. They don't understand about us. Promise me..."

Peter sent back his promise, and after that it was quiet in the Mews.

CHAPTER TWENTY-TWO

Jennie Makes a Decision

PETER WAS SO stunned by everything that had transpired in the Mews, the disappearance of his parents, and subsequently the loss of Jennie due to her finding *her* family again, that he did not go immediately to the hostel at Number 38 Cavendish Square, the bombed-out house where the stray cats of the neighbourhood foregathered, but instead wandered in a dazed manner in and about the square.

He watched the children playing hopscotch on the walk inside the park, leaping on one foot over the chalk marks from one square into another, and he could not help but think how short a time ago it was that he himself had been hopping there with them in the same manner. He recognised several of them and wondered what they would say if they knew that he had suddenly been turned into a cat.

He saw Mr Wiggo, the constable, his thumbs smartly inserted in his belt, conversing with somebody's nursemaid, and remembered that he used to stand in exactly the same way when he talked to Nanny and himself when they would come into the gardens, saying, "Well, and good morning to you, Master Brown. And how are you this fine day, Mrs

McInnis?" which was Nanny's name. Peter realised that if Mr Wiggo saw him now he would chase him, as neither dogs nor cats were permitted inside the enclosure, and the constable would never suspect that the big white cat that was trespassing was Peter Brown to whom he used to wish such a cheery good morning.

To forestall this catastrophe, Peter slunk under a bush and hid until Mr Wiggo passed on along the pram-lined walk on his rounds. But just the fact that he had to slink and hide from the policeman made Peter feel his plight and loneliness all the more.

Sparrows twittered in the shrubs and hopped and pecked about the street. Taxicabs coming around the corner went "Honk-honk" as their drivers squeezed the rubber bulb of their horns; from Oxford Street came the hum of the heavy traffic. Although it was getting on in the afternoon, there was still a sun shining, the trees in the square were freshly green, and the air had lost its sharpness. It was May in London, but not for Peter.

He thought of Jennie safe and happy at last with Buff and the Penny family she loved so much, how she would be taken care of now, have her comfortable basket again to sleep in, fresh milk to drink, and all the good things to eat she wanted, with never again a worry or a care, and Peter wondered whether it might not be best if he were simply to vanish out of Jennie's life and never turn up at the hostel at all. Then she would no longer have to trouble or bother about him.

The more he thought about this, the more he considered putting it into execution for Jennie's sake. He had but to turn and run away from Cavendish Square as he had done once before and the city would swallow him up for ever. Jennie would grieve for him at first when he did not keep the rendezvous at the hostel, but in her happiness with Buff she would get over missing him after a time, just as his mother had. What became of him was not important as long as Jennie was well off. With his new-found self-reliance and all that he had learned from Jennie, he would make out somehow.

In spite of the pang of loneliness at his heart and the misery induced by the thought of never seeing Jennie again, Peter rather fancied the sacrifice he was considering, and its nobility had a certain attractiveness that tended to obscure his better sense.

He was saved from this foolish step when it came to him, just in time, that he had promised to meet Jennie. And he remembered from when he had been a boy that nothing in the whole world hurt quite so much as a broken word. Once his mother had promised him that on his birthday she would spend the entire day with him. And then in the last moment something had come up which had prevented her from keeping it. Remembrance of the pain this had caused him was so keen that, huddled under the bush, Peter shook himself to try to drive it away. Then, quickly pulling himself together lest he should yet succumb to the temptation, he went around to Number 38 Cavendish

Square, located the place where the board was loose at the bottom of the door, and slipped inside.

And when he got there he found Jennie waiting for him.

He was so glad he could have run up and kissed her. As a matter of fact he did, in spite of the assortment of strays of all sizes, kinds and colours sitting or lying about in odd nooks, crannies and perches of the burned-out house, that is, he rushed up and touched noses with her and began washing her face as Jennie laughed and said:

"Well! I thought you were never coming. I've been here just hours. I was beginning to get worried that something had happened to you..."

"But, Jennie," Peter said – "I never thought you would be here so soon."

"Ho!" she scoffed. "You know me and being kept indoors. When I make up my mind I want to get out – well! Anyway, now you're here, you must come and meet everyone. There are some really interesting cats here. I've been having a chat with them while I waited for you. Let's see, we'll start at the bottom and go around. This is Hector, here – the name, of course, doesn't fit him a bit. He once belonged to a coal miner, and he's actually been way down deep in a mine. Later on you must get him to tell you all about it."

Hector was a lemon-yellow cat with a faint white stripe and a somewhat sour expression on his face, and who, Peter noticed, was not too clean. But he was evidently so pleased by the introduction that Jennie had given him that he was disposed to be pleasant and gave him rather a lengthy greeting which enabled Peter to look about and see the kind of place to which he had come.

The house had been gutted by the blaze that followed the firebomb that dropped on it during the war, and there was little left but the four walls and a few of the larger beams going across from one side to the other. However, the steps leading to the second floor were of stone and they had been preserved, as well as part of the stone landing which still clung to the wall. There were cats up on the landing, and several squatted comfortably on the stairs from which vantage point they could look down with their big green or yellow eyes and take note of everything that was going on.

But really the best places were in the ruins of the foundations. Some of the cellar walls and partitions were still standing, now overgrown with weeds and the purple fire-flowers, and some of the corners were covered over, which was fortunate as there was no roof to the house and when it rained these nooks gave some shelter. But the way they were cut up by cross-walls and parts of the older foundation it was almost like small private flats, and the nice thing was that one always had a little piece of wall at one's back, or a corner in which to curl up, and to cats living the life of strays this was doubly important.

But Hector was finished saying how pleased he was to meet as travelled a cat as Peter (Jennie had evidently been laying it on thick in his absence) and Jennie was now continuing:

"Well now, this is Mickey Riley who was thrown out in the streets when he was a kitten and who *never* had a home. If there's anything you ever want to know about London and the best places to go to make a living, ask Mickey. There's just *nothing* he doesn't know…"

Mickey, a big dark chap with a tiger stripe and an enormous square head, lapped up Jennie's flattery and practically took a bow as he said: "Quite, quite. Be glad to answer your questions. As Jennie Baldrin says, there isn't much I haven't seen or done. Though I will admit I've never been to Glasgow on a boat, or fallen overboard. I'd like to hear about that sometime, youngster."

How wonderful Jennie was, Peter thought, at always saying just the right thing and making everybody feel good and purry.

"This is Ebony," Jennie said, introducing Peter to a lean-flanked, jet-black cat. "Isn't she beautiful? Not a touch of white on her anywhere, not a single hair. That's quite unusual, you know. Ebony used to belong to an old widow, a tobacconist in Edgware Road. When she died, nobody took her on. She had been devoted to her too. Eight years. You would think the woman would have made some provisions for her. Ebony learned the streets the hard way, didn't you, dear?"

Ebony showed a tiny piece of pink tongue at the centre of her coal-black mask and quickly gave herself a couple of self-conscious licks. She was so pleased she didn't know whether to stand up or lie down.

"And this" (who proved to be a brindle cat with white face and whiskers somehow reminiscent of Father Christmas) "is G. Pounce Andrews, who *really* has had a lot of hard luck. Started in a butcher's shop and it closed down, got a job with a tailor and he went out of business, then went into a boarding-house and it burned down, and then a private house where he was staying was hit by a bomb – the only one in the block. Well, you know how people talk and how ridiculously superstitious they are, especially about cats. Word got around, and nobody, but literally nobody, would have Pounce around, no matter how many mice he brought in. He's been on his own ever since. And he does deserve better, because none of it was his fault...

"Oh, and of course," Jennie continued, "I mustn't forget. This sweet little grey girl is Limpy. She *has* had a hard time of it. Orphan. Never even knew who her mother was. Lost her in a flood almost before her eyes were open. Country cat, you know. How she ever survived I'll never know. AND then getting her foot caught in a trap. And actually moved to the city and learned to make a go of it. When you are talking about real, true-blue courage... well—"

Limpy fell over on her side and did some violent washing. It was true. Peter saw the toes of her left hind foot had been crushed. But he was given no time to linger over this tragedy, for Jennie was spinning merrily on –

"Now these two dears are sisters, Putzi and Mutzi. From the Continent. Vienna, I think they said. They have known true sorrow. Came over here in 1938 with some refugees.

Their house caught it in 'forty-four. Flying-bomb. Luckily Putzi and Mutzi were out visiting in another block. When they came back there was nothing, just a hole. They didn't even find any small pieces of their people. And after that, nobody thought of taking them in. The wonder is that they got on so well in London, I mean being really foreigners and not knowing our ways at all. Darlings, I think you are really marvellous..."

Putzi and Mutzi, who were a pair of quite ordinary short-haired tabbies with identical looks and expressions, except that one was a little thinner in the face than the other, purred modestly, and Putzi said: "Ach, it is really nothing. What shall one do? One does the best one can, no?"

And so, one after the other, Peter met them all, including Tiggo, a half-Persian with a white mask who had had a home and was now a stray because he liked it and preferred to vagabond it than live the soft life, and Smiley, who was a big, cheerful-looking mottled grey-and-white tomcat who had belonged to a bachelor who had got married to a woman who could not abide cats.

At the end of Jennie's list of introductions and her recital of the accomplishments, trials, tribulations and individual virtues of each inhabitant of the hostel, there was not a cat in the place but was reduced to a state of complete adoration of her. And thus Peter learned that there was more than one way of extracting a living and a night's shelter and safety from the streets of London, and that a winning nature and blarneying tongue were quite as valuable as a sharp claw in a swift paw.

For they soon found themselves settled by the mutual consent and urging, as it were, of all the residents of the hostel, in the best ground-floor suite of the ruined building, a secluded little dugout made by the rear stairs leading to the cellar and a corner of a brick wall. The steps were already overgrown with a kind of fungus-like moss that made a soft bed, and they were sheltered on three sides by the remains of a brick wall with a ledge overhead in case it rained. It had been occupied previously by the two Viennese sisters and Ebony and Limpy who, however, insisted that Peter and Jennie take it over all to themselves.

And as for dinner, it was a question of choosing from the many gifts brought to them, and dividing up the rest so that everybody had something. Mickey Riley brought a bone, G. Pounce Andrews had a mouse put away that had not been too much used, Limpy contributed a fish head, and Tiggo had salvaged an entire half lobster carcase, legs attached and all, out of a nearby dustbin.

After supper was over, they all had a general community wash-up and get together talk-feast, after which some of the strays who liked night prowling went out through the place where the board was loose. Others stayed around to chat a little longer and exchange experiences, and then wandered off to their various quarters to sleep.

Down through the top of the roofless house shone a three-quarter moon, its silvered disc filling the inside of the building with soft light that made the angles of the ruins stand out sharply shadowed, and reflected in cold pools of emerald and topaz from the eyes of the cats who were still awake and had them open.

Peter, snug against his bit of wall, heard the clock strike eleven from nearby All Souls' church tower. His heart was heavy within him, for any moment now he knew that Jennie would have to be leaving him and returning to her people. She seemed, however, to be quite content to remain where she was, and when she neither made any move to go, nor any mention of having to do so, Peter himself, no longer able to bear the suspense, brought up the subject.

"Jennie," he said, "won't you be, I mean, oughtn't you to be getting back to Buff and the Pennys? Surely Buff will have missed you when she went to bed...!"

Jennie did not reply for a moment. However, she raised her sleek head and Peter saw the soft moonshine on her white throat and mask, and the glitter of her eyes. Then she spoke, saying in a strange kind of voice, "Peter, I've been out on my own too long to go back. I shan't be returning. I've come back to you to stay. Do you mind very much?"

How very much like Jennie for her to put it that way. Did he mind her coming back! And dismissing with the simple declaration that she had been a free cat too long to be able to return to domestication, the depth of the sacrifice she was making for him.

For Peter had no doubt whatsoever that had the Pennys understood that he and Jennie were together and taken him in with her she would have been happy to remain there with the child who had been her first and only real love among human beings. What she was saying so simply and without any fuss whatsoever was that she was giving up everything she loved for him.

And he was deeply touched by it. But being that inside of him he still thought like a little boy, he could not help but think of the sorrow and disappointment that must be the share of Buff, the little girl with the long brown ringlets and the sweet face.

Aloud, he said to Jennie – "Jennie, dear. It was so lonely without you. Nothing seemed the same any more, and I thought that was how it was always going to be, and I didn't know what to do. But won't it be just too dreadful for poor Buff? She was so happy to have found you again. Jennie, why does *someone* always have to be unhappy?"

Peter saw the shining in Jennie's eyes before she turned her head away for a few washes as seemed indicated by the emotional content of the moment, and they were brighter and more glistening than even the moon could have evoked. But she said after she had smoothed her fur down somewhat and gained control of herself and her voice:

"Buff isn't a child any longer, Peter, and doesn't need me as much as she once did. She is almost fifteen now. People change too, Peter, and as they grow older things no longer mean the same to them. She will cry when I don't come back, but she will get over it, because she has other things that interest her now, and above all she will remember that I did come back once and that I understand that she didn't abandon me on purpose. And actually," she added with that queer and sometimes frightening wisdom she seemed to possess, "what made Buff most unhappy all the three years was the thought that I believed she had deserted me. Which of course I did, because I was a fool, until *you* came along and taught me what people really can be like…"

She gave herself a long stretch and an inverted 'U' bend, and concluded, "Well, anyway, that's all over and done with. And now here we are together again. But oh, Peter, for a little you gave me a bad turn. I was so afraid you might be going to do something foolish for my sake and not keep your promise to come and meet me here. Never, *never*, do that, Peter…"

Peter thought it best not to say that he had been tempted for Jennie's sake. Instead he gave a great sigh. He was very happy now. They lay down side by side, curled up together, and soon went fast to sleep. As the disc of the moon slid away from the opening of the roof, the soft light went out from the inside of the bombed house and all its ruins and sleeping cats vanished in the shadows of the night.

CHAPTER TWENTY-THREE

Lulu – or, Fishface for Short

THE NEXT MORNING was a fine day. Peter awakened to find Jennie curled up in a tight ball, one paw over her eyes to keep out the light, and emitting just the tiniest of snores. Although the roof overhead was now the blue sky, and soon the sun would be streaming into the hostel, she was still fast asleep. Most of the other cats were already up and about their business. Some had departed, others were sitting about making their toilet with a serious wash, or giving themselves a lick and a promise, depending upon the state of their personal pride and how low they had come down in the world.

Peter thought he would go out and forage. It would be nice if when Jennie woke up there he would be with maybe a mouse, if he could find one, or perhaps a bone dug out of last night's refuse from some of the better houses on the square, or even a bit of melon rind of which Jennie was extraordinarily fond.

And so, moving quietly in order not to waken her, he stole away from her side, bade an amiable good morning to Putzi and Mutzi who were tidying up close to the door, slipped through the narrow spot at the bottom, and found himself in Cavendish Square just as the All Souls' clock struck nine.

Simultaneously with the chime of the steeple clock, Peter was aware of a little shriek close by and then the most extraordinary voice he had ever heard: "Oh, I say. You did give me a turn. I wasn't expecting anyone. Lumme, but you are tall, white and handsome. Whoooooooooooeee! Where do you think we all ought to go, then?"

Peter himself was startled, because the voice was so deep, husky and disturbing, and turned around quickly to see who it was had spoken. And what he saw was the most astonishing and beautiful creature on which he had ever laid eyes, either as boy or cat.

She was a small puss, much smaller than Jennie, but with a wonderfully firm and compact body that was coloured a kind of smoky pearl, or biscuit, or maybe it was more cream-coloured, or the colour of coffee with a lot of milk in it, and he had never in all his life seen a cat exactly that shade.

But this was only the beginning of the surprises for Peter, for she had a seal-coloured face and mask, coal-black triangle of a nose, cream head and dark brown ears. She also had four almost black feet and tail. But the most marvellous and beautiful of all, out from the middle of the dark face gleamed two of the loveliest, shining, liquid and deep blue eyes he had ever seen. They weren't violet and they weren't sapphire; they weren't really the colour of the sea, nor did they quite match the sky; one couldn't exactly describe what shade of blue they were, except that having once seen them one could only think of blue being *that colour* thereafter. Peter also noticed that they were slightly crossed, but this in a way added, rather than detracted, from the interest and beauties of her countenance. He was quite aware that he was standing there dumbstruck staring at this lovely vision, and also that it seemed as if he could do nothing else.

The spell was broken by the little creature herself who skipped three steps sideways and three steps back again, bushed her tail, and said, "Good evening! I know it's morning, but I don't care. I say what I please. In the evening I say 'Good morning' if I feel like it, and I never say 'Good afternoon'. Well?"

The last being a direct question addressed to him, Peter felt he must reply, but was so bewildered by the charm of the cat as well as her odd way of speech that he could think of nothing to say but "Good evening, Miss," which brought another shriek from her and this time she jumped straight up into the air, and when she came down she cried – "Oh, I say, you are going to be fun. My name is Lulu, but all my friends call me Fishface for short. That's because when I eat bloaters, or kippers, or have a little hake, brill, cod or pollock my breath always smells of fish. Here, I'll show you. SMELL?" And she came over quite close to Peter and breathed in his face. The aroma of fish was unmistakable, but somehow, perhaps now that he was a cat, Peter did not find it unpleasant.

He smiled and said, "My name is Peter, and—" but could get no further, for Lulu made a backwards and forwards dash almost simultaneously and cried "Peter, Peter! There was a poem that started that way, but I've forgotten the rest. Anyway, I think up my own poetry. I am thinking of one now about thimbles. Very well then, I'll recite it for you," and here she sat down with her tail folded about her and a most sanctified look on her face that reminded Peter of some of the saints he had seen on the stained-glass windows in church, and recited as follows:

> "Thimble,
> Thimble,
>   Thimble,
> Thimble,
> THIMBLE!

"You see," Lulu explained to him after she had finished, "unlike most poetry, it ALL rhymes. Whoooooeeee!" With a leap and a bound she was away, chasing a wholly imaginary leaf, whirling, striking at it with her swift, dark paws, then finally imagining that it had been blown back close to Peter where she landed on it with a terrific pounce and crouched there, looking up intensely into Peter's face as she said: "Do you like tea? Do you like coffee? I *love* olives. Wasn't it a nice day next Thursday?"

"Never mind answering!" she cried in her deep voice before Peter could even so much as think of a reply, and got up and danced away from him with one shoulder all hunched up and crooked – "Come on, dance with me, all sideways and twist-about. Up you go, and *down* you go, and AROUND you go; now *RUN!!*"

Swept away, Peter found himself dancing sideways beside her, then leaping up in the air and turning all about before he came down, and then when he landed on the pavement, running, running, running with her as hard as he could. He could not remember when he had ever had so much fun or been in the presence of such a wholly fascinating and enchanting creature.

They did this several times, after which Lulu threw herself down on her side, stared at Peter out of luminous blue eyes and announced: "Of course, you know I'm Siamese. My father was a King and my mother a Queen, and all my brothers and sisters Princes and Princesses. I am a princess myself. Aren't you glad?"

And again, before Peter could reply that he was indeed very glad, she half sat up and recited as though it was something she had once learned out of a book – "I'm not like a cat; I'm not like a dog; I'm more like a monkey, really, but *mostly* I'm like ME, and nothing else. I get along with EVERYBODY." Then she concluded rather irrelevantly – "I can wear hair ribbons," and got up and began walking down the block in the direction of Portland Street. When she had proceeded some distance, she stopped and looked back over her shoulder.

"Coming?" she called to Peter.

Without a second thought, indeed, he could not have helped himself had he wished it, so enchanted with her had he become, Peter went trotting after her.

"Where are we going?" he asked.

"Oh," cried Lulu with one of her little side jumps. "How will we be able to tell until we get there? Some place exciting. I haven't been off like this for ages. I'm so glad I found you. We can do everything together…"

Progress with Lulu, Peter found, was wonderful, enthralling, exciting, and somewhat nervewracking. One moment she would be shrieking with laughter and leaping along the street stiff-legged, or flying along the top of a fence at full speed, her ears laid back, tail streaming out behind her, commanding Peter to a game of 'Follow My Leader', and the next she would be sitting down in front of a perfectly strange house, miserably sad and woebegone, with the tears streaming from her magnificent eyes and announcing to Peter in heartbreaking tones that she was all alone in a strange country, thousands and thousands of miles away from Siam and all the Siamese. "You don't know, you cannot know what it is to be so far away, so very far away from everyone…"

Peter felt his own heart would break too, she was so pathetic in her plight and separation from her loved ones. He tried to comfort her by saying, "Oh, poor Lulu. Tell me about your far-off home and where you were born. Perhaps talking about it will make you feel better."

"Who me?" Lulu chirped, her tears as suddenly drying

up as they had started. "Why, I was born in London, of course. Where else would anybody of importance be born? My whole family too. We have a pedigree longer than our tails. I told you, all Kings and Queens, didn't I? Have you a pedigree? Well, never mind. Your being cute makes up for a lot of things. You came along at just the right moment. You know, I was *so* bored." Here her hoarse voice sank to a quite confidential whisper – "I live with very rich people on the Square. Number 35. VERY rich. He has Shares. Don't look so sad, Peter. I'm really quite marvellously happy now." And off she would go, leaping, twisting, dancing and shouting at the top of her lungs, and of course Peter would be after her full tilt, laughing madly at her funny ways.

Thus in many starts and stops they found themselves at last, after climbing steadily for some time and proceeding up many curvy blocks of small houses one just like another, on a sort of plateau, an open space with a rail around it, almost like being on the top of a mountain. For when you looked over the edge, there was all of London spread out beneath your feet and stretching for mile upon mile of streets and houses and spires, and the silver winding of the Thames, and the millions and millions of chimneypots on the rooftops, the endless rows of grey houses, and in the distance the occasional spots of green that marked the little parks in the squares. There was the big patch of green that was Regent's Park, another that was Hyde Park, and a third that was Kensington Gardens; tall chimneys and cranes far off that marked the docks and factories and warehouses on the Thames and, after that, the whole trailing off and vanishing into a kind of blueish haze of distance and mist and smoke.

"Hampstead Heath!" Lulu announced. "Isn't it picturesque? I often like to come up here just to meditate," and with that she threw herself down on the ground, closed her eyes, and was quiet for just five seconds, when she was up again, gave herself a couple of fierce and energetic washes on both sides of her neck and said, "There! Now that I've meditated, where shall we go next? Oh, I want to have fun, fun, fun! One can't be serious all the time you know…"

It was well on towards noon, for the journey up to the Heath had taken considerable time, and Peter ventured to remind Lulu that it was getting late. "Oughtn't you to be thinking about getting back?" he asked — "I mean, your people, you know. Won't they miss you?"

Lulu stopped and looked at him as though she could not believe her ears.

"Miss me? Of course they will. They'll *bust* when I don't come back. Why, that's half the sport. What fun would it be if they didn't care? I'm sure they'll have notified Mr Wiggo the Constable already. They hate me to be out. Sometimes I don't come back for days if I don't feel like it. I think I don't feel like it right now. I think I feel like staying away for maybe three whole days, just to see what that would be like. I've never done *that* before. They *will* be upset. Oh listen, Peter. It sounds like music somewhere. Let's go THERE!"

It was quite true. As Peter pitched his ears forward to listen, he could hear borne on the wind the strains of the gay and strident music that sometimes comes from a carousel. Somewhere in the vicinity there was a Fun Fair.

They set off, following the direction of the sound, and sure enough pretty soon they came to a large collection of tents from which gay pennants were flying, booths, roundabouts, coconut shies, ice-cream counters, aeroplane whirls, auto dodgems, shooting galleries, shove-ha'penny boards, darts games, sideshows with dancing girls, fortune tellers, strength-testing machines, and all the gay and noisy paraphernalia of the itinerant Carnival.

There were crowds of people thronging the fairgrounds. "Hurry, hurry!" Lulu shouted to Peter, scampering along and looking back over her shoulder at him every so often. "Isn't this luck? I've never been to anything like this. I'll bet there are all sorts of good things to eat inside. Here we are. You lead the way just in case anything should go wrong, and I'll follow you…"

Peter *had* been to a small fun fair once when he had been by the seashore on holiday, but he had certainly never been to one by himself, that is, without somebody holding him by the hand and telling him where to go and where not to go, and of course never had he been anywhere in the company of a creature so beautiful, charming and wholly captivating as Lulu.

They went by a man who specialised in selling big inflated balloons attached to a stick coloured red, yellow, blue and green for the young folk, and of course Lulu had to reach up and bat one with her paw, and since she had neglected, or even out of pure mischief refrained from pulling in her needle-sharp claws, the balloon, a large crimson one, went off with an appalling explosion, knocking Lulu head over heels and frightening her so that when she got to her feet she tried to go in three directions at once, with the result that she went nowhere at all, but remained practically in one spot, causing Peter to shout with laughter. But the man who was selling the balloons did not think it was at all amusing to have a sixpenny one ruined and dangling a limp bit of torn rubber on the end of a stick, and he snatched it up and would have beaten Lulu with it except at just that moment she found her feet and went darting away like an arrow out of a bow with Peter after her, still laughing. When he caught up with her finally, however, she was furious at him, not only for laughing at her, but also for breaking the balloon which she accused him of having done just to frighten her, and which of course was quite untrue.

But so under her spell was Peter that he did not even mind that, though when he had been a boy, nothing had made him quite so miserable or unhappy as to be unjustly accused. Instead, he apologised to her just a though he *had* done it, and to make up for it offered to take her where they might get some ice cream.

Lulu, who never seemed to be able to stay in any mood very long, at once stopped being angry and even rubbed up against Peter twice, most lovingly, and said: "Ice cream! Oh, ice cream! I just LOVE ice cream. If you can get me some ice cream I'll never forget you as long as I live," and then she added quickly: "You know, we have ice cream *every* day at our house, every single day and twice on Sunday. That's because my people are so rich. Shares, you know. Or did I tell you?"

Peter did not *quite* believe this, else why would she be so very eager to have some, but he was not able to find fault with anything that Lulu chose to do or say, and besides, he did think he knew where to get it. His sharp eyes, now trained never to miss an opportunity for a snack or a full meal, had noticed that right in the vicinity of where they had stopped was an ice-cream booth served by a girl in a white apron, with bright yellow hair the colour of straw, jaws that never stood still, and eyes that also moved constantly roving over the crowd. The jaw movement no doubt was due to the use of American chewing gum, but since her eyes were constantly wandering over the crowd looking for a personable young man, she did not quite pay attention to what she was doing, with the result that every time she served up a gobbet of ice cream, which she got out of a cylinder-shaped tin with a metal scoop and flopped it on to the wafer cornet before handing it to a customer in exchange for threepence, large dribbets of it would fall to the floor behind the counter at her feet. It was on these drippings that Peter intended to concentrate.

The problem was how to get behind the counter without

being noticed, but that was not too difficult when it developed that it was only oilcloth around the bottom of the booth, and not fastened too securely at that. In a moment he had showed Lulu where to nip under, and only after she had achieved it safely without attracting any attention did he follow her himself.

There was one opening on the other side by the feet of the girl and this was immediately filled by Lulu whose dark tail stuck out straight behind her as she squatted there and licked and lapped and sucked up all the ices that dropped down beside her like manna from heaven. While Peter waited patiently for his turn, she had some chocolate and vanilla and some cherry flavour, then a bit of pineapple and strawberry, followed by orange, pistache, coffee and lemon, as well as raspberry, peach and blackberry. This took quite a long time, as sometimes there would be a considerable wait between customers and nothing would come down. But it was steady feasting at that, and from where he sat and waited, Peter was sure that he could actually *see* Lulu's sides distending.

Had Peter thought of Jennie at that moment, which he did not, he might have wondered that Lulu had not offered to make a little room for him so that he too could enjoy the delights his wits had provided. But the sad truth was that not once since he had first laid eyes on Lulu had Jennie crossed Peter's mind. He was completely bedazzled by the gay, fascinating and irresponsible little Siamese.

Not only did Lulu fail to offer to share, but when her sides were really so ballooned out that Peter was beginning to be afraid that she might burst, she emitted a resounding burp, followed by a deep sigh, and turning away from the hole said to Peter: "Oh! I simply couldn't lap another tongueful. That was delish. Where do we go now? I think I'd like to see the animals if it was quite safe. Come on. You lead the way. You're so clever."

Peter would have loved to have had some ice cream, and, as it happened, a big, thick, gooey gob of chocolate dropped into the opening at that moment, but Lulu had already turned and ducked out of the booth by the opening through which they had come and Peter perforce had to let the treat go and follow her, for he could not bear to let her out of his sight.

Opposite was a large tent with some glaring posters outside depicting in four colours the wild denizens of the African jungle, and they had no difficulty whatsoever slipping under the sides of the tent.

Within, it was not quite as exciting as outside, for the advertised denizens of the jungle proved to be but three in number. The show consisted of three cages built into wagons, containing one thin and shabby-looking lion who looked in need of reupholstering, a mangy hyena, who smelled bad, and a small Capuchin monkey with a sad face and unhappy eyes who hung by his tail from a bar.

However, there was nothing anaemic about the roar the lion let out when he saw Lulu and Peter, and he paced up and down his cage, pushing his shoulder against the bars and rubbing his already worn pelt to further tatters.

Trembling with fear, Lulu crowded as close as she could to Peter and said, "Oh! Isn't it wonderful to be so frightened? Don't you *love* it? I could just stay here the rest of my life and tremble. Isn't it thrilling?"

But soon she said: "I'm afraid; I want to sleep against you."

They went round behind the lion's cage and, obediently, Peter lay down beside her. She immediately whipped around, curled against him, put both paws in his face and went to sleep. Peter held himself statue-still, for he did not want to disturb her, but the paws were tickling him and one of them was interfering with his breathing and so at last he shifted ever so slightly which brought an immediate and raucous protest from Lulu.

"No, no, NO!" she cried, her blue eyes coming wide awake at once and glaring at Peter reproachfully. "I LIKE sleeping with my paws in your face. It's so much softer. Do hold still." This time she managed to put them in his ears, but he dared not move, and eventually the long, exciting day through which he had been took its toll and he fell asleep too, but not very soundly.

The following morning, awakened by the roaring of the lion who was shouting for his breakfast in exceeding bad temper, Peter saw that not only was Lulu sitting up, not at all frightened, but she was yawning so that he could see right to the back of her pink throat.

"Aren't you frightened any longer?" he asked her.

"What, of that poor old thing in a cage?" Lulu replied.

"That was yesterday, and yesterday is never the same as today. Don't you think tomorrow is really the best of all? Today I'm not frightened of the lion any longer, I don't want any more ice cream, and I'm tired of the fun fair. Let's go somewhere else. You know about everything. YOU lead the way."

But as he started to crawl out from beneath the tent, she went by him with a whisk, a roll and a flash, and was ten yards ahead of him and waiting by the time he had got free of the canvas.

"Goodness," she said, "I've been waiting for hours. I thought you were never coming. Do you *hate* rain?"

There was some logic in her last remark, for now that he was outside the tent, Peter found that it was a grey, unpleasant day with a fine, early-morning drizzle coming down from the sky.

He replied, "Yes, indeed I do. I don't like it at all. My fur gets all wet and cakey, and then it gets dirty and—"

"Pity," Lulu interrupted. "I LOVE the rain. All cats hate water but me – us, I mean. I once dived right off a punt into the Thames at Henley. It was Regatta Day and everybody applauded. Rain makes my eyes bluer. Come on, let's take a nice long walk in it."

They left the fun fair and the Heath and promenaded steadily north through Highgate to Queen's Wood Priory Road. Here the drizzle changed to a downpour, but Lulu, who ordinarily proceeded only by leaps and frisks, now seemed to enjoy walking at a sedate stroll while blinking her eyes up into the downpour so that, as she apparently believed, they would get bluer. Peter was hideously wet; he had never been quite so thorough rained on before, and yet somehow wandering along beside Lulu it didn't seem to matter too much. If it *really* did make her eyes bluer, it was quite worth it.

Towards early afternoon the rain stopped, the sun came out again, and nothing would do for Lulu but they must go on, and so they wandered across Finsbury Park and east through Clapton to the Leyton Marshes, where they played for a while in the vicinity of the waterworks before they struck north again as far as Epping Forest, which they reached by nightfall and where they found an astonishing amount of trees and foliage considering that they were yet within the limits of London.

Peter was beginning to be tired and quite hungry, for somehow it always worked out that there was somewhere they had to go or something immediate they had to do just as he was about to catch a bite or a snooze for himself, but Lulu was too excited and enthralled at being in the woods and country, and fairly begged him to join her in the excitement.

For the stars had come out overhead and the moon was now nearly full, and so bright that one could hardly bear to look it in the face.

The moonlight, of course, had a most marvellous effect on Lulu. She leaped; she danced; she shouted; she turned somersaults and ran up one side of a tree and down the other without ever stopping, her cream body flashing in the silver light. And whatever she did, Peter had to come and do it too, and they chased in and out the trees and shrubs until Peter thought he would drop, at which point Lulu cried –

"Now! We're going to run right up a moonbeam. I'm the only one who knows how to do it. Follow me!"

Of course she didn't, but the way she gathered and hurled herself moonwards, her little feet working furiously in the air, it seemed to Peter as though she actually were, and he wore himself breathless and ragged trying to follow and imitate her. Finally she seemed to exhaust herself for a moment and lay panting at the foot of a great beech, but only for a moment, for when Peter threw himself on the turf beside her, ready to drop off to sleep, she said: "Moonlight makes me SO sentimental. Would you like me to sing you a Siamese song?" And without waiting for him to answer, she sang in her odd, cracked little voice:

"Eeny-meeny-miney-MO
Hokey-Pokey Bangkok Joe!"

She repeated it several times, but her voice was growing sleepy. Finally she said: "There! Tomorrow I'll teach it to you. Now it's bedtime. Watch over me, Peter. Strange places make me nervous at night. Somebody ought to keep an eye out while we're sleeping. You do it." She lay over on her side and soon the regular movement of her flanks showed that she was off. Peter gazed down at her and thought he had never seen anyone sleep so gracefully, and the position of trust she had endowed him with as her guardian thrilled him to the core. Let anything come out of the forest, no matter what, a lion, a tiger, or even an elephant, and he would protect her – that is, provided he could manage to keep awake.

Fortunately there were only a few hours left of the luminous night, and shortly after the moon dipped beneath the trees, the sun once more mounted the sky, and Lulu awoke. She stretched, blinked, and gave one of her paws a nip as Peter watched her enchanting movements. And then with a swift stirring, as though she had suddenly remembered something, she sat bolt upright and stared at Peter in the strangest imaginable way, almost as though she had never seen him before in her life. She even got up and walked over to him and peered at him. Then she shook herself once and asked in a kind of dazed and faraway voice: "Where on earth are we? Where have you brought me to? What has happened to me?" And although she actually did not pass her paw across her brow, the expression on her face was exactly as though she had.

Peter, taken aback by this strange behaviour of his erstwhile gay and carefree companion, said: "I'm not certain, but I think we're in Epping Forest…"

Lulu gave a little shriek and sprang away from him as though he were contaminated. "Gracious! I remember nothing. I must have been drugged. What day is this, and since when?"

Peter counted. It had been Tuesday, he remembered, when they had gone away together. "Thursday or Friday, I think. I'm not sure."

Lulu gave a loud cry – "Thursday or FRIDAY! Oh, what have you done? My poor people. I must get back at once. The poor, poor dears; how very upset they will be. I mean more to them than anything. They will be worried ill, you wretch…"

"But… but…" stammered Peter, commencing now to be completely bewildered, "you told me yourself that you wanted them to worry, that that was half the fun, and that—"

"Oh!" Lulu said in a shocked voice. "How can you be so horrid and so wicked? Luring me away from home with soft words and promises, plying me with ice cream to stupefy me and then trying to shift the blame on to *me*; having all the fun and then making ME responsible. I don't think I ever want to see or speak to you again. I'm going home at once. The mercy is they'll be so glad to see me they won't scold me at all perhaps when I come back. By now they'll surely think I'm dead. And I might be for all of you."

Peter was stunned by the attack and even more so by the sudden fear of losing Lulu.

"Lulu!" he pleaded, "don't go back. Stay with me – for ever. I'll get you ice cream every day, and mice, and wash you as often as you like, only don't leave me…"

"Oh!" said Lulu again, and once more, "OHHHHHHHH!" and now her voice was really shocked as well as angry. "How dare you? How do you imagine such a thing? Don't you know that I'm a princess? Stay with you indeed! What I ought to do is hand you over to the nearest policeman. I shan't do it, because I am too good-hearted. Everybody says I have the disposition of a saint. But don't you dare to presume upon it. I am going home at once now, and don't wish to be followed. Goodbye."

And with that she turned and went scampering off through the trees in swift, galloping leaps, leaving Peter sitting there, too dazed and stricken to speak, move or even call after her. But after she had gone about twenty yards she paused suddenly and looked around, and called back: "It *was* fun, though, wasn't it?" Then she turned once more and ran and ran as fast as she could, her tail streaming out behind her, and in a few moments she was quite out of sight.

And that was the last time that Peter ever laid eyes on her.

CHAPTER TWENTY-FOUR

The Informers

YES, WHEN LULU'S dark tail vanished around a clump of shrubbery, that was the last of her, and when Peter, hurt and bewildered no less by the sudden desertion of his new-found friend and comrade as by the accusations she had made against him, trotted to the edge of the park where the monotonous line of two-family houses, as alike as two peas in a pod, began once more, and looked down the street, there was no sign of her. She had not reconsidered. She had not waited for him. She had not changed her mind. She had gone home without him.

And quite naturally now that he was alone for the first time and the peculiar spell of Lulu over him was broken, or at least loosened somewhat, since even though she was no longer there, the echoes of her presence, the faintly crossed blue eyes glowing out of the dark, velvety mask, the compact, tight little cream body with the dark feet and tail and ears, and above all the hoarse, haunting, challenging voice, were all about him, Peter thought about Jennie Baldrin, and once he did think about her and remembered how he had left her without a word as to where he had gone or when he would be back, it had to be admitted that his conscience was very bad indeed.

He thought of her waking up in the hostel and not seeing him at her side and then going out to look for him and not finding him, and no one about to tell her where he had gone or give her a message from him. Then she would look for him all over in the square and about the neighbourhood, and when she failed to locate him and he had not come back at night, or the next night, either, goodness knows *what* she might think. She might believe that he had gone off so that she could go back to Buff; or even worse, she might fear or suspect that he, Peter, for whom she had just made the supreme sacrifice of leaving the family she loved so much for his sake, had the very next morning run off with someone else.

Of course, Peter told himself, actually this was not so, and he heard himself making a speech to her when he should return to the hostel and find her waiting for him, in which he explained everything to her exactly how it had happened so that she would not misunderstand, and in which he began with: "You see, I thought it would be nice if when you woke up I had a fresh mouse for you and so I went outside to have a look around and see where I might find one. Well, there she was, just the other side of the door, this extraordinary, beautiful, gay, mad person. Really, Jennie, I had never encountered anyone like her before and she lured me away by coaxing me to dance with he and we went to a fun fair together and slept in the animal tent, and after that we stayed in a stable and…" But Peter never got much beyond that because it had a kind of a hollow ring, and worse, it sounded perfectly absurd, not to mention cruel and fickle on his part, and he could not imagine himself really saying anything like that to Jennie for all the world. Well, then, what *would* he say?

And the more he thought about it, the less certain and happy he became about the whole business, because it wasn't as though he had just stayed away for a few hours, or a day at the most, but *three days*. And the really dreadful thing was that just before Lulu had deserted him he had begged her not to return home to her people, but to go off with him on a kind of perpetual outing and holiday-camping trip. Of course Jennie need not know about that, but the fact remained that *he* knew it, whatever happened, and at the moment he felt that it was not a very nice thing to know.

For a while he succumbed to the temptation of thinking up a story to tell Jennie that would cover his heartless desertion of her, something dramatic, possibly with catnappers, two spivs with checkered caps and neckerchiefs who had scooped him up from the square with a net just as he had been about to pounce on a fine medium-sized mouse which he intended to bring to her, and who had then whisked him off in a high-powered car.

There would then be a good deal more about a mysterious house with drawn blinds in Soho, a silent, evil-looking Chinaman with a long knife who was his jailer, and the masked leader of the gang with the villainous leer and the scar on his face who had bargained with the dealer in illicit furs, a fat, greasy-looking fellow with a bulbous nose and bloated face. With the odds at more than twenty to one against him, he, Peter, had finally managed to elude his captors and fight his way out of the dungeon and escape from the house to return to her at last.

But he knew that he could not do that, either. First of all, he was quite well aware that it would not be possible for him to lie to Jennie, even if he really wished to do so, which, deep down, he did not. And, secondly, the story was not a very good one.

And the conclusion to which he finally came was that there was only one thing to do and that was to go back to Cavendish Square – though goodness knows actually where he was now and how long it would take him to find his way, and once he had got there to march into the hostel, confront Jennie, and make a clean breast of the whole business and ask her to forgive him.

He found he felt a little better immediately he had come to this decision, and not pausing even to make his toilet or forage for something to eat, he set off at a swift trot, alternating with darts and rushes, in the direction his instinct told him was south by south-west and Cavendish Square. But he had not realised actually how far it was possible to come in three days, even stopping off as often as he and Lulu had, and it was close to nightfall before, tired, hungry and footsore, the tender pads on his feet worn almost to bleeding from pounding along the hard stone pavement, Peter arrived at last at his destination. Entering the square from the north, along Harley Street, he turned at once to the hostel at Number 38 and, squeezing in through the narrow opening, found himself once more inside, his heart beating in his throat and a very uncomfortable feeling in his middle.

When he discovered inside did not tend to make him feel much more comfortable. It *was* the hostel all right; he had made no mistake in the address, and besides, there was but one bombed house in the row, and yet it was *not* the same at all. It looked as it had before in the twilight with the shadows falling over the walls and cornices and overgrown bits of rubble and ruin, but it felt quite different.

And then Peter saw why. The inhabitants seemed all to have changed. The lemon-yellow Hector was no longer there, nor was Mickey Riley. He failed to see Ebony, or G. Pounce Andrews, or little grey Limpy, Tiggo or Smiley. There seemed to be as many cats in and about the place, and some of them even resembled his old friends, but when he saw them closer he noted differences in colour and marking, shape and size, but above all in their behaviour towards him. He was a stranger. They did not know him. There had been apparently a turn-over in the population of the hostel.

With a sinking heart Peter went back to the snug little den that he and Jennie had occupied the night of their arrival. There was someone in it, but the eyes that glared out at him from under the shelter of the cornice were not the soft, liquid, melting ones of Jennie, but two cold, amber-coloured, hostile orbs, and he was greeted as he approached with a low growl, and the old, well-remembered cry – "'Ware! You're trespassing."

The hostel was free ground and open to all, but Peter was not in a mood to argue the point with the new occupier, a big, hard-faced, cherry-coloured tom with dirty white saddle markings and battle scars.

"Excuse me," Peter said, "I didn't mean to. I was looking for a friend. We were here together – I mean we had that place three days ago, and—"

"Well, you haven't now," the cherry-coloured cat said unpleasantly. "I was assigned to this by old Black himself. If you want to make something of it, go and see him..."

"Yes," said Peter, "I know. But I was really only looking for my friend. Do you happen by any chance to know where she is? Her name is Jennie Baldrin."

"Never heard of her," the cherry-coloured cat said curtly. "But then I've only been here since yesterday. There was no one here by that name when I came."

Peter felt himself growing sicker and sicker, and the empty, scared feeling about his heart grew greater all the time. Picking his way carefully through the hostel, upstairs as well as down, he searched it thoroughly from top to bottom. But there was no Jennie Baldrin, nor anyone who remembered her or had seen her. One brindle tabby did recall somebody mentioning Jennie's name, and that was all. This seemed to have happened two days ago. Peter had the horrid feeling that somehow he had been bewitched, that not three days but three years or perhaps even three centuries had passed, that in some manner he had left the planet to wander elsewhere and now that he had returned everything had changed and, most terrible of all changes, Jennie Baldrin was no longer there. She had vanished and no one knew where she had gone or what had become of her.

Just at that moment his ears were caught by the faint scraping sound as two cats made their way into the hostel from outside, two twin tabbies with identical markings and expressions, except that one was slightly thinner in the face than the other. Dark as it was growing, with a great leap of his heart Peter recognised them, and with a glad shout ran over to them calling – "Putzi! Mutzi! Oh, how glad I am to see you both. It's me, Peter. You remember me, don't you?"

The pair stopped at this approach and stared first at him and then they exchanged a look between themselves. They did not seem at all to share his enthusiasm at seeing them, or to return it. For a moment it appeared even that they were going to turn away without speaking to him, but then Putzi eyed him coldly and said: "Oh ho! So you have come back, have you?"

But Peter was too elated to have found someone who knew him and who would be able to tell him where Jennie had gone, to notice anything, and said:

"Yes. And I'm looking for Jennie Baldrin, but I can't find her anywhere. Can you tell me where she is?"

Putzi and Mutzi exchanged another look, and now it

was Mutzi who replied in a voice that was filled with primness and distaste. "No, we cannot. And even if we knew, we would not tell you, so there."

The little pang of fear and discomfort was returning to Peter now, and besides, he was feeling quite bewildered. "But why?" he asked. "I don't understand. Where did she go? And why wouldn't you tell me?"

"Because," replied both Putzi and Mutzi together now in chorus, "*we saw you!*"

All the worst possibilities now crowded to Peter's mind, but he managed to stammer – "You saw me what...?"

"You and that *foreigner* from Siam," Putzi replied, lifting her nose high in the air, in which scornful motion she was joined by Mutzi – which was a little strange seeing that they too were both foreigners. "Your dancing with her and carrying on right in the middle of the street, and staring like wass coming right out from your head your eyes. Oh yess. We saw you."

"And putting your nose right up to hers and listening to the silly poetry. We heard you too," Mutzi chimed in.

"Und then so to running off with her," Putzi continued. "We went at once and told Jennie."

"Oh!" said Peter, feeling now quite sick and sad in his heart. "What did she say?"

The sisters smiled prim little satisfied smiles. Putzi announced: "She said she didn't believe us, and that it iss some kind of a mistake."

Mutzi added: "We advised her to go right away because

you were not good enough for her. In spite of everything we tell her she says she will stay and wait because she knows you will come back soon."

"But WE knew you wouldn't," Putzi said triumphantly. "We told her so. That Foreigner! Everybody in this neighbourhood knows *her*. Ach! Only a man could be so stupid. So now you have it. In the night she realise how we are right, because in the morning she iss gone. We have not seen her since, und we think it serves you right."

Mutzi added acidly: "I suppose now you want her back."

"Oh yes," said Peter, not even caring that this self-righteous, gossipy pair should see his pain and his misery – "Yes, I do want her back. Most awfully."

"Well," said both in chorus again, "you won't get her. She's gone away for good." And then turned away with their tails high in the air and twitching slightly with their indignation as they picked their way over the rubble and through the weeds to the rear of the hostel, leaving Peter alone.

Never had he felt so badly, not even when he had been turned into a cat and Nanny had pitched him out into the Mews. For that had been before he had met Jennie Baldrin. He knew now how much lonelier and unhappy one can feel after one has lost someone who has grown dear, than ever could have been possible before. And he knew, of course, that he deserved it.

But the real ache in his heart was for Jennie, who had thought only of him even to the point of leaving home and loved ones with whom she had just reunited, for his sake. For Peter had not been deceived by the casual manner in which she had dismissed her gesture. He knew that Jennie had made a decision that had cost her much, but she had been able to do it because she loved him. And this was how she had been repaid.

Peter went out from the hostel hardly realizing what he was doing, or seeing where he was going, for he was quite blinded by tears of remorse for his thoughtlessness and irresponsible behaviour, and as the lamps came alight in Cavendish Square, he walked slowly along making a vow that somewhere, somehow, he would find her if he had to search for her the rest of his life, just so that with his last breath he could tell her that he had meant nothing by what he had done and that he cared for her and for her only.

Surely some place he *would* find her again, but his spirits sank when he thought of the magnitude of the city of London with its teeming millions of people and houses, and *all* the places where a small tabby cat with a white throat and mask, and gentle, loving eyes could crawl away to hide a broken heart.

Still, there must be a beginning made. And perhaps, oh perhaps, she had gone back to Buff around the corner in the Mews. Why had he not thought of that before? Surely, surely, deserted by him, that is what Jennie would have done.

Hope lifted him again, and with a little run and a skip he went dashing across the Mews, to see.

CHAPTER TWENTY-FIVE

The Search

PETER SAT ON the pavement and watched outside Buff's house in the Mews, all through the long night with a heavy heart, for while it did not seem as though Jennie were there, he could not really be sure until the next day.

Lights were on in the house, first on the lower floors, then later spreading to the upstairs parts, and once he saw Buff's brown head framed by the window and against the yellow lamplight, but there seemed to be no Jennie draped about her shoulders.

Then one by one the windows went dark, not only in Penny's house, but all over the Mews, until soon the only illumination came from the street lamp at the corner and the moon overhead. Peter began calling to Jennie, softly at first, then louder and with all the misery and mournfulness that was in his heart, but there was no reply from her and not even the faintest hint of her presence coming in over the sensitive receiving-set of his whiskers and vibrissae. The only result of his wailing was that a window on the Mews was opened and someone cried – "Oh hush up, kitty. Be quiet! Go away!"

Thereafter he dared not call any longer, for he remembered the strictures placed by Mr Black on their welcome in the neighbourhood depending upon their remaining quiet and not disturbing the residents. But remain there he must, just in case Jennie had not replied because she was angry with him and thus there might still be hope of seeing or learning something about her on the morrow.

It was a long and lonely vigil out there on the pavement, but it passed at last with the coming of the milkman, and the darkness lifted from the east and turned first to grey, then to pearly pink, and thereafter shortly the sun arrived and brought with it the daylight.

There were yet many weary hours to wait until the Mews woke up, prior to beginning the new day.

At last the door to Number 2 opened and a gentleman wearing an important-looking homburg hat and carrying a black leather dispatch case emerged and hurried off in the direction of the Square. Peter judged that this was probably Buff's father on the way to his business. Anyway, there was not much to be learned from him, but a short time later the door opened again and this time it was Buff who came out, accompanied by her mother. She was carrying her school bag, books, and lunch.

So excited and eager did Peter become at the sight of her that he quite forgot himself and ran across the street to them crying – "Buff! Buff, please. Have you seen Jennie? Do you know where she is? I've been horrid to her and I must find her and tell her I'm sorry."

But of course Buff could not understand a word he was saying. All she saw was a large and somewhat soiled-looking white cat running across the street to them mewing piteously. For a moment there seemed to be something familiar about him as though she had seen him somewhere before, and she gave Peter a long and fixed look as she passed by as though she was trying to remember something.

But Peter heard her say to her mother, "Mummy, why do you suppose that Jennie went away again after coming to find me? And do you think she will ever come back again? It's been days now…?"

He heard her mother reply: "Buff, are you sure it really *was* Jennie? After all those years… It may have been only another cat that was like Jennie."

"Oh, Mummy, now… There was only one cat in the whole world like Jennie—" And here her voice trailed off as she and her mother walked out of earshot and turned the corner into the Square, leaving Peter's heart as cold and weighted as the cobblestone on which he crouched, and in his ears the echo of Buff's last remark: "…there was only one cat in the whole world like Jennie." How well he knew this to be true now that he had lost her, perhaps for ever.

There was no use waiting or looking any longer in the Mews. And besides, deep down, Peter had always known that even if Jennie had been angry at him she would have answered his call had she been there.

But where to search next? In a panic lest she might have returned to the hostel in the meantime, he went charging around the corner and in through the broken board, almost tearing an ear in his haste, but of course she was not there. He would even have been glad to have been abused by the two sisters once more just because they had last had contact with Jennie, but they had gone out and there were only a few strangers in the hostel, most of the residents having gone about the business of the day.

It was then the conviction came over him that he must look elsewhere, and probably far from there, that she must have left the neighbourhood which had brought her unhappiness.

He thought now that he would go back and look around their old haunts on the docks as the most likely place where Jennie might go. He moved both by day and night, and because his mind was so occupied by his quest, Peter was not even aware what an experienced and practised London cat he had become thanks to Jennie's teaching and training. Sighs and sounds and sudden noises no longer frightened him; he seemed to know how to avoid trouble automatically; he could melt away and hide at a moment's notice, instinctively, no matter where he was he always picked out and marked a place of safety to which to go in case of sudden danger, something to get under, or on top. But of course he was doing these things without realising it at all. For right then he was going through that awful stage of seeing Jennie in every tabby cat curled up in a shop doorway, or washing in a window, or gliding across the top of a fence or hoarding.

Because the yearning for her was ever in his mind, it seemed to him that each time he turned a corner, his heart leaped high with hope that he *might* come upon Jennie, and if there was a cat there at all tiger-striped, no matter what her size, shape or colour, he suffered first from the hope-born illusion that it was Jennie and then from the oft-repeated disappointment when it was not.

And from this he passed to the stage where he had the strongest feeling that surely now he must and would find her just around the next corner, and so he would dash at full speed to get there and look. There would be nobody there, only some children playing in the gutter, or women queueing up at the fish store or the local sweet shop, or perhaps only a dog scavenging in the streets. Then the conviction would seize hold of Peter that he had just managed to miss her, that she *had* been there but probably had just nipped around the *next* corner, and that if he ran as fast as he could he might be in time to catch her there.

This sort of thing of course soon led to a state approaching exhaustion, particularly since he was not stopping to eat or drink, except as he came upon a pool of dirty water still remaining from the last rain in some depression of the street, and whatever scraps of anything edible happened to come his way during his pell-mell, headlong, conscience-driven search. He had let himself go physically and personally as well, not stopping to wash or clean up, and soon his white fur lost its gloss and became matted and dirty, his pink skin began to collect grime and itch him, and it was not long before he was the counterpart of the scrawniest, mangiest stray that ever slunk along the backwaters of London Town and the river reaches.

And still he kept on, with night merging into day and day into night again. He slept when he could not go on any longer out of sheer weariness, and wherever he happened to be, and always when he had had a little rest there was the memory of the sweet and unforgettable face of Jennie with its white throat and soft pink-lined muzzle, and the glowing, liquid, tender eyes, as well as all her individual mannerisms; her smile, the quick way she would look over at him to make sure that everything was well with him, her dear motions when she washed herself, her gay carriage. And there were her little weaknesses such as her family and ancestry and her desire to show off and look well before Peter's eyes, and at the same time all her strength, her lithe sureness, muscular paws, and quiet, efficient action when it came to the hunt, or any kind of emergency. And it drove him on and on and on, ever searching.

When he reached the dock section once more he found that he remembered his way about somewhat better, and he went to the shack where Mr Grims had lived on the chance that Jennie might possibly have returned there to mourn for her friend, or drawn by her memories of the old man.

It was a grey, cold day, and raining again, when Peter went slinking along beneath the cover of the lined-up goods wagons in the late afternoon as he had that day so long ago with Jennie and thus came at last to the shack with the tin roof and the crooked-pipe chimney sticking out of it.

But, alas, what a difference. Gone were the red-blooming geraniums from either side of the door and from the windows. It looked dirty, dismal and more tumbledown than ever, and when Peter crept near and looked inside through the half-opened door he could see a mean-eyed, snivelling-looking little fellow wearing a dirty neckcloth, sitting on the cot with an upraised gin bottle held to his mouth, and the whole place smelled of gin and sweat and dirt. And of course there was no sign of Jennie.

The man removed the bottle from his lips, and since he had drained it empty, he sent it flying through the door where it crashed into a thousand pieces almost where Peter was sitting. Had it been another inch or two to the left, it would have hit him. Peter wished it had. He dragged himself away from there...

As a kind of last hope, he found his steps turning towards the basin, east of the London docks, where the *Countess of Greenock* had been berthed. Surely, oh surely that was where Jennie must have gone. And the terrible part of his punishment was that each time he had such a thought about where she might be, it became at once the place where she *must* be and then he became all of a fever to get there, and as he went his mind would delude him with the picture of exactly where he would find Jennie, and how she would look, and what he would say to her, and what she would reply.

And soon he would convince himself that it was all true and that he had only to hasten his steps to reach the *Countess* to find all as it was before – Mr Strachan slashing at his dummy with a sword, Mr Carluke cocking his fingers and firing off imaginary pistols at imaginary bad men and Indians, the crash of smashing crockery emanating from Captain Sourlies's cabin, and Jennie perched up on her favourite place – the flag locker on the after-deck.

The *Countess* was indeed in port, warped to her dock in the usual slovenly manner, but outside of the mournful strains of singing coming from amidships, there were no signs of life aboard her, the entire crew and officers having apparently gone ashore leaving no kind of watch whatsoever and no one aboard except Mealie, the cook.

He was sitting on a stool on deck at the head of the gangway, shining black and round-eyed, chanting a doleful blues, but his sharp and rolling eyes missed nothing, and when Peter poked his head around the corner of the gangplank and looked up, he ceased singing at once and shouted down – "Hollo, you Whitey! Hollo you. I know you. I know you. I never forget NO one. Where you been, hey? Where you gorl friend? You looking for you gorl friend, hey? She ain' been aroun' here… Why you both no come back? We got plandy mouse and rot on board again."

Peter was so stunned by the news that Jennie was not there, that for the moment there was nothing he could do but stand, almost frozen by despair. He had been so certain that Jennie would be at the ship, that this was truly the last place where she could be, and he could only look up at Mealie in silent misery.

It was astonishing how the big negro seemed to understand him. He arose from his stool, shaking his head and saying: "Don't you look at me thot way, big Whitey. I tol' you I ain' seen your gorl friend. Where you leave her, hey? Maybe she come along later…" Now he made clucking noises and advanced halfway down the gangplank and called: "You Whitey! You come bock and work, hey? I pay you good wages for cotching rot and mouse. Roas' lamb on Sunday and watchu like… Plandy milk too. What you say, Whitey? You look like you plandy hongry inside…"

Now Peter became afraid that Mealie might pick him up, take him back aboard the *Countess*, and lock him up in the galley, and so before the cook could come any nearer he turned away and ran and ran, his eyes again scalded by tears of misery and disappointment. He ran as fast and as far as he could, but it was no great distance, for it had been so long since he had eaten anything that he was quite weak and even felt that he was perhaps going a trifle light in the head since he now began to take to imagining things.

This took strange forms, such as finding himself at places with the feeling that he had been there before, and of course in the company of Jennie. Under the spell of this imagining, Peter would even turn to speak to Jennie, only to find that she was not there and the street a strange one in the wilderness of London.

He was staggering late one night, still looking, hunting

and searching in the grim neighbourhood of the great warehouses and storage yards and buildings near the basins and the river by Wapping, when again he was impressed with the sense of familiarity as he passed a large hoarding advertising Bovril, not far from a pillar box. Surely he had been here before, but in his exhausted condition he could not remember when.

He felt ill and weak, and was sure that another imagining was upon him. But he gave himself up to it because of the strong feeling that Jennie was somewhere nearby and the comfort it brought him for the moment.

He had had so many bad dreams and horrid nightmares during the endless days and nights of looking for Jennie, that he welcomed this good one that seemed to have been granted him for the moment, and this was that the drab, grimy, blackened brick wall of the warehouse along which he was dragging himself at the moment would soon contain an aperture or hole, about the size of a dinner plate, a foot or two above the pavement, and that the grating which belonged over it would have rusted at the catches and fallen away so that if one wanted one could get out of the hole – or into it…

Yes, it was a good dream that had come over him, for sure enough, there was the so-familiar hole, metal lined, and on either side the small indentations to show where once the grating had fitted over it.

Such a dream, Peter felt sure, was meant to be followed, and with an effort he leaped upward and into the entrance.

Oh yes, indeed, no more than three feet along inside the iron pipe and there was the rusted-out spot, a smaller hole leading off into the dark tunnel at the left, just as he had known it would be.

It was so good, and so comforting, not to feel quite so lost and aimless any more, to seem to be knowing where he was, or at least which way to go at the behest of this kindly, benevolent fantasy, left – now right and then left again, and if the dream was truly his friend and comforter, surely there would be the bin with a little light filtering into it from a grimy window near the top that had one pane out of it, and it would be filled with red and gilt furniture, covered with dust sheets piled right to the ceiling. In the centre would be an enormous bed with a red silk cover on it and a high canopy at one end with folds of yellow silk coming down from a kind of large oval medallion with the single letter 'N' over it in script, with a crown above...

Sweet and dear dream, thought Peter, for there indeed was the room, exactly as it had been before. And would the dream hold now, would it grant him the final grace by letting him imagine that he had but to leap up on to the red silk cover to find Jennie waiting there for him, or would he waken or return to his senses to find himself cold, hungry, miserable, wet and shivering in some wretched alley in the slums, alone and no nearer to Jennie than he had been at the beginning of his search?

For a moment almost he dared not move lest it fade,

and then came the queerest feeling that he was no longer dreaming, but that maybe... maybe...

The next instant he made one leap up on to the bed, and found himself face to face with Jennie. *And it was no dream.* No, not even an imagining. It was true. He had found her at last.

"Jennie! Jennie!" Peter cried – "Oh, Jennie, I've looked and looked for you. Jennie, have I really found you?"

Jennie said: "Hello, Peter. I'm glad to see you. I've been waiting such a long time. I knew you'd come here in the end to find me." And then she went over to him and touched noses and kissed his eyes. But the next moment she said: "Peter... How thin you've grown. And your coat! Oh, my Peter, what has been happening to you? You haven't been eating. You're starved. Peter, you must let me give you some mouse at once. I've a lovely one I caught earlier in the day..." She leaped down to where she had cached the prize and returned to the bed with it and laid it in front of Peter. "See, he's just the right size, and nice and fat too. But don't eat too fast, Peter, if you haven't had anything for a long time."

There was a quiet pride in her eyes when Peter carefully took it down on to the floor to eat, and even more when after he had finished half he withdrew and offered her the rest. "No, my dear," she said, "you finish it. You need it more. I've had plenty..."

Peter felt strengthened at once. He was so wildly happy at having found Jennie, at seeing her once more, or he would have been had he not felt so ashamed and worried about how he would explain to Jennie, and what he should say and how to begin.

But somehow the final miracle happened too, for it just never came to that at all. Because when he started to wash after his meal, partly from realizing what a mess he was again and how he must look to Jennie, and partly because of his embarrassment, Jennie came over to him and said: "Peter, you're so tired. Let me do it for you. Just lie down and close your eyes…"

It was plain to Peter now that she had forgiven him, and all the shame and misery and conscience feeling that was in him seemed to be swept away by a great flood of loving her that seemed to pour through him and dispel all the darkness, unhappiness, and sorrow that had been his share for so long.

He lay on his side and, closing his eyes as she had bade him, gave himself up to the delicious medicine and balm of her rough, busy little tongue, soothing, massaging, healing his worn, tired, aching limbs as she washed him thoroughly and lovingly from head to tail-tip just as though nothing at all had happened.

CHAPTER TWENTY-SIX

Jennie, Come Out

AND JUST – WELL, *almost* – as though nothing had happened. Peter and Jennie resumed life among the Napoleon furniture in the storage bin.

Without mentioning *why* she had left the hostel on Cavendish Square by herself, Jennie merely recounted that she had made her way back to the warehouse almost directly, and to her surprise when she arrived there had found all the furniture back again and the bin exactly as it was before. It seemed probable that it had been removed originally to be presented at some exhibition or other and had been returned when the exhibition closed.

She did not tell Peter the reason why she had come there, namely because this was where they had first met, as it were, and where they had been so happy together in the early days of their friendship when Peter was learning how to be a cat. But there was no need to do so, for Peter quite well understood, and he was ashamed that *he* had not thought of the same thing, and had not come back to their first home immediately to see if she were there instead of running almost blindly and unreasoningly about London, searching for her everywhere she was not. He was of course too young to understand that there was an essential difference in the way that she thought about things as compared to the way that he did and that could not be accounted for. Nevertheless he was instinctively wise enough to permit her to labour under the little white deception that having exhausted all the other familiar and remembered places where she might have been, he had come to their own home on purpose, instead of staggering upon it almost by accident in a kind of dream-delirium induced by not having enough to eat.

Important was that they were together again and that Jennie seemed to bear him no grudge of any kind. She listened with great interest to the tales he had to tell her of what he had overheard Buff say to her mother, of the melancholy change that had come over the shack of their departed friend, Mr Grims, and the new and unpleasant occupant thereof, and about the *Countess of Greenock* and Mealie, and she laughed when he told her of Mealie's complaint that there were again plenty of mice and rats aboard and that they were wanted back on the job.

No, the difference, and Peter was quite well aware that there *was* a difference, lay not in Jennie's comportment and demeanour towards him, but in a certain preoccupation, an occasional absent-mindedness and staring off into the distance with a worried expression on her countenance, certain unexplained absences from their home by herself from which she returned even more disturbed and filled with an underlying sadness.

If anything, she was even kinder and more loving towards Peter than she had been before, more generous, thoughtful and solicitous about his welfare and health (which now that he was eating regularly again, bloomed up quite rapidly), quick to smile upon him or try to anticipate anything he might wish to do. Sometimes, he noticed, that for what appeared to be no particular reason, Jennie might suddenly get up and come over to him and give him two or three little licks over his eyes or the sides of his cheeks, or between the ears. Then she would look down upon him with the tenderest and most loving expression imaginable, but also with a great sadness that seemed to lie behind her lustrous liquid eyes. It was clear that Jennie again had something preying on her mind, something secret that was troubling her deeply and Peter could not fathom what.

And it was also true that since the episode of his adventure with Lulu a certain shyness and reserve had come between them in that they did not care to enquire too closely into one another's thoughts lest they invade some compartment marked 'Private', the opening of which might permit the escape of old and wounding memories. And for this reason Peter felt in a way shut off from coming right out and asking her what was the matter and whether there was not something he might do to help. For as the time went by she seemed to be growing more and more unhappy.

And then one day, after Jennie had been away for a particularly long time, she returned home more than usually troubled. She greeted him kindly, but almost immediately retired to a corner of the bed and crouched there, her forefeet tucked under her, staring straight ahead, the way he knew one did as a cat when one was miserable or did not feel very well. Only from time to time would she turn her head slightly to look at him, and then Peter noticed that her eyes were swimming with tears and that she was looking utterly despairing.

Thereupon, he could stand it no longer. He went over to her and washed her face tenderly, tasting the salt of her tears on his tongue, and said to her: "Jennie, dear. What *is* the matter? You are so unhappy. Won't you tell me? Perhaps there is something I could do to help you. There is nothing I would not try to do to make you happy again…"

But Jennie only cried the harder and crawled nearer to him and gave herself up to his ministrations for a little until he had soothed her. She seemed then to recover somewhat and also to come to a decision, for she arose, shook herself, and made a few tongue strokes down her back as though to win herself a few more moments of respite to reflect over what she was going to say. Then at last she turned to Peter, her face grave and filled with concern, but now backed with what seemed to be a decision that could be no longer postponed, and she said:

"Peter… Listen to me and do not be hurt. Something has happened… The time has come when I must leave you…"

Peter felt a pang at his heart as though a knife had been inserted in it at these words.

"Leave me, Jennie? But why? How can you? I don't understand. Where would you go? Why can't I come with you? Wherever you go, that's where I want to be…"

Jennie hesitated before replying as though she were searching within herself if there were yet not some way of escape, or even some manner of telling it that might hurt Peter less, or which he could be made more easily to understand. Then she sighed and said:

"Peter, I cannot help it. I must. Dempsey has spoken for me. I must go away with him."

For a moment, Peter did not even know of whom or what she was speaking. And then suddenly he emitted a long, low growl and his tail began lashing furiously. For now he remembered the big, cruel yellow cat he had encountered in the grain warehouse right at the beginning of his strange adventure, the lean, hard fellow with the scar on his face. He recalled his arrogant, truculent voice and his brutal attack upon him. He was reliving the stunning buffets and the terrible charge that had bowled him over, the sharp teeth that had ripped his ear, and the claws like a hundred knives tearing at his chest and stomach, and in particular there came back the mocking, sneering cry of the big tomcat as Peter had painfully dragged himself away, torn and beaten to within an inch of his life: "…and don't come back. Because next time you do, I'll surely kill you…"

But mixed in with his anger at the memory of the pain and humiliation he had suffered was still bewilderment at what Jennie was saying, for he did not quite understand.

He said: "Jennie! Go away with Dempsey? But I don't understand why. I don't want you to leave me…"

She replied: "It's our law, Peter. When you are spoken for by Dempsey or someone like him you must go with him. He refuses to wait any longer, and so I must."

"But, Jennie," Peter protested, "*I* will speak for you. I have, long ago, haven't I? You belong to me…"

Strangely, Jennie made no reply to this, but just stared at Peter miserably. He asked her: "Jennie, do you *want* to go away with him?" and this brought an anguished wail of protest from Jennie.

"Peter! How can you ask such a thing? I *hate* him. I have begged him to let me go a hundred times, but he will not. He says his mind is made up and I must come with him, and this is the law. Don't you see, Peter, I can do no other than obey…"

And now for the first time Peter had the odd feeling that there was something that Jennie was holding back, that she was not telling him the whole story, and that in some manner she was still protecting him. He knew many of the laws that regulated the life and living of cats that Jennie had taught him through their days together, and all of them seemed right and logical and were easy to understand after you learned the reason why they were made, all except this one, and he felt certain that there must be something else about it that Jennie had not told him.

He said, "I don't want you to go. I won't let you go, Jennie, because I love you. What can I do under The Law to make you stay with me? Jennie, tell me the truth, or I will go to Dempsey and ask him…"

And now Jennie saw that Peter had grown and changed. He loved her very dearly, and because of this she could no longer conceal the truth from him, much as she would have wished to do so, and she replied finally in a small, frightened voice: "If you really want me, Peter, under The Law, you may fight Dempsey, and if you beat him then I need not go with him, but can come with you wherever you go," and with that she began to cry bitterly again.

Peter, however, said at once: "Then I will fight with Dempsey, because I want you to stay with me always, Jennie. I can fight, because you taught me how."

And here, to his surprise, Jennie wept more miserably than ever until he begged her to stop and tell him why, whereupon she explained: "I'm so frightened, Peter… if you fight him. For this is different from anything else. He has spoken for me, and you must either kill him or he will kill you. It can end in no other way. And oh, Peter, Dempsey is so big and strong and terrible, and no one has ever been able to beat him. If he were to kill you, I should die. And that's why I think it would be better if I went away with him. Peter, I couldn't bear to have anything happen to you, don't you see? Let me go…"

"I am strong too," Peter said.

"Of course you are," Jennie said quickly, "but oh, my Peter, you have a secret that only I know, that you are not really a cat, but a boy, which, perhaps, I think is why I love you all the more. Dempsey is all cat and knows every foul trick of fighting and killing. No, Peter, I won't let you. You'll be able to forget me in a while after I'm gone…"

"No," Peter said, "I will not let you go. I will fight for you under The Law, and I will kill Dempsey," and then he added, in spite of himself, "or he will kill me…" because the truth was that he did not feel too confident that he might win. A certain understanding had come to him and he knew now that it was one thing to engage in play fights or even half serious ones in arguments over priorities or squatters' rights, or passage through certain disputed territories, in which the battles were all conducted strictly under the Rules of the Game, and could even be broken off, and quite another to face Dempsey to decide with whom Jennie Baldrin was to remain for ever.

Ah yes, this would be quite different. For in this one there would be no rules or etiquette whatsoever, no pretending, no looking away, no washing when it was needful to call a halt, no playful giving of handicaps or advantages to make the sport more thrilling and exciting, no generous gestures or chivalrous behaviour – just rip and tear with tooth and claw, until one or the other was finished for ever – kill or be killed.

And he understood now too, everything about Jennie Baldrin's behaviour, how much she loved him, her terrible dilemma, and how she had tried to solve it by giving up everything to shield him. But he knew also that there remained nothing else for him to do but fight Dempsey and, for Jennie's sake as well as his own, strive with his utmost to the very last that was in him, to conquer.

And Peter was conscious of yet another emotion. Although he was not at all certain that he *could* triumph over such a seasoned and formidable opponent, as he thought back over the hurt, humiliation and indignities that Dempsey had inflicted upon him in their first meeting, Peter discovered that whatever the outcome might be, destroy or be destroyed, he was not at all averse to the encounter and, almost, he looked forward to it. It would be something to get a little of his own back from Dempsey before he perished...

"Don't worry, Jennie," Peter said. "You shan't have to go away with Dempsey. I'm not afraid of him."

And here it was that Jennie turned quite suddenly from protectress to the protected, for she stopped crying and came over and looked up at Peter with almost a worshipful expression in her eyes as she said; "Oh, Peter, I know you are not. You never were afraid of anything, right from the beginning. I am sure that is what I first liked about you. Oh, it is so good to have someone one can *rely* on."

At her words, something transpired in Peter now, a kind of calm acceptance of whatever it was that fate had in store for him. For not only was a life lived without Jennie unthinkable and certainly not much worth preserving, which he had known from the very first and which had been confirmed over and over during the long days and nights of his search for her, but there was also the personal matter of the little score he had to settle with the big, ugly yellow tom who was a sneak and a bully as well as a tyrant and a despot. For he, Peter Brown, for all of his white tail, four feet and furry ears, his cat's eyes and whiskers and body, was still inside of it and in his thoughts and ways very much the human being, a small boy and the son of a soldier. His father had taught him never to accept an insult and to fight for what he thought was right and against any kind of oppression, no matter what the odds were. Important was that here was clearly a case where he must fight, and therefore the consequences became quite secondary.

He explained this to Jennie, or at least tried to as best he could, and to his surprise, once he had put it that way, she dried her tears, ceased her objections and self-accusations, and almost from one minute to the other became an entirely different person. What Peter had won back by the moment and method of his decision was his old comrade, partner and standby, the Jennie he had first met and knew and come to love − loyal, steady, faithful, coolly intelligent, and as always wise and efficient, and thoroughly capable and self-possessed.

"Very well, Peter," she said in quite a different tone of voice, for the time for weeping, fretting and sentimentally lamenting was over for her now, "there is at least one way in which I *can* help you. I can show you a few things you won't find in the book, and maybe that Dempsey hasn't seen either, and prepare you. You will have to harden yourself, Peter, and forget everything, because I am going to hurt you and you must be prepared to hurt me, for this is serious.

When the time comes, and you face him, there will be no quarter given or asked. We have a little less than three days, for that is when Dempsey has said he will be coming to get me. It isn't much, but at least we can get in some training and hard work. Dempsey doesn't know about you, so *he* won't prepare, though he's fighting nearly all the time and is always in condition. Still…"

"When and how will it be when he comes?" Peter asked.

"At night," Jennie replied. "At night of the third day. He will come and call to me at the mouth of the iron pipe from the street. He will be angry and impatient for me to come. Anything or anyone who gets in his way at that moment he will try to kill."

"Ah," said Peter, "I see. You won't come out, but I will. There's room in the street…"

"That will be in Dempsey's favour," Jennie said, "he's the greatest street-fighter ever seen in this neighbourhood for generations back. But that can't be helped. He's too experienced an old campaigner to be lured in here. Otherwise you could try to ambush him in the tunnel and kill him there."

Peter stared for an instant in astonishment at his friend and companion, and then said – "But that wouldn't be fair. I couldn't do that."

Jennie said: "Oh, Peter, in this kind of battle there is no such thing as fair and unfair. There is only life and death, the vanquished and the survivor. Rest assured that Dempsey won't trouble about being 'fair'…"

"Well," said Peter, "I don't care about him. I shall."

Jennie emitted a great sigh. There were certain things in Peter, certain facets of being human that she could never learn to understand. They just had to be accepted.

"Very well," she said, "let's go into the gymnasium and begin…"

The gymnasium proved to be a large and wholly empty storage bin about five down from where they had their home, and to which they repaired at once.

"Now," Jennie said, withdrawing a slight distance from him, "I'm coming at you. Give a little with the charge, and stop me *with claws out*. Hit hard, Peter!" She flew at him like a small cannonball of furred fury.

Peter yielded ground as she had directed, but he countered her attack with no more than a gentle play-pat, a buffet only half delivered with all talons sheathed. He on his part suddenly felt a sharp stab of pain in his right flank and a stinging in his nose. He backed away, blinking. His tender nose *was* scratched, and when he turned his head to look, a small fleck of red was already showing near his shoulder where Jennie's claws had dug.

Jennie was standing a few feet away from him, her eyes narrowed down to slits, her tail bushed and lashing. "I warned you!" she said. And then, only for an instant, and the last time, she softened and the love-sound was in her throat. "Oh, my Peter," she said, "you must… It's for YOUR sake…" Then she cried — "'Ware!" and charged again.

This time Peter defended himself with tooth and claw.

Then began what was a kind of nightmare to Peter – three days of grim and bitter lessons in the art of self-preservation and other-destruction. From the lore of cats from time immemorial culled from jungle, rocky mountain caves and desert, Jennie brought up her memories of every trick of attack and defence, augmented by her deep knowledge and experience of the seamy side of London and the hardbitten customers to be encountered there.

It was not that Peter could not take it, but when he first saw the telltale flecks of crimson on Jennie's white throat and sweet muzzle and mask, for which he knew he was responsible, he came close to breaking down and weeping because so deeply and tenderly did he love her that he could not bear to hurt her.

But she was as hard as steel, and far more tough than he at that moment, for she knew that her own skin was of no account at this time and that he needed the training if he was to survive the battle to come. And she was merciless to him too: she *made* him protect his vital spots, or suffer the consequences. Herself, her own person, she offered to the augmenting of his skill in combat almost as a sacrifice to ensure his victory. Since she could not by their Law enter the fray and battle at his side, she took her hurts in this manner and cherished them, because each drop she shed, each nick or bite, cut or scratch she suffered for him and thus it was no suffering at all.

At night they lay down side by side on the great Napoleon bed and washed and licked one another's wounds so that they would be clean and healed by the next day when the horrid lessons resumed, and Peter, learning quickly,, now improved by leaps and bounds in speed, deadliness and agility… And if he noticed that he was less injured now during the training affrays, while Jennie's face and body was a mass of bites, cuts, scars and bruises, he said nothing, for she had likewise managed to instil in him a feeling of the danger and the deadly earnestness of the fight into which he was going. Time was so short, and it would be for her happiness as well as his that he would be doing battle.

But the third day there was no training, nor would Jennie let Peter eat anything, for she knew that one fought best on an empty stomach. But all day long she made him sleep, curled up and relaxed on their bed, and when he showed signs of being fretful or restless as the hour approached she soothed him with washing and massage until he slept again.

And so the sun girded that part of the hemisphere and the light faded away from the broken pane of glass in the tiny window in their bin and Peter slept, calmly and deeply, the sleep that repairs all ravages to mind and body and brings renewed strength.

It was shortly before Dempsey came and called that Peter roused out of the depths of his sleep at once, and awake all over, alive and clear-headed, and tingling in every nerve and muscle. It was pitch dark, but the light of a single star that came in through the broken pane was enough for his cat-sensitive eyes to orient themselves. Jennie was nearby.

He felt her presence rather than saw her. He stretched once, and then crouched and listened.

Then he heard it, muffled by its passage through the walls and windings of the warehouse, via the tunnel and aisles, but unmistakably the voice of Dempsey. Peter remembered it now. He would have known it anywhere. And it was calling to Jennie. "Come out... Jennie, come aaaaaaaout naaaaow! Naaaaaaaow, Jennie, come aaaaaaaout..."

A low, deep, nearly inaudible grown formed itself in Peter's throat. He flattened himself almost on to his stomach and began to slink forward. The last thing he heard was Jennie's deep sigh from the bed, and he felt rather than heard her wish to him – "Good hunting, oh, my Peter..."

Then, he was down from the bed, and with the fur from his belly almost brushing the floor, every movement controlled to that he seemed to flow along the ground, he went down the dark aisle of the warehouse in the direction of the tunnel from whence came that call that raised every hackle and hair on his body –

"Jennie, come aaaaaaaaaout naaaaaaow, come aaaaaaout, come aaaaaaaaaaout!"

CHAPTER TWENTY-SEVEN

The Last Fight

'MY JENNIE, COME aaaaaaaout! Naaaaaaow naaaaaaow come aaaaaout!"

The low-pitched, insistent cry from the street penetrated the pitch-black tunnel where Peter was crawling slowly but steadily towards the exit orifice. And now that the moment was so close at hand when he must face Dempsey, Peter knew that he was very lonely and very much afraid. Nevertheless, he kept on.

When he had been together with Jennie, in the safety and security of their home, he had had the comfort and aid of her presence to keep him from dwelling too long in his mind or imagination upon the consequences of the encounter that lay ahead of him. Also, for the world he would not have let Jennie see that he perhaps might be worried or apprehensive.

But here in the dark of the tunnel, by himself, with no one to see him, with none for whom to put up the front of bravery and careless courage, he could yield to being horribly afraid. He *was* frightened of what awaited him on the outside in the street. Nevertheless, he kept on moving in that direction.

He felt fear of everything that might be about to happen, the lacerating pains of bite and tear, the dizzying buffets and crushing holds, the indignities of the assaults about to be launched upon his person as well as his own loss of humanity in that in a few moments he would be trying his best to destroy the life of a fellow. He did not realise it at the moment that these were quite human thoughts, for in spite of his cat body and keen eyes and ears, sharp claws and teeth, he was still Peter, and it was really a boy who would some day become a man, and not a cat at all, who was preparing to go into a fight. But even had he so realised, it would not have helped him very much, or minimised the dangers, or the awful figure of Dempsey that loomed up in his mind.

For there in the darkness, creeping ever nearer to his enemy, Peter found himself magnifying the powers and proportions of Dempsey beyond all bounds. In his mind he became as large as the lion he had seen at the fun fair, with claws of steel, curved and as long and sharp as surgeons' knives, and with terrible yellow fangs dripping poison. Dempsey's eyes were larger around than dinner plates, and devastating lightnings flashed therefrom. Nevertheless, without ever for a moment halting, or even contemplating turning back, Peter continued to move steadily onward in that wonderfully controlled slow-motion approach that Jennie had taught him when there was something to stalk, and always closer to the battleground where the horrible apparition he was thinking up for himself awaited him.

Thus he came from the tunnel behind the baseboard to the hole where the intake pipe was rusted through, and thence into the pipe itself where a few feet ahead he could see the exit into the street illuminated by the pale rays from the lamp a little down the block.

And at this point, quite suddenly he ceased to be afraid, or rather, to be more accurate, he stopped bothering about it, for now he had other and more important things on his mind – which was to make his exit on to the street and face Dempsey without being caught at a disadvantage. He contemplated what might happen if Dempsey suddenly took a notion to stick his head into the entrance of the pipe to see whether or not Jennie was coming, and he had a momentary vision of the entire diameter of the pipe filled with the huge, square, scarred, sneering face. But then he remembered Jennie's assurance that Dempsey was too old and experienced a customer to go sticking his head into anything he did not know, particularly at night, and besides at that moment he heard the old fighter's cry again – "Come aaaaaaout, Jennie…"

Peter, therefore, as he had been taught to do, settled down almost at the mouth of the pipe to sniff things out and receive through the ends of his whiskers all the messages of where and how things were and what were the conditions on the battleground-to-be.

The church-tower clock of St Dunstan's began to chime and Peter counted the strokes almost automatically. "Six-seven-eight-nine-ten-eleven-twelve." Midnight, then.

He twitched his sensitive moustaches and felt the presence of Dempsey, but not in the immediate vicinity of the exit from the warehouse. He could not tell exactly how far, but he felt sure that his enemy was squatted some little distance away from the aperture, at least a few yards.

His whiskers told him there was not a human in the street, and not another animal, dog or cat, or sleeping sparrow.

There was no footfall. No vehicle moved. The sky was overcast with the stars and the waning moon hidden, and there was a hint of rain to come.

"Come aaaaaaout naaaaaaaaow, my Jennie, come—"

Peter stepped out into the street and Dempsey's call was cut off as though someone had slipped a noose around his throat. He was sitting several yards from the mouth of the hole leading into the warehouse. He did not look as big as a lion. He did not look like anything but what he was, a strong, compactly built tomcat with a broad, flat head and powerful shoulders. He did not look any larger or stronger than Peter himself, for in the days of his vagabondage and travels with Jennie, Peter had grown, filled out and strengthened.

There he sat, the street lamp showing up his dirty yellow colour and the scar that ran across his nose, and the battle-torn ears, lean and raking and sinister enough, but at that moment frozen into immobility by sheer surprise. And for that brief second, Peter had the advantage and should have hurled himself across the intervening space straight at Dempsey's throat before he could recover from his astonishment, or even realise that a battle was impending. But this Peter could not bring himself to do. Instead he said – "Jennie isn't coming. But I'm here…"

The growl of rage and hatred that came from the throat of Dempsey as he arose and backed away from the wall sounded almost infeline in its quivering depth, passion and intensity. Then hoarsely he enquired – "You! Who are YOU?"

Peter was not at all afraid any more. At the moment Dempsey was nothing more than a rather ordinary-looking alley cat put considerably out of countenance. Peter had seen *bigger* cats on his travels. He said to him: "Look again. You ought to remember me after doing me the dirty as you did. I'm taking care of Jennie Baldrin now."

Another terrible growl, more fiend than feline, issued from Dempsey's throat, and he spat: "Oh… YOU!" I remember you now! My warehouse. Trespassing. I warned you then if ever you crossed my path again I would kill you. I'm going to kill you now!" And with that he began to go crooked, bush his tail and swell up until he really did begin to look enormous, menacing and twice his size.

But Peter said – "Pooh! I know that trick. There isn't actually any more of you. It's nothing but wind, really," and he began to blow and swell up himself until he too was Dempsey's size, and for a few moment they faced one another thus until Dempsey, looking a little nonplussed at being met at his own game, deflated, and Peter rather carelessly did the same, but without paying too much attention to where he was or in what position.

And in this, and also in rather underestimating his foe now that he saw him face to face and discovered that he was no super-cat, Peter made his mistake. He should have remembered at all times that Dempsey was the veteran and the victor in hundreds of battles, and that not for nothing does one win such a reputation as was his in one of the hardest neighbourhoods in all the world.

For quietly and cleverly, without in the least giving himself away, the cunning old champion had manoeuvred himself out along the pavement close to the gutter and away from the wall, putting Peter between him and the sheer, dark sides of the warehouse, cutting off one of the cardinal planes in which Peter needed to move. And the next instant, without another sound, threat, warning or battle cry, Dempsey launched his attack, and a few desperate moments later Peter found himself fighting for his life.

Lightning-fast as Dempsey had been, Peter had still anticipated the rush and accurately gauged its length and power. But, alas, when he went to give and roll with it to rob it of its initial force and sting, preparatory to launching his own counter, he found himself blocked by the wall just behind him. The shock of the contact with the object he had not realised was there or that he was so close to it, further distracted him, and Dempsey was in on him with two brutal, sweeping blows and a bite. Because the blows rocked Peter's head from side to side, the bite following too swiftly missed its mark of the throat, but sank deep into his shoulder.

Peter felt an agonising pain as the bone snapped, followed by something, in the circumstances, much worse – a horrible numbness and loss of feeling. His own right paw and shoulder, his best weapon, was useless.

He was badly hurt and handicapped from the outset, and *Dempsey knew it.*

Now the attacks came with a dreadful and horrid insistence: tooth, nail and blow, bite, scratch, kick and buffet that yielded not a moment of respite. Gone were all of Peter's carefully laid and rehearsed plans of combat, of defence and attack, of clever duelling and manoeuvring. Battered, dizzied, panic close at hand, Peter could only reply weakly with a kind of despairing, scrambling, futile blows with his good paw that had no power behind them, weak evasions and ever more desperate twists and lurches, as pinned against the wall by the vicious and never-ending surge of Dempsey's attack he could feel his strength ebbing from him and knew that in a short time he must be done for.

There was blood in Peter's eyes now, blinding him, his flesh had been ripped in a dozen places, there was an injury to one of his hind legs as well, he could hardly breathe so raw and burning was the sensation in his chest; in less than a minute he had been all but destroyed, and still the relentless attacks continued without let-up.

And this then was to be the finish of the proud undertaking to protect and defend Jennie Baldrin from the tyrannical brute who had claimed her for his own. The end would be soon for him, he knew, but at least one could struggle and fight to the finish. And he *was* still fighting, he realised, not too effectively, and taking ten times more injury and punishment than he could mete out, and yet, even in his desperation, he had apparently accomplished something – for Dempsey also was now no longer whole or free from wounds. An eye was damaged, an ear further torn, one paw bitten through and bleeding heavily. These things Peter noted almost like flashes in a dream, the awful nightmare of what was happening to him. But they did serve to give him courage and he even then was able to win a moment's respite when, squirming and slipping down along the wall against which he was pinned, he managed to get on to his back, and when Dempsey hurled himself upon him, Peter raked him fore and aft with his one good hind leg and ripped at his head with his left paw, until at last it was so that Dempsey had enough of that and broke off the combat long enough to tear himself away from Peter's painful embrace.

But now it was the presence of that same wall that suddenly served to embarrass and distract Dempsey, and before the big tom could quite recover himself to launch the final attack which would surely have spelled the end for his opponent, Peter managed to pull himself around and on to his feet, away from that deadly contact, and with his bared white teeth showing in an angry and menacing snarl, and left paw upraised, at least he stopped Dempsey for the moment and caused him to pause and study his adversary for his weakest points before again advancing to the kill.

No more pitiful figure could be imagined than Peter, slashed from head to foot, his fur stained and matted, back on his haunches, shaking and trembling, one paw out of commission but the other still upraised to do battle. And it was to make an end of him that Dempsey now advanced for the last time.

His brain clearing for a moment, Peter saw him coming, his narrow, slanted eyes slitted with hatred, his moustache pushed forward, and for an instant he was struck by the strange resemblance that Dempsey looked not at all like a cat but like a rat. And he thought of the rat that he, Peter, had fought so well and successfully deep down in the bowels of the *Countess of Greenock*, and what he had done, and with his last remaining strength, as Dempsey charged him, he leaped into the air, twisted his body around and came down squarely on Dempsey's back.

And as he did so, he buried his teeth deep into the back of Dempsey's neck, and with all his might and main strove to reach the same vital spot in the spine that had spelled the finish for the rat.

Dempsey gave a shattering cry of anguish and fright, for in all his hundreds of battles he had never once been attacked in this fashion before. Then he began to struggle madly to dislodge Peter. Right and left he leaped, up and down. He rolled over. He smashed himself up against the wall. He stood clawing and screaming on his hind legs. And always deeper and deeper Peter pressed his jaws, searching, probing, clinging with might and main, dizzied and sickened by the battering he was receiving, for Dempsey was many times stronger than the rat had been and there were times when he felt he must be flung off, and that he had not one ounce of strength left to hang on. And just at those times he became stubborn, and where his strength lacked, his courage and spirit did not.

And quite suddenly, and even unexpectedly, he found bone and nerve and gave a crunch, and Dempsey without another struggle fell over on his side, limp. His legs and tail twitched once, and after that he never moved again.

Peter had won. But at what a cost. For, stretched out now across Dempsey's still and rigid body, bleeding from a hundred wounds, Peter knew that his own course had but a short time to run. He had triumphed and saved Jennie, but his own end was only a matter of minutes. He had been too badly bitten and mauled to survive. Wherever it was that his enemy had preceded him, he, Peter, would not be long in following. Victor and vanquished would soon be lying side by side upon the same dust heap.

Nor did Peter find that he minded particularly. He was so tired and hurt in so many places. When death came there would surely be rest and an end to pain. But before it happened, he wanted to see Jennie Baldrin just once more to say goodbye.

With a supreme effort, he lifted himself up from his still and fallen foe, and for the last time looked down upon one who had named himself his enemy and had dealt with him so harshly. He was filled with the pity that the soldier who has triumphed in battle feels for his vanquished enemy who has fought valiantly and to the death, a pity which to Peter's surprise was almost akin to love. The poor, still form that had been so handsomely alive with shining eyes and vibrant muscles rippling beneath the tawny pelt was now a grotesque sack of skin and bones, and Peter, looking at his work, felt the strong wish for an instant that somehow he might undo it and bring him back to life again. Then he remembered that he too must die because of this quarrel, and so with what little remained of his ebbing strength he commenced the long, tortuous crawl in through the pipe and along the dark tunnel to their home.

Because his right shoulder was broken and his left hind leg injured, Peter could no longer stand, but had painfully to drag himself inch by inch through the dirt and dust and cobwebs across the floor of the tunnel until he came to the hole in the baseboard. He wondered why Jennie did not come to help him, until he remembered that under The Law of Fair Combat she must not, but was constrained to remain where she was until one or the other of them came to fetch her.

Besides, he knew he was too weak even to cry out to her. He inched forward down the dark and gloomy aisles until finally after what seemed like many hours he came to the bin that had been their home, and with the goal in sight he now summoned his last reserve of strength, and squeezing through the slats he pulled himself up on to the bed and collapsed over on to his side to the edge as Jennie rushed to him crying – "Peter! Peter! Oh, my poor, poor Peter! What has been done to you?"

Then she was washing and licking his wounds, ministering, gentling and crying over him.

Peter raised his head and gasped, "I've killed Dempsey. But I think he has killed me too. Goodbye, Jennie."

And then a little later he said, "Jennie... Jennie... where are you? I can't see you..."

For the bed, the room, the piled-up furniture, the canopy, everything began to turn and spin about him and lose clarity. He seemed to go shuddering off into a kind of groaning darkness from which he tried to fight his way back just once more to see the love and tenderness glowing in Jennie's tear-filled eyes.

Then the darkness wholly engulfed him, but even though he could no longer see her, he heard her anguished, frightened, pleading voice reaching through the heavy, swimming murk, calling him back to her, begging him not to go away...

"Peter, my Peter, don't leave me! Don't leave me now, Peter..."

Chapter Twenty-Eight

How It All Ended

"PETER! PETER, MY darling! Don't leave me. Don't leave me now…"

Through the darkness Peter heard Jennie Baldrin calling to him again. Or was it Jennie? The words of the pleading cry seemed still to be hers and yet the voice somehow sounded different, though no less filled with love and heartbreak. And never before had she called him her darling…

"Peter! Peter, darling! Cannot you hear me?"

How tenuous the thread of her voice trying to hold him. It was so much easier to drift off into the soothing darkness and the mists where there was no longer any pain, nor battles, hunger or thirst, or the wet, shivering misery of homeless nights. To let this friendly blackness enfold him for ever in eternal sleep was what he most desired. He was so tired. But again the voice penetrated to him, calling him to return.

"Peter… Peter… Come back to me…"

Someone was sobbing, but it was not like Jennie's gentle lament that used so to touch his heart. These sounds were filled with deep pain and suffering that told him of someone who was desperately unhappy, unhappier even than he had been. He opened his eyes to see who it was.

The room was spinning about him, the white, bright ceiling, lights, faces, people and, for an instant, it seemed that he saw his mother.

He lowered his lids momentarily to escape from the dazzling brightness, and when he looked again found that he was indeed gazing into his mother's eyes. How soft, liquid and deeply tender they were, and as loving as Jennie's when she gazed at him. Now they were filled with tears too, as Jennie's had been...

"Peter! My darling, my darling! You do know me..." This was his mother's voice. And there was an odd kind of murmuring that reached his ears, for there seemed to be others in the room as well, and for a moment he thought he saw his father.

But if it was so and he was back with them again, how were they able to recognise him when he was not Peter at all, but a cat? It was certain that he had not changed, because now that he was looking about and had somewhat accustomed himself to the light, he could see his white forelegs and paws on the counterpane. It was all so very confusing.

He was still a cat, but somehow they seemed to have found him and brought him to wherever he was and put him to bed, and his mother knew him again and was crying over him. Sudden panic gripped him. Where was Jennie

Baldrin? Why had they not brought her too? Or was this vision of his mother's face gazing down at him only a part of another dream from which he would awake to find Jennie once more at his side? If this *was* a fantasy, it was a most vivid one, for Peter felt two of the tears falling from her eyes strike gently on his cheek. He shut his eyes quickly again to give the dream a chance to change and bring his Jennie back to him.

This time the mists were only grey and luminous, and nowhere could he find Jennie. But then a curious thing happened to him. He was unable to see through the pale void in which momentarily he seemed to be suspended, nor was it penetrated by any sound. And yet all of it and him as well appeared suddenly to be permeated with Jennie Baldrin. He could not find her face or form, or any longer hear her voice, and yet, unseen, unheard, she was so strongly felt that it was almost as though the greyness enveloping him *was* Jennie, or she a part of it, that he was somehow inside of her and then again it would appear to him that Jennie was all locked away within himself. For a moment he gave himself up to the enthralling sweetness of the emotion. Jennie… Jennie…

But the other dream would persist, and when he returned to it again by opening his eyes once more he saw that strangers were bending over him, a woman in starchy white with a white cap on her head and a man in a linen coat. Why, it must be a doctor and a nurse. This seemed quite clear. He had been injured in his fight with Dempsey, and of course they were attending him. He remembered now. He could not move his left hind leg, or front right paw, because Dempsey had bitten them through and broken them.

The nurse leaned to him. She was wearing a shiny breastpin with a smooth, flat surface, and with a shock Peter saw himself in it. For he was not a cat any longer. *HE WAS HIMSELF AGAIN!*

Or at least he was *half* himself, for in the tiny mirror he had seen his face, and it was the face of Peter the boy. How frightening and confusing it all was, because while the features were as he used to be, he seemed to be still partly white cat about the head. And what was the meaning of the white paws on the counterpane?

The doctor bent closer and looked into his eyes in a kindly and searching fashion. Then he said: "He has passed it. He has come back. He is going to be all right now." Peter heard his mother, who was standing just behind him, crying softly, thanking God and calling him darling over and over again.

All that part of it was true, then. His father was there too. He was wearing his uniform and looking very grim and pale. He came over to the bed now and said to Peter: "I'm proud of you. You made a good fight, old man…"

Peter wondered what his father knew about his battle with Dempsey and how when beaten and nearly dead he, Peter, had rallied and turned the tables on his terrible opponent. Surely his father had not been there. How was one to know or understand anything?

Peter raised one of his paws, his left one, and saw to his intense surprise that there were not sharp, curved claws at the end of it, but instead, five pink fingers. In amazement he moved them and then touched the fur of his injured right limb. But it was not fur at all he was feeling. It was rather something stiff and harsh, the texture of which he remembered – or would remember in a moment…

And then it came to him. It was tightly wrapped *bandage*.

Now he knew for certain. He was cat no longer, anywhere. He was all boy. And then, rushing, tumbling, cascading like water when the sluicegates are opened, everything seemed to come flooding back to him: Scotch Nanny, the morning in the Square, the striped tabby kitten sunning itself by the park, his running across the street and Nanny's shriek; then the grinding bump and thud of the accident. And thereupon Peter burst into tears and cried and cried most bitterly, as though his heart would break.

He wept for many reasons, none of which he wholly understood: for his parting from Jennie Baldrin and the world in which she lived, the sense of loss of a beloved companion, fright due to what had happened, his present plight of finding himself in cast and bandages, but mostly, perhaps, his tears were shed because it was his first encounter with that depth of human sadness that comes with waking from a dream of aching and throat-catching beauty to find it already fading and the dear partner thereof lost beyond recall. For this it seemed to him, now that he returned once and for all, had been the true substance of Jennie, and the long figment through which they had adventured together so gallantly and tenderly was done, and he was never to see her again.

There was a kind of commotion, and through his tears Peter saw that Scotch Nanny had come into the hospital room and now approached his bedside holding something in her arms, something that moved and struggled there. It was a black-and-white cat, a young one, barely out of the kitten stage, with lean, stringy flanks, three white feet and one black, and a queer black smudge just above the muzzle of its black-and-white face as though it had just dipped its nose in the inkpot.

Nanny was bending over him and trying to put it beside him, saying: "There, ma puir, bonny jo. Dinna ye greet so. Look ye, this wee poussie baudron's for ye tae keep for your ain."

But Peter only turned his head and cried – "Take it away! I don't want it. I want Jennie Baldrin. Jennie, Jennie! Jennie!" and he would not leave off crying.

His mother knelt by his bedside, took him to her breast, and laid her cheek to his and held him there in her arms gently and lovingly while she whispered:

"There, there, my darling. Don't cry so, my dearest. Who was it you wanted? Was there someone? Tell your mother. You are safe here, my Peter. Oh, so safe. There is nothing I will not try to do to make you happy if you will just get strong and well once more. There now, my darling, see

– nothing hurts any more…" and she kissed his tearstained eyes.

And for Peter, for an instant, it seemed as though Jennie had returned and had kissed him over the eyes as she used to do, and again he was filled with an overpowering sense of her presence somewhere, everywhere, the dear, tender, loving spirit, the essence of her that remained to fill the awful gap of his loss of her and for which he had wept so bitterly. Yes, now he was certain. Jennie was gone, the sweet companion of his adventures. Her physical presence, the soft, gentle, yet wiry little furred body, the white feet with their telltale black underpads confirming her superior ancestry, the lightning speed and graceful carriage, the small aristocratic head, her luminous eyes and the peculiarly endearing expression of her face, these things he saw and remembered for the last time before they faded away and vanished, and in their stead left something that was neither memory nor dream nor fantasy but only a wonderfully soothing sense of homecoming, well-being and happiness.

It was true that nothing hurt any more, nothing at all, anywhere, not even the loss of Jennie Baldrin, for it seemed as though he had found her once and for all and would never again be wholly without her, now that she was all about him in the gentle, loving pressure of his mother's arms cradling him to her, the velvet of her fragrant cheek against his, the expression of her face and the soft touch of her lips to his eyelids.

And then a most strange thing happened, though perhaps

not so strange at all when one considers. The black-and-white kitten in Nanny's arms, and which he had rejected, gave a little cry, and Peter heard her and understood.

He understood, and he knew – oh, not what she was actually saying, for with his return to being a boy all knowledge of the language of cats had been wiped from his memory as though it had never existed. But he recognised the wistful melody of the plaintive little mew, the cry of the waif, the stray, the unloved, and the homeless that he had come to know so well. It was the forlorn and lonely heart begging to be taken to his own, there to be warmed and cherished.

In it, he felt, was contained all of the misery, hurt and longing he seemed to have known for so long, and, for a moment, harsh, vivid memories of things that had happened to him and places where he had been during his illness came back for the last time.

It was as though it was crying to him to be saved from those very terrors he had left behind him, the appalling fear engendered by finding oneself one small, helpless object loosed in a gigantic and overpowering world, the desperate hunger and thirst that surpassed any other, the yearning, and the need to belong, to be loved, to be surpassingly important to someone. Hers was the call of the loneliness of the rejected, the outcast of the granite heart of the unheeding city.

For that instant, all the sights and sounds and smells were there again, the filthy cobbled street, the running gutters, the terrifying shouts and cries and street noises, the crash and clatter of things being hurled at one, and the dreadful blind panic of endlessly fleeing. It was as though the cry of the waif had made it possible just once more for him to peer through the closing door into that other world he had left for ever, to see the shadowy four-footed figures slipping soundlessly from cover to cover in the streets of the hard city, standing on hind legs outlined against the faint silver cylinder of some dustbin to scavenge for a meal, or licking their wounds and sores in the shelter of a deserted ruin. And then it was gone. The door shut and he could see no more.

Again Peter heard the plaintive note of the black-and-white kitten, but now it no longer evoked the dark phantasms. It only went directly to his core. Why, why had he ever rejected her the first time? He could not seem even to remember that now as he focused his attention on the forlorn little animal. He felt only that he must have her now, that he loved her already.

"Oh, Nanny, give her to me, please. I want her…"

Nanny came back and placed the cat on his bed. She crawled at once on to Peter's chest, placed her head beneath his chin, as so many cats were to do all through Peter's later life, as though they knew and understood him at once as one of their own. And there it cuddled and started so loud and contented a purr that it seemed to shake the whole bed.

Peter lifted the good arm that he could still use and

with the fingers that emerged from the ends of the bandage he gently stroked the kitten's head, rubbed the side of her cheek and scratched her under the chin, as though seemingly by instinct he knew all the things to do and places to touch to make a cat the most pleased and comforted.

The nondescript black-and-white purred louder and longer and more ecstatically, and moved her little body even closer and more lovingly to his neck and face in complete and worshipful surrender.

Peter's mother said: "Why, she's a darling. What will you call her?"

Peter thought for a moment, searching his mind for what to call her. Surely there was something he had once heard or thought of should he ever have a cat, a name with which he had been so familiar and had known almost as well as his own.

He looked at his mother and then at the little stray again, and nothing, not so much as a faint echo, came welling up out of the past to aid him. Now he was not even sure that he ever had known a name.

But with the closing of the door had come a wonderful sense of peace and security. Behind it were locked all the dark terrors conjured up by his fantasies and his fears. He was afraid of nothing any longer, not the strange hospital room in which he found himself, or the dull ache of his injuries, or loneliness, or anything. It was as though during the long hours that he had been asleep and dreamed the dream that he could no longer remember, they had taken fear away from him and he could never again experience it in the same form as before. He felt that never in his life had he been quite so happy.

At last he said, speaking from the innocence and comfort that filled him now, "Oh, Mummy! Isn't she sweet! Look how she loves me. I shall call her Smudgie because of the black spot on her nose. And please, may she sleep with me?"

And he smiled up at all the people crowded around his bed.

Thomasina

Paul Gallico

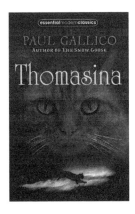

"I was always aware, from the very beginning, that I was a most unusual cat…"

When young Mary Ruadh's beloved pet Thomasina is put down, she pines for the cat and falls dangerously ill herself. Meanwhile, Thomasina is rescued by a strange young woman the townsfolk believe to be a witch. Could she hold the key to saving both Mary Ruadh and Thomasina?

978-0-00-739518-7

the Silver Brumby

Elyne Mitchell

A silver brumby is a very special and valuable horse…

Thowra, the magnificent silver stallion, is locked in a battle to become King of the Brumbies. But a terrible danger is coming, and Thowra faces a threat even greater than the rival King: the menace of Man.

978-0-00-742520-4

T.H. White

When Merlyn the magician comes to tutor Sir Ector's sons, Kay and the Wart, schoolwork suddenly becomes much more fun. After all, who wouldn't enjoy being turned into a fish, or a badger, or a snake?

But Wart is destined for great things and Merlyn's magical teachings are only the beginning of his amazing future…

978-0-00-726349-3